Bridle Path
Press

Also by M.K. Graff

The Nora Tierney Mysteries:
The Blue Virgin
The Green Remains
The Scarlet Wench

Co-author, *Writing in a Changing World*

DEATH
UNSCRIPTED

—— *A Trudy Genova Manhattan Mystery* ——

For Cathy,
Lover of dogs.

With all best regards
Marni Graff
7 Sept 2021

M.K. GRAFF

Bridle Path Press, LLC
8419 Stevenson Road
Baltimore, MD 21208

www.bridlepathpress.com

Direct orders to the above address.

Printed in the United States of America.
First Edition.
ISBN: 978-0-9908287-2-3

Library of Congress Control Number: 2015943544

Book Design by Elizabeth Ryan Cole
Cover photo by Joshua Haviv/Shutterstock

Bridle Path
Press

For P. D. James
Baroness James of Holland Park OBE
1920-2014
Mentor and Friend

And so I greet you . . . with profound esteem
and with the prayer that for you, now and forever,
the day breaks and the shadows flee away.

Fra Giovanni, Letter to a Friend, 1513

DEATH UNSCRIPTED CAST OF CHARACTERS

In Order of Appearance:

REECE HUNTER, *Thornfield Place* Actor playing Bryce Kenyon

MISTY RAINES, *Thornfield Place* Actor playing Savannah Dale

TRUDY GENOVA, RN, *Thornfield Place* Medical Consultant

RON DOWLING, *Thornfield Place* Director

FRANK RESNICK, *Thornfield Place* Stage Manager

NIKKI OLIVIER, *Thornfield Place* star playing Vikki Starr

GRIFF KENNEDY, *Thornfield Place* Actor playing Griff Kennedy

MEG PITMAN, *Thornfield Place* Production Assistant; Trudy's best friend

EVA HENRICKSEN, *Thornfield Place* Hairdresser

WILKIE COLLINS, Trudy's ginger cat

SAL, Trudy's doorman

DETECTIVE NED O'MALLEY, 20th Precinct, NYPD

DETECTIVE TONY BORELLI, his partner, 20th Precinct, NYPD

DR. BYRON BURKNIKOFF, NYC Medical Examiner

GARY KNOWLES, *Thornfield Place* Property Master

LI YUNG, *Thornfield Place* Makeup

EDITH CARLISLE, *Thornfield Place* Wardrobe Mistress

A. J. EAGEN, *Thornfield Place* Head Producer

MARIT VON AKEN, Pitman legal team, counsel for Trudy

ALLISON STEWART, *Thornfield Place* teen actor

MONICA STEWART, her mother

MEREDITH BAUMAN, Ned's cousin

OFFICER DAMON, NYPD, part of Ned's team

MELISSA WEST, sister of Dave West, beating victim

HILDA GENOVA, Trudy's mother

BEN GENOVA, Trudy's brother

OFFICER RON HANSON, Schoharie, NYPD

LUKE ROMANO, former NYPD on Ned's team

REGAN MCKENZIE, Director, Westside Woman's Clinic

Evil is unspectacular and always human,
and shares our bed and eats at our table.

W. H. Auden

DEATH UNSCRIPTED

Chapter One

"Y ou're a self-centered bitch." The pronouncement was at odds with Bryce Kenyon's handsome face, his chin as sharp as the tips of his tooled leather cowboy boots. Folding his arms across his chest, straining the material over his biceps, Bryce leaned against the ornate marble mantel where two rounded cherubs held a mirror over the fireplace. Dark, hooded bedroom eyes narrowed as he waited for the woman's response.

"I *loathe* you!" Savannah Dale's curves matched the complicated swirls of the mantel that looked imported from a European castle. She swung her brunette curls over a shoulder, pointedly ignoring Bryce. The room oozed elegance, with burgundy-striped wallpaper and heavy crown molding picked out in creamy paint. Windows flanked each side of the fireplace, accented on each side with falls of off-white raw silk drapes that puddled on the floor. Two gold love seats placed at right angles to the fireplace were covered in what was surely real silk damask. There was money here and plenty of it.

Sinking gracefully onto one sofa, Savannah leaned forward, a pained expression on the flawlessly made-up face that enhanced her beauty. Her magenta dress was cut to reveal creamy cleavage that matched the lush feel of the room in color and tone.

Bryce sighed and shook his head. He crossed quickly to stand in front of her, adjusting the crisp pleat in his tailored slacks. Savannah stared at his knees. An antique mantel clock ticked loudly.

Suddenly Bryce grasped her wrists and drew Savannah roughly to her feet, tilting her chin to look at him. Her wide eyes searched his face. Her hands crept around to encircle his neck and she tilted her head up as their lips met, locking in a fierce kiss. Finally they drew apart, panting, and Savannah touched his lips with her index finger. She turned on her heel and walked away to a set of French doors.

"Savannah!" he called, his voice choked with emotion.

Refusing to look back, she grabbed the door handle and twisted. Pushed. Shoved. The door stayed solidly shut.

"Shit! It's stuck again, Frank!" she snapped.

"CUT!" The Stage Manager's voice boomed overhead. "Can someone please fix that damn door!"

I watched a Props man hurry onto the living room set with a screwdriver and a can of WD-40. One of the perks of working on a soap opera filmed for the Internet is watching the drama on and off camera. Things can suddenly go off kilter. Call it a side perk for the medical consultant. My name is Trudy Genova, RN, and that's my job on this lovely spring morning in May.

"Nice job, people." Ron Dowling, true Napoleon of soap directors, appeared from behind the cameras, consulting his script and ignoring me.

"Reece, don't forget to touch your mouth in wonder as she walks away," Dowling instructed the muscled actor. "And Misty, not so much tongue, dear. You're making up after a fight, not meeting after the Titanic has sunk." He consulted his huge diving watch. "Downstairs to rehearse the hospital scene."

The Stage Manager's voice rang out. "Hospital scene to rehearsal, five minutes please." The lights went out with a loud thunk, the vivid colors of the brightly lit set immediately fading. Muted lighting provided a pathway over thick electrical cables, pointing the way to the sound stage door past other sets, all fully dressed and waiting for action, as they say in show business.

Gathering my sweater and backpack, I followed the actors, Reece Hunter and Misty Raines, downstairs. Misty's name has a definite porn star ring to it, but then I'm not her agent.

Each morning two huge food trays are delivered to the set from a local deli. One is a fruit tray, melons peeled and sliced in long fingers, bunches of glossy grapes, mounds of huge strawberries and even the occasional mango. The other holds the crap most of us wolf down—tiny iced pastries, sliced pound cake and freshly baked cookies. A coffee urn sits next to a metal tub filled with ice and bottles of designer water. I stopped at the catering table to scoop up a few juicy strawberries and an oatmeal cookie, reflecting on my good fortune in having this job. Not bad for a country girl whose family owned an apple orchard.

How many nurses get to work in The Big Apple where no one is really hurt or dying, and the rocks in a landslide are made of cocoa-covered Styrofoam and oatmeal? Working for a movie studio means no more night shifts or dirty bedpans, no stinky vomit on my white nursing shoes, no real tears, no suffering, no death. Some days I work from home in my pajamas, correcting faxed script pages from movie and television medical scenes.

I never know if my script suggestions will be used. I'll be watching a television episode or a feature film when suddenly my idea appears on the screen. Like that scene in the movie *Lars and the Real Girl* when Patricia Clarkson's doctor character tells Ryan Gosling that his mail-order doll girlfriend suffers from low blood pressure and he must bring her in weekly so the doc can really chat with Lars—that was all mine.

Other days I work on the sets of medical scenes filming in Manhattan for television and the occasional movie, most often a soap opera. I routinely take the calls to *Thornfield Place* and have come to know the cast and crew, part-time regular that I am, as well as the idiosyncrasies found only in the artificial world of soaps.

A cluster of people held us up at the stage door. The smokers run outside to brave the crowds of waiting fans and always make fast for the front door.

"Hi, Trudy. Rehearsal for the medical scene downstairs in five." Frank Resnick, the Stage Manager, zoomed past me.

"Got it," I saluted. "Keep the crew happy" is my motto.

Thornfield Place is taped at Studio 12 on West 66th Street down a side street from Lincoln Center, in an old armory building that resembles a red brick castle from the outside. It stands directly across from the Passion Broadcasting Junction building, which takes up an entire city block and contains their offices and several other studios.

It gave me a real kick when I received my first paycheck to see *PBJ* emblazoned across the top. Some studio head had coined a name whose initials represented many children's favorite sandwich, but the checks were legit and the pay better than any hospital I've worked in. I smiled all the way to the bank. And since I'm never on camera, I wear jeans and whatever I like, no uniforms or scrubs anymore. No hours at Hair and Makeup that the actors have to endure, either—just my kind of job.

When I receive a call out, I show up for rehearsal and listen to the episode's director explain his or her vision for the medical scenes. A rotating stable of five directors all strive for an episode that might garner them a Daytime Emmy nomination. Then I work with the actor to blend what would really happen with the dramatic idea the director has imagined. I try to merge both into a rough semblance of the reality of the particular accident, emergency or disease of the day. Frankly, it's an uphill battle, dealing with egos as huge as those of politicians. Often my objections are overruled with a shrug, accompanied by the blithe statement: "Artistic license." But I learned early on that even if my suggestions aren't used, I still get paid.

Finally able to hit the stairs, I trooped down and entered the stuffy waiting room where the U-5's slouched on droopy couches, fervently studying their scripts, hoping to find a way to be discovered entering a fake elevator or passing by in a street scene. U-5's have under five lines, hence their name, and thus are paid the lowest daily rate from the Screen Actor's Guild. These transients of soaps only reappear if one of them catches a specific director's eye. This often translates to having lunch together in a quiet, locked room. If lunch is very good, the U-5 might merit a bit part with at least six lines here or there as a reward. Since there are both male and female directors in the rotation, those lunch retreats reflect all of the varied couplings imaginable. And then some.

Today's U-5's were garbed in hospital scrubs. The men all took stock of Misty Raines.

"Want some, Trudy?" Misty asked, holding out a Ziplock bag of cut up veggies. "Y'all know carrots have less calories than that cookie." She cocked an eyebrow but smiled to show me she was being kind. The Georgia actress tossed her shiny brunette curls over her shoulder as she offered me a carrot from a bag she usually carried around.

I'm convinced Misty's too-blue eyes are contacts and her breasts have definitely been . . . embellished, let's say, but the woman has a naturally lithe figure. My friend Meg swears I have a perfect hourglass shape, but I know my heritage of Italian hips and German breasts would never look remotely lithe on camera. Thinnies like Misty are always trying to get me to diet. Somehow I manage to find the strength to ignore them.

"No thanks." I smiled a polite refusal.

"Saw you upstairs," Misty said. "Same door problem, can you believe it?"

I nodded in sympathy. "Props will sort it out before taping," I assured Misty, grabbing new script pages from my cubbyhole.

Yellow pages meant there were changes to the script I'd seen last night. "Uh-oh, Ron and Griff battling again?"

Misty munched a carrot stick. "Big Griff and Director Himself were going at it before that last scene. Griff wants to fall out of bed, full crash cart, the works," she drawled. "Ron wants him staring moodily out the window, with voice-overs of Nikki professing her love, then Griff clutches his chest and sinks to the ground."

Great. Dueling egos today and on top of that, I had to work with Griff Kennedy, my least favorite actor. He'd come on to me a few times too many. The ladies man seemed to think any female should be happy to be groped by him. Several weeks ago I'd found myself alone in the rehearsal room with him after turning down yet another invitation for a drink after work. He'd had the temerity to fondle my breast as he tried to change my mind.

I'd shouted loud enough for the U-5's outside the door to hear: "Hands off, slimeball!" That line, plus a knee in the right place, had stopped him in his tracks and he'd left the rehearsal room to a series of titters from those lounging outside.

The incident left a residual tension when we worked together. If it happened again, I'd go straight to PBJ management, whether Griff is a senior cast member or not. I sighed and entered the rehearsal room.

Inside, the windowless room held a few tables and folding chairs. Nikki Olivier, the star who played Vikki Starr and was the big draw of *Thornfield Place*, was stirring a cup of tea, her wet hair wrapped in a towel. The star had the uncanny ability to ignore people she knew well if the mood struck her, but I'd learned to read her moods and stayed out of her way, so we'd always gotten along well. On the show for almost twenty years, the blonde had a shelf of Emmy statues at home and over that time had probably suffered every known ailment and accident the writers could conceive, including a split personality and demonic possession. It was amazing what viewers would tolerate if they liked the actor. Suspension of belief, and all that jazz.

Beside Nikki sat my nemesis, Griff Kennedy, but with Nikki present, I didn't have to worry about him taking liberties again.

"C'mere gorgeous," he stage whispered in Nikki's ear and threw his arm over her shoulder. Griff sipped from his ever-present plastic Emmy cup, a relic from the one time he'd been a presenter. Covered with a plastic lid, its contents were usually some variation of adult beverage, a grownup's sippy cup. The burly, hard-drinking actor had been a stage star in his younger days, a fact everyone he met was made aware of in the first three minutes. I know I should feel sorry for him, with his star over the horizon and all that. But after his third attempt to put a check mark by my name on his conquest list, there had been that knee incident and I'd been decidedly cold toward him. His hair-transplant plugs are obvious, his gut straining at his belt, and the thought of coupling with him, of *anyone* coupling with him, gives me the willies.

"Hello, Trudy." Nikki deigned to be polite today and nudged Griff, who added his own "Hi there" without meeting my eyes.

I murmured my own greetings and read the yellow pages over—nothing I couldn't handle—and flicked my eyes to take in Nikki and Griff's cooing.

In real life Griff and Nikki are divorced, but rumor has it they are still lovers off and on. On the show, the number of times they've been married and divorced was too numerous to count. Today my job was to teach Griff how to fake a heart attack while the computer worked its magic to reflect a myocardial infarction on his hospital monitor.

Ron Dowling entered and arranged three folding chairs side-by-side into a makeshift bed, motioning Griff into position. The short, intense director scowls entirely too often and has a cocky attitude. I'm short—although I prefer petite—and too often we meet eye-to-eye when disagreeing. He likes to call me "Nurse Nancy." After more than two years of working with him and other directors who are far nicer, I decided this is his attempt to keep me in my place, directly beneath his tiny, Birkenstock-shod feet. I tend to get touchy over men with attitudes, in positions of power or not, and have my own way of letting them know that.

A king to his subjects, Dowling pretended to look around the small room for me. "Nancy?" He beckoned me closer.

"Trudy," I corrected for the umpteenth time, taking my place near Griff. I took his cup and placed it on a nearby shelf while he slid carefully down across the chairs.

"Whatever," Dowling answered. "We've decided to go for a situation where Griff first feels his chest pain in the bed, stumbles out of it to the window as the symptoms progress, and we insert voice-overs with Nikki. Then he realizes he's in trouble, turns back to reach for the call bell, but falls short of it to the floor. Alarm bells ring as the scene closes."

They sure weren't going for reality today. "What about his monitor?" I reminded Dowling. "You had him hooked up to a heart monitor in Friday's scene and it has to show a change in heart rhythm." Part of my job is to stay on top of this stuff. Viewers hate to see reality thrust at them by a loss of continuity. The phone calls and emails arrive in droves to PBJ when that happens.

Dowling scowled but quickly recovered. "He disconnects it when he gets out of bed."

I squashed that one immediately. "The alarm would go off and staff would rush in."

Dowling crossed his arms over his chest. This was going to be a battle of the wills and he was determined "Nancy" was not going to win. "The doctor comes in earlier and tells him he's getting better and disconnects it then."

Over to me; I shook my head. "If he was that much better, he wouldn't be in ICU. He'd have been moved to a step-down unit—it's a protocol matter." I shrugged my shoulders.

Dowling crushed the pages of his notes while I watched his crooked toes curl in his sandals. I firmly believe someone with toes like that has no business wearing sandals without socks unless they're playing a Hobbit in a *Lord of the Rings* movie.

Griff, who had started to doze on his makeshift bed, mumbled: "Move the bed closer to the window."

The Stage Manager was summoned. Frank Resnick took

the message upstairs to the Props Department to make the adjustment. Strict union rules prohibits anyone not from their department from moving things around on the set. Props would move the bed close enough to the window to allow Griff to slip from the bed and gaze out without disconnecting his monitor.

While that was happening, I spoke to Griff about what he would be feeling and how to react if he were really having a heart attack. Then we all trooped up to the frigid sound stage for blocking, where Dowling would work out where the actors would stand and move, and which cameras would focus on which actor at what time. A good director has this all storyboarded out to match the script. Dowling often leaves a lot to be decided on the spot because he makes so many last-minute changes.

When we reached the soundstage I grabbed a bottle of water—and in defiance of Misty's advice, another cookie—and headed down to the hospital set.

Watching blocking is a bit like watching the blind leading the blind. Those numerous throw pillows on couches, chairs and beds in soaps? They all have scripts hidden behind them, thrust there by the actors as they stumble through rehearsal. Most have only received those scripts the night before as they leave the studio, anytime between six and eight on a normal evening. That doesn't leave them a lot of time to learn their lines for the next day. On a show airing daily, actors have to film a complete show each day, about three weeks ahead of what is airing. And if a holiday like Christmas falls in the middle of a week, scenes for *that* show have to be added onto the regular scenes filmed in prior weeks. Then they would have a show ready to air on the holiday and the cast and crew could have the day off. They really do work hard; that's why they get the big bucks.

"Hey, Trudy."

"Good to see you, Trudy."

I smiled hellos to the cameramen, who had been fans of mine since the slimeball-knee incident spread around the studio like a flash fire. I sipped my water and munched my cookie through the beginning of the scene. On the other side of the hospital set was the set representing the hall of Nikki's house. Nikki pretended to take a telephone call telling her to hurry to Griff's bedside. I'm always impressed with the range of facial emotions Nikki can summon despite her Botox injections. Finally we got to Griff's hospital room scene, where he waited in bed for me. Oh, joy.

While Dowling talked to the cameramen about the shots he wanted, I lengthened the monitor leads taped to Griff's chest. He bantered with the cameraman and left me alone, knowing Nikki was off camera. In reality, no hospital would ever move a bed so close to a window. Griff performed admirably, slipping out of bed, gazing out the window, clutching his chest as he mimicked the crushing chest pain I'd described: "Imagine an elephant sitting on your chest."

I hit a button on my computer remote, the monitor close-up showed an erratic heartbeat, alarm bells sounded on cue, and Griff fell gracelessly to the ground.

Frank's voice rang out: "CUT! Lunch!"

My hand hovered over the hot pastrami sandwich on offer at the huge, marble-columned PBJ cafeteria across the street from Studio 12. I watched Meg and followed her example, settling for the chicken salad.

"Griff behaving today?" Meg asked.

"Nikki was around so I was safe. Let's hope it lasts." Swiping my credit card, I followed Meg to a table. There was one near the door, a table for four with only an Asian woman reading emails on her phone.

"All right if we sit here?" Meg smiled her sunny smile and the woman nodded and pointed to the open seats.

Meg Pitman is the reason I have my great job. We were roommates when I first moved to Manhattan from upstate New York to work at St. Vincent's busy Emergency Room, brought together by a Craig's List ad I found when I came down for the interview and decided to give the Big Apple a fling. The work was more challenging than the medical or surgical units in Albany, and at first I'd felt a real thrill at working in a big city hospital. But shift work drove me crazy. I had trouble sleeping during the day when I was on night shifts. The days and nights ran together and I felt like I lived in a perpetual fog, not a good place to be when I needed a clear head to function safely. Just as the situation began to really worry me, Meg mentioned an opening for a nurse consultant. I jumped at the opportunity. We no longer live together, but do try to eat lunch when I work Studio 12. I consider Meg a great person and my best friend.

"I have the yellow pages for today. Any more coming down the pipeline?" I wanted to be prepared if Dowling had any plans for last minute changes before taping started.

Meg forked a chunk of celery before answering. "All quiet and set for taping. He's already working on next week's script and giving the writers fits about what he calls their lack of creative dialogue."

"Endearing himself as usual."

Meg laughed. She's the glue in the third floor office, doing everything from secretarial chores to keeping the writers soothed and their many script changes in everyone's hands. Her parents detest her working here. The philanthropic Pitmans are benefactors to museums and have several foundations. Meg could have her pick of the one she wanted to run, but she'd found this production assistant position on her own. Her parents didn't understand why their daughter insisted on earning her own way—which told me a lot about Meg.

I learned early on in our friendship not to be jealous of Meg's slender frame and silky blonde hair, or those large honey-colored eyes with thick lashes. Yes, Meg is gorgeous and rich, but she's also a supportive friend with a killer smile and a streak of wickedness I adore.

"Dowling and Griff get today's scene ironed out?" Meg asked, sipping ice water.

I described the way the scene was set to work. "If all goes well, I should be able to leave right around five. Want to catch an early movie?" There's a cinema a few blocks from the studio where it's cheaper before six PM.

Meg nodded. "I'll Google the schedule when we get back. Whose turn is it?"

We take turns choosing the movies we watch. I like comedies, mysteries, and even the occasional well-acted period drama. Meg goes for romances and arty movies. One time she made me sit through this famous Swedish director's film—Gustav Andersenbergstrom, or some such long Scandinavian name—a nut job whose actors rarely spoke a line of dialogue. Instead they communicated angst through raised eyebrows, pouts and glares. Botox would kill any of their careers. Such highbrow crap fortunately is rare. We both enjoy classic movies, and those we watch at one of our apartments with a big bowl of popcorn. It helps that neither of us has a significant other at the moment. After I'd moved in with Jake, Meg found a new roomie who's a flight attendant on a Paris to JFK route and stays more in France than in New York. I would, too.

"Yours," I admitted, hoping Gustav was not in town.

"I'll check the listing. Look, there's Perry King," Meg said under her breath, shifting her eyes to the right.

I glanced over and saw the host of PBJ's popular morning show, "King and Kiley," dining with several studio bosses. A perennial favorite, King is on his third co-host in as many years.

"Probably trying to get Kiley fired," I said, eating the last of my chicken salad. I looked with longing at the slice of coconut pie on our neighbor's tray. The woman had taken one forkful and abandoned a perfectly good piece of pie. What a waste.

"I've heard he really likes Kiley," Meg said. "Maybe he's trying to get a raise."

"Maybe he's just hungry," I said, and we both laughed until Meg looked up just as a meaty hand fell on my shoulder.

I turned to see Griff Kennedy leering down. "Nice lunch, Nancy?" His hand moved to knead the back of my neck and I saw red.

I stood up so fast my chair overturned, stopping the noisy flow of conversation around us. Even as I felt a flush rise to my cheeks I shouted: "Don't touch me again!"

Griff stepped back, looking around at people with a wide smile. "Hey, relax. I was just being nice." He held his hands up in a gesture that said he didn't understand what the fuss was about.

I stood on tiptoe to point in his face. I didn't care if I was making a scene. "I should bring charges against you, Griff Kennedy." I felt Meg tugging my sleeve, trying to drag me away.

"Touchy broad," Griff said to the crowd staring at us. "That's not what you said last week, but okay, if that's the way you want to play it . . . " He shook his head, still laughing, and clutching his plastic cup, turned to saunter away.

I didn't think, just reacted. I grabbed the uneaten pie off the tray from the startled woman next to us and dumped it on Griff Kennedy's head.

"I meant what I said. You stay away from me—or else!" I stomped away before Griff had time to muster a comeback or let a curse slip out.

I fled to the ladies room, shaking in anger. Meg followed, and as I ran cold water over my face, Meg rubbed my back.

"I couldn't help it. It's a good thing I'm shorter than him or I swear my hands would have gone around his ugly throat and squeezed the smarmy life out of him."

"Asshole," Meg agreed.

I love that she cursed for me.

A woman fixing her makeup touched me on the arm on her way out. "The pie was priceless."

"You did what a lot of other women wish they had," Meg said.

"I know he's one of the stars, Meg, but that doesn't give him the right to manhandle us. If he touches me again I'm reporting him to the studio heads."

I pulled paper towels to dry my face and saw Meg's grimace in the mirror. "What?"

"You're absolutely right, Trudy, but I'm afraid the person who would be let go would be you. Griff Kennedy brings in the ratings and sponsors want good ratings."

I balled my paper towel and threw it in the garbage. "You're right, of course. Who am I? Just a lowly Nancy. I get it—want the job, ignore Griff, right?"

"Good luck with that," piped up a voice from one of the stalls.

DEATH UNSCRIPTED

CHAPTER TWO

When my scene was called to tape, I had to grit my teeth to leave the safety of the downstairs waiting room, where I whiled away time between my scenes by reading. I stowed the new John Sandford in my backpack, then went upstairs to run a brush through my hair and shove my backpack in my locker. Periodically I debate cutting my hair, but Meg insists the reddish highlights in my dark blonde hair would be lost if I did.

Meg also insists men favor women with long hair. I keep reminding Meg that having a man in one's life is not all it's cracked up to be. Maybe after Jake Forester and that debacle I need to remind myself.

I scooped my hair up in a clip to keep it out of my face during taping and grabbed my sweater for the perpetually cold sound stage, glad I'd worn my warm Uggs. It will be too warm to wear them soon, but they feel good at work and keep my toes cozy. Opening the heavy metal door, I walked down the center aisle to the hospital room set, past Nikki's living room, an outdoor patio, Nikki's hall, and the hospital waiting room.

Each set is decorated in grand style, little nuggets of color in the otherwise drab sound stage with its gray cement floor and high ceilings draped with klieg lights, wires, and cables. Most sets overflow with fresh flowers on mantels, tables or in pots on the fake patio floors. Prop Master Gary Knowles has one of the biggest budgets on soap sets, with rumors that the cost of his fresh flowers run in the thousands every month, compared to the $300 spent on plastic plants over at the soap *Time Will Tell.* Only the Wardrobe Mistress, Edith Carlisle, has a bigger budget, with her designer suits for men and couture clothes for the women. It was amazing to learn what is spent on dressing those sets.

The hospital set had a cluster of the usual people ringed around it: two camera men, prop crew, lighting and audio, the Stage Manager, and the show's hair and makeup crew. All of the equipment is genuine rented medical equipment, right down to the crash cart and the monitors. But in this case, the monitor's rigged to a computer that allows my remote to change the tracing with the push of a button. Magic.

Griff Kennedy was being helped into bed. This would not be pretty after the pie incident. *Be professional* was my mantra as I plastered a blank look on my face. I liked this job and needed it. Next week would bring a different director, and if I were lucky, a different actor.

Approaching the bed, I kept from making eye contact with Griff as I readied my supplies. The actor wore a hospital gown over a pair of gym shorts, and I thought Li's makeup had done an admirable job getting his face a nice pallid white as I slid my eyes sideways to check him out. There were no signs of pie in his hair. Now if he could just keep his mouth shut and his hands off me, we can do our scene and I can get the hell out of here.

I cracked open a fresh vial of atropine eye drops and Griff leaned his head back and let me administer a drop in each eye while he kibitzed with Frank. The atropine would dilate his pupils for his close shots. Next I taped fresh monitor leads onto his chest where live ones would be, waiting for the comments I knew he wouldn't be able to hold back, pie or no pie.

"Hey, pretty green-eyed Nancy, I love having you work me over in bed," Griff slurred. "I even brought my own dessert." He giggled.

Must have been a two-cup lunch. If I'd been hoping for an apology, I'd obviously be waiting a long time. I reminded myself to take the high road and ignored Griff, turning away from the cloud of alcohol and minty mouthwash that hung around him. "Just remember the elephant," I reinforced, the ultimate professional as I taped an intravenous tube to his arm.

Griff seemed uncharacteristically shaky. Sweat poured from his forehead and upper lip, although his skin felt cool and even a bit clammy to my touch. Maybe he was coming down with something. It would serve him right.

"I don't feel too good, Nurse Nancy," he whined, patting the mattress next to him. "Why don't you join me—ouch!"

Did this guy ever give up? I'd torn off a lead, ripping a few chest hairs with it. "Sorry—had to be repositioned." Two could play this game. I noticed red blotches on Griff's chest and thought he might be sensitive to the adhesive on the lead pads. I made a mental note to use paper tape to attach future leads if we had to reshoot this scene. I could only hope we didn't.

After turning on the computer module, I checked my remote batteries for a full charge, ready to turn Griff's monitor from normal sinus rhythm to ST segment elevations, a classic heart attack tracing for those medical people in the viewing audience who would object if we did it wrong. Griff was getting into character, staring across the set at a blank wall, muttering his lines.

He rubbed his temple. "Hey, cut those lights already—I'm getting a monster headache."

"No can do." Dowling's voice boomed over a speaker from the control room where he sat at a bank of monitors. "Are you ready to try this?"

"One take, flat out," Griff replied.

The crew snickered as I moved out of camera range. Griff was usually good for five or six takes until he got it right. Frank Resnick held the black and white clapperboard in front of Camera One and clicked it closed.

"Action!"

Griff rubbed his chest. I frowned when his hand slipped decidedly lower than we'd rehearsed, nearer his stomach than his heart. Now he pressed both his hands clearly on his paunch instead of mid-chest. At least he hadn't dislodged the monitor leads.

The actor threw back the covers with more than a hint of impatience and took a step to the window, still rubbing his stomach. He stared out the fake window, and in a bit of ad-libbing, touched it, as taped voice-overs of Nikki professing her love for him were spliced in. This was my cue. Let the magic begin. I hit the proper button on the remote and

Camera Two closed in for a tight shot of the erratic rhythm change. My eyes followed to be certain it worked. Mission accomplished.

When Camera One lit back on Griff, he was supposed to be clutching his chest dramatically before sliding to the floor. Instead, Griff whirled around, beads of sweat flying off his face. This wasn't right. I frowned. Griff was either heavily over-acting or something was seriously wrong.

The atropine was clearly working. His pupils were seriously dilated. But his eyes had a wild look. One hand clutched at his stomach. The other was raised and shook as he looked around in panic. A large glob of saliva slipped from his mouth.

Then Griff pointed right at me. "You—YOU!"

Everyone froze in stunned silence and I felt people look at me. My face flamed as I sucked in a breath. What was he playing at now? Was this when he was going to accuse me of dumping that stupid pie on him, on tape and in front of everyone? Dowling would hit the roof. I'd lose my job for certain.

"You . . . " Griff croaked out as his eyes rolled back in his head and he fell to the floor in a dead faint.

"CUT! Great work, Griff!" came from the control room.

A few people clapped, then stopped as I rushed over to Griff's inert form, noting a small amount of vomit on the floor. I felt for a pulse in his neck. "Call 911! And get me that Ambu bag off the cart!" I yelled.

Frank shouted into his cell phone for an ambulance as I grabbed a stethoscope hanging around the neck of a stunned U-5 nurse and a pair of gloves from a box on the wall.

I knelt next to Griff's chest and with my hands on top

of one another, locked my wrists and did about thirty brisk chest compressions, leaning into them and letting my weight push my hands into his sternum to restart his heart.

I listened for his heartbeat. Nothing. No respirations, either. Despite the profuse sweating, Griff's skin was ice cold. I slipped on the gloves, tilted his neck back and cleared his mouth and airway, noting the red patches had spread up his chest to his neck as Frank handed me the Ambu bag.

Ignoring the copious amounts of saliva mixed with alcohol and vomit fumes, I leaned over Griff's inert body, fit the mask over his face and squeezed the bag to force air into his lungs. One of the grips fell to his knees beside me before I could get back to Griff's chest.

"I'm CPR certified," he said, and on my nod, he started chest compressions, counting so I could keep a respiratory rhythm of twenty breaths a minute in between his continuous compressions, two breaths every thirty pumps. We worked together: my bag pushing air into Griff's lungs, making his chest rise and fall, followed by the compressions designed to restart his heart.

Bystanders clustered around and I heard their frantic whispers as I concentrated, noting that Griff's pupils, dilated by the atropine drops, were fixed without movement. This was not good. I prayed for the paramedics to arrive. The studio door slammed as Nikki Olivier ran onto the set, screaming.

"Griff! What happened?" Her scream echoed to the rafters.

Nikki must have been watching the video monitor downstairs. I saw Frank run to hold Nikki from getting in the way. Nikki stood over us, her weeping setting the makeup and hair gals sniffling and crying.

DEATH UNSCRIPTED

I saw the grip was tiring and caught his eyes. With a nod, we exchanged places. I felt for a carotid pulse. Nothing.

I shook my head and we resumed CPR. I leaned into the compressions, my hands wrapped around each other on Griff's sternum. I looked up and saw Meg and the writers from upstairs arrive. A weird silence settled over the ring of onlookers, punctuated by Nikki's crying as I leaned into Griff's chest over and over, pushing fast and hard.

Minutes later the paramedics arrived. When they peeled us away from the still form, there was little doubt in anyone's mind that Griff Kennedy was dead.

Chapter Three

The paramedics departed, rushing Griff to the hospital, continuing resuscitation despite my conviction the actor was dead. Two PBJ honchos from across the street arrived and instructed everyone to wait on the sound stage. Only Nikki Olivier left, riding to the hospital behind the ambulance in her limo with one of the studio heads as her escort.

The departing ambulance's siren echoed eerily throughout the cold, cavernous sound stage. I found myself sitting alone on the foot of the hospital bed Griff had just vacated, wiping the sweat from my face with a clean towel Frank Resnick handed me.

"Thanks very much for the help," I told the shaken grip. "You did everything right. At least we tried."

The white-faced young man nodded and hurried over to a group of his crew, who consoled him on his efforts. It was one thing to take a CPR course on a dummy and an entirely different thing to perform it on human being.

Meg ran over. "Are you all right? I came down as soon as I heard what was going on. Upstairs is buzzing with your attempts to save Griff."

"Attempt being the key word," I pointed out. Despite my training I'd been unable to save the man's life and it rankled.

"Still, you were very professional, kicked right into action," Meg insisted.

"No one deserves to die like that." I threw the crumpled towel down in disgust at my failure to save him. I felt guilty for the horrid things I thought about the man, despite the fact he deserved them at the time. And to think that just hours before I'd humiliated him by dumping pie on his head. Hardly a good last memory—even if he'd asked for it.

"Let me get you a bottle of water." Meg left to scrounge the catering table.

I shook my hair out of the ponytail, which was giving me a headache. My hands had stopped trembling from the adrenaline surge. The accompanying wave of nausea subsided. Everyone left me alone, but was that to allow me to collect my thoughts, or because of the way Griff had pointed at me? Did they feel I was responsible for his collapse?

I shook the paranoia off. Everyone was just stunned. No one could think I was really responsible for Griff's death. I remembered the first time I'd performed cardiopulmonary resuscitation on a human and knew how the grip had felt: I never forgot the sensation of the woman's ribs and sternum giving under the pressure of my hands as I leaned into the compressions, nor the hiss the air made as it rushed out of her lungs.

It was completely different from learning on a Resusci Annie dummy the way I had. That dummy had given me the willies in school due to the legend that the dolls were made in the image of their inventor's daughter, who had died tragically but might have been saved if CPR had been performed.

Recently I'd read an article in *Nursing Spectrum* magazine

and learned the truth and a French phrase all in one day. Asmund Laerdal, whose company had designed the dummy, stated the dummy's face was based on "Inconnue del la Seine," or "the Unknown of the Seine," an unfortunate young woman who drowned in the Seine around 1900 and was never identified. At that time the morgue next to Notre-Dame Cathedral was a tourist attraction, the draw being the viewing of unidentified corpses on black marble slabs in a window, in hopes of them being claimed. One cadaver's angelic visage so captivated people that a death mask was made and copies of her lovely face were displayed in many fine homes across the continent.

That story slightly improved my feelings about the dummy. Maybe I'd tell it to the grip, go and see how he was doing. I glanced to where he was surrounded by his buddies, but they all had their backs turned from me and I felt the chill of exclusion. Maybe another time, then.

The stage door opened and Ron Dowling came in with two PBJ execs just as Meg handed me a cold water bottle. The small man looked even more diminished and I could swear he'd been crying.

"Can I have your attention please?" Dowling's voice quavered. He waited until the cast and crew gathered around him in a wide semicircle. One of the execs gave him the nod to continue.

"I'm sorry to tell you that Griff Kennedy has been pronounced dead at the hospital." He stopped, unsure what to say next. The exec to his left whispered in his ear.

"We will dim the studio lights now and close tomorrow as a sign of respect and take up again on Wednesday. Leave the sets as they are until we decide how to handle the, uh, change in the storyline due to Griff's death. Any questions?"

People broke away, gathering up sweaters and water bottles, heading out to lockers and home. Most rushed past me except for Eva, the hairdresser, who cried into a sodden tissue and hugged me. Why was everyone else avoiding me? One of the writers stopped Meg at the door and she mimed calling me later.

I gathered my things and flung my backpack on my shoulder. The studio's security guard wouldn't meet my gaze at the door. I didn't feel I deserved special status as the woman who'd tried to save the victim's life, but surely someone could have thanked me for trying. But then I remembered my efforts had failed.

I might have despised Griff Kennedy, but I couldn't help feeling sorry for the man. I'd seen a lot of deaths in my life, but this had to be one of the worst. I also couldn't help wondering why he'd died. What could have caused such a sudden collapse? I shook off the musing. It wasn't my concern. They'd do an autopsy, find out at the hospital, and contact the family—if he had any besides Nikki.

Outside it was twilight, the dusk sending pink rays over skyscrapers into the Manhattan sky above Lincoln Center. Up on Broadway the traffic moved sluggishly, red brake lights punctuating the shadows.

No movie tonight. It was amazing how quickly the most mundane day could turn tragic. I strode up the block, deciding to walk home, a light breeze ruffling my hair as I tried to sort my emotions. Cherry trees set at the curb were just starting to bloom and I drew a deep breath, happy to be alive to see those trees and hear the traffic noise. It was a lovely spring night, but not for Griff Kennedy.

CHAPTER FOUR

That evening Meg called to check on me. "You feeling any better, Trudy?"

"I keep picking things up and putting them down, can't seem to concentrate." I stroked my cat's ears absently, his green eyes narrowing to slits as he purred.

"It's shock. After all, you were right there in the thick of it. Did you eat?"

"Now that's a change—you worried about me eating. Reminds me I need to feed Wilkie."

"Want me to bring you takeout? Chinese?"

My stomach roiled at the thought of heavy food. "No, thanks, I'll rustle up something here. Talk to you tomorrow."

"Trudy? I don't want to pry, but why did Griff point at you like that? I heard all about it upstairs after they took him away."

"I don't know, Meg. I thought maybe the eye drops were hurting him. He seemed off from right after lunch—but he never mentioned the pie incident."

"That's because he knew he was wrong and was protecting himself from gossip spreading."

After Meg rang off I fed Wilkie and tried doing a crossword

puzzle, more of my self-education process for becoming a writer, but the words swam in front of my eyes and Meg's words echoed. Finally I made tea, then rooted around in the fridge, pulling out a wedge of cheddar and some grapes. I added the tail end of a box of Triscuits and sat in the living room in front of the television watching *30 Rock*, its humor washing over me. I ate with the volume low until the nightly news came on, when I turned up the volume and found myself glued to the set.

Griff's death was the lead story in local news, complete with a shot of the paramedics wheeling his stretcher down the stone steps of Studio 12 to the ambulance backed up to them. I noted a uniformed cop just to the right of the door making notes as he spoke to the security guard. It was a strange feeling to have been so present at the death of someone and so unable to prevent it.

With a sigh, I turned off the set and padded into the kitchen. I rinsed my plate and reached up into the cabinet over the stove where I kept spices and moved things around, past the cooking sherry, until I came up with two small sample bottles of Amaretto. Pouring them both over ice, I took them to bed to finish the John Sandford, hoping Lucas Davenport would be able to blot out the awful day.

DEATH UNSCRIPTED

Wednesday, May 5th

Most mornings when I wake I lie in bed for a few minutes and listen to the city noises while I organize my thoughts for the day. I savor the warmth of the bed and the huge orange cat lying behind my knees. I'm optimistic by nature, that glass half full idea, and all feels pretty darn good when I prepare to face another day—usually.

Today was nothing like that. Sleep hadn't come easily. I couldn't stop going over the details of Griff Kennedy's death. The feeling that he hadn't had a sudden heart attack, life imitating art, picked away at me. There was his profuse sweating and salivating, that wild look in his eyes, and the way he'd looked at the window as though he were hallucinating. He had definitely been rubbing his stomach, not his chest, and there were those red spots, too, almost hive-like. Could there have been something in the eye drops he'd had an allergic reaction to?

When I had finally fallen asleep, it was to dream of Griff in a hospital gown, onstage at Radio City Music Hall. Surrounded by a dancing line of leggy Rockettes in nurse's uniforms, he kicked with the best of them, while pointing his finger at me in the front row of the audience, yelling "YOU! YOU! YOU!" in time to the music.

In my nursing career, plenty of people had died, but most of them were ill and their deaths expected. Maybe that's why my desire to work in an Emergency Room paled after a year. There were too many chances I'd face an accident or tragedy with a sudden death, one that didn't allow time for the adjustment or acceptance of loss. My past with my father hadn't prepared me to deal well with abrupt, unexpected news.

Wilkie meowed loudly and pattered into the kitchen. I followed the ginger cat, yawning, lack of rest giving me a muggy feeling as I trudged after him. Opening the window the six inches my safety bars allowed, I watched him move in a series of calculated leaps down the fire escape from the fifth floor until, with a final flick of his striped tail, he disappeared around a corner and out of sight. He would be meeting and greeting his friends in the neighborhood for hours. A breeze drifted in and I closed the window, leaving it open enough for him to squeeze back in, and rested my head against the cool glass. Get a grip, Trudy.

I rubbed my eyes and scratched my scalp until my hair stood up untidily, then poured a glass of orange juice and drank half down, taking the glass with me into the large front room. Looking out the windows onto West 98th Street, I watched the morning traffic move slowly up the block from Riverside Drive toward West End Avenue, the blare of horns a constant backdrop that would swell as the day ran on. I tried to dispel my ugly mood and looked past the accumulated pigeon droppings on the window ledge down to a group of barking dogs dragging a paid walker toward the doggie playground at Riverside Park. City noises took getting used to—now I didn't think I could fall asleep without the whoosh of traffic and staccato siren bleeps.

Turning my back to the window, I drained my glass. This room has high ceilings, thick crown molding and tall windows around two sides, with oak floors darkened from the patina of many owners. A stuffed bookcase holds an assortment of the Scottie dogs I collect running across its top. I liked their jaunty look although I'd never wanted to own the breed. The books on the shelves are a mix of medical books but mostly my beloved mysteries. I always have a book in progress in my backpack and another on my nightstand. One of these days I'll think seriously about writing one, but for now reading is educating me in the genre while it entertains me. Writing is for when I need a break from nursing, down the road. My violin sat in the corner, chiding me for its dusty case, but I didn't have the energy to clean it.

I love this apartment, despite its oddly shaped bathroom. Meg tells me often enough that the apartment is one of two good things Jake Forster left me, and eventually I had to agree. The other was the cat he'd named after my favorite author, Wilkie Collins, to impress me. The naming had worked at the time, but thinking of Jake now added to my dark mood.

I jumped in the shower while my mind kept itself in overdrive. If this had been a mystery novel, I thought as I washed my hair, Griff's finger-pointing would have been an important clue—that was, if Griff had been murdered. But that's absurd. There had to be a medical abnormality behind the things he'd displayed.

No, I decided, rinsing the shampoo from my hair, there was something off about Griff's death. With a renewed sense of purpose, I decided to research his symptoms.

As I toweled off I scrutinized myself in the full-length mirror. My eyes look green, but they're really teal, blue on the outside, green inside with gold dots nearer the pupil. I know this because in an effort to get me out of my Jake depression, Meg had taken me to Bloomingdales for all new makeup that I hardly ever wore. But in choosing my eyeshadow colors, the technician had me look in the biggest magnifying mirror I'd ever seen. She told me those colors in my eyes, or their opposites on the color wheel, are the best colors for me to wear. She went on to insist some people actually structure their entire wardrobe around their colors. Some people also have entirely too much time and money on their hands.

At twenty-six, my face has mild lines outside the corners of my eyes, but I call those laugh lines. I slapped on some moisturizer, added a tinted lips gloss and was done. The whole makeup thing passes me by unless it's a dressy occasion, like a wedding or a date. Since I haven't been on a date in over eight months, and no one I know is getting married, that leaves me with a quick and easy morning routine.

Dressing in my favorite comfort clothes was a no-brainer: soft washed-out yoga pants and a faded blue tee shirt advertising my family's business, "Genova's Apple Orchard, Schoharie, NY." Turning on my iPod and its Pandora app, I used my mini Bluetooth speaker dock to fill the room with music. I decided I couldn't handle Katie Perry today, and chose my jazz station. Ella Fitzgerald's smooth rendition of "Embraceable You" proved an immediate balm to my frazzled nerves. I should have played music last night to fall asleep. I grabbed my laptop from the desk and pulled up the online *Merck Manual*, browsing through Griff's symptoms at the kitchen table.

An hour later I was finishing an English muffin smeared with orange marmalade when the apartment buzzer sounded. I glanced at my Wordsmith calendar on my way to the door, wiping crumbs off my mouth. Upgrading my vocabulary is part of my ongoing self-education program, a campaign of sorts to eradicate what my mom calls my truck driver mouth. Despite my decent education, the influence of growing up with two brothers had left its mark. I noted today's Word of the Day was "thanatophobia: fear of death or the dead." I tore it off and crumpled the page. I wouldn't be working hard to make that one part of my vocabulary after yesterday and Griff's sudden death.

"Yes, Sal."

The doorman's voice boomed from the speaker. "Trudy, two men here with badges want to talk witchu." The doorman's voice boomed over the speaker.

"Okay, send them up."

Hmm. I took a deep breath and blew it out. Two policemen here to see me? I didn't own a car in the city so it certainly wasn't about parking tickets. I doubted they were here to collect for the policeman's ball. I took a comb from my backpack and ran it through my hair. I didn't even jump subway turnstiles.

Even though I expected it, I still started when the knock came. After my father's death, I wasn't a fan of police at the best of times. I peered out the peephole and saw two plainclothes officers. Detectives? What the hell was going on?

I yanked open the door, practicing creating characters for my future mystery. I think I'm a good judge of people, like the profilers I read about, and quickly appraised the two men to see if either one of them could be a model for my project. The shorter one was olive-skinned with black curly hair, and wore an off-the-rack dark blue suit with a red and blue striped tie. I'd bet Meg a vodka gimlet his last name ended in a vowel. The taller man carried a folder. He had a craggy squared face, light brown hair and dressed his lanky frame in an immaculate grey suit with a subtle plaid tie. Definitely a few pay grades and years of experience over the shorter man.

"Can I help you?"

"Gertrude Genova?" The taller man spoke up.

"Trudy." I kept on a wide smile and felt like a grinning Cheshire cat.

"Detective Ned O'Malley, and this is Detective Tony Borelli from the 2-0. We'd like to ask you a few questions about Griff Kennedy."

"Of course. Please come in." I pointed the way to the living room and followed the men in. With Borelli right in front of me, I noticed his pants were a little shiny; time for a new blue suit. I pictured two others hanging in his closet, tan and black, with a few sports jackets he alternated with chinos and an assortment of solid shirts and striped ties. The thoughts distracted me from my inner voice, which was shocked and yelling at me: *THIS IS NOT GOOD.* But then Griff *had* died suddenly. They probably just want my take on his condition.

I decided to plunge in and take the lead. "I'm actually glad you're here." I didn't miss the look Borelli threw O'Malley. "I've been going over Griff's death and I'm not sure it was natural." I watched them take in my grandfather's oak desk and the vintage movie posters on the walls. Pointing to the futon, covered in a bright quilt my mother had made, I plunked down in a wide tiger oak rocker I'd refinished myself and curled one leg under me to appear relaxed.

"Why do you think something wasn't right about his death?" Borelli asked, taking out his notebook and choosing to sit with one hip on the wide windowsill.

I counted off the reasons on my fingers. "First, his gestures were off from what we'd rehearsed. I'd told him to picture an elephant sitting in the middle of his chest, squeezing the air out, but instead he seemed to be rubbing his stomach. Second, he was touching the window almost as if he were hallucinating. Third, there was his skin: profuse diaphoresis—sweating—in spite of the cool feel of his skin, and red patches on his chest and neck. Fourth, his excessive drooling, and fifth . . . he just acted weird. I thought about the eye drops I used being tainted, but I'd broken the seal myself."

O'Malley tented his fingers and sat silently throughout this recitation. Now he tapped them together as though making up his mind on a point.

"The medical examiner seems to agree with you, Miss Genova. He's running toxicology tests, but thinks Mr. Kennedy might have been poisoned. We'll know more after the autopsy later today."

"Poisoned?" I raised my eyebrows in surprise, then nodded. That actually made sense. "That would fit his symptoms more. I've been doing my own research. But who would have poisoned him, and why?"

"We were hoping you could tell us that, Miss Genova," said Borelli.

Wasn't he the smug one. "Trudy. It wasn't me, if that's what you're implying," I said in a crisp tone, but inside I felt stunned. Then the more I thought about it, the angrier I became. I was the professional who'd tried to save Griff's life and shouldn't be treated as a suspect. This stopped now. I sat up straighter and directed my question to O'Malley. "When will you identify the poison?"

"How about we ask the questions, Miss Genova?" O'Malley frowned and consulted his own notebook. "It says here," he said, consulting his file, "your real name is Gertrude Genova."

"It's called a nickname." Did he think I was using an alias? I guess he has to check facts. Just the facts, ma'am, but this guy was seriously uptight. "Gertrude Sofia Genova, to be exact. German mom, Italian dad. Wouldn't you rather be called Trudy?"

He ignored my attempts to be friendly and to be treated as his equal. "And that you are employed as a medical consultant. What exactly does that entail?"

I gave him a succinct run down of my script and on set duties, ending with Griff Kennedy's scene. The detectives listened and O'Malley jotted an occasional note; Borelli wrote copiously, tapping his pen periodically, jiggling one knee. I amended Borelli's profile to add: caffeine addict, currently in need of a fix.

"And then I put his eye drops in—atropine to dilate his pupils for a close-up—and taped heart monitor leads on him. The monitor connects to a computer. With a remote I change the tracing. Which I did, when it was the right time in the script, I mean." They seemed to be following this, but in the retelling my hands started to shake with anger and maybe just a touch of fear.

"What happened to those eye drops?" O'Malley asked.

"I left them on the crash cart on the hospital set, unless someone's moved them."

"Get Damon to find those and bag them," O'Malley instructed his partner. He turned back to me. "Shortly afterwards Mr. Kennedy collapsed, is that right?" he asked, making eye contact.

I slid each hand under the corresponding thigh, stilling the tremors. It wouldn't do to let my emotions out now. I wasn't even certain which was ahead, anger or fear. "At first people thought he was just overacting, but it wasn't what he was supposed to do. I had a feeling he was really ill." I described searching for a pulse, and how a certified crewman had assisted in CPR until the paramedics arrived.

"How well did you know the decedent?" O'Malley asked when I fell silent.

"Only from work, not outside the studio."

"Not outside work at all?"

"That's what I said," I repeated through gritted teeth.

"In talking with the producer, a Mr. Egan, he indicated Mr. Kennedy was something of a womanizer. Yesterday there was an incident in the lunchroom with you . . . " He pointed to me.

Great, Egan had seen the pie incident. "I never said he didn't *try* to see me outside the studio, I said I never did." My voice was becoming strident. A curse was not far behind. "Yesterday was the culmination of one too many times he'd manhandled me. I reacted with what was closest to hand—a piece of coconut pie." I watched Borelli smirk and was glad I left out saying I'd wished I'd throttled Griff instead. Oh, boy, just how many people had heard me say that?

"So you didn't have a personal relationship with Mr. Kennedy?" O'Malley persisted.

This guy was obtuse. "Not at all. Listen, Detective, there are two kinds of people working in soap operas . . . " I leaned forward, the tremors gone and my anger and fear under control.

O'Malley sat back, never losing hold of his notebook, and popped a mint in his mouth after offering me one. "Tell me."

"The first are glad to have a steady job with great pay, a fan club, and a home life. They're the backbone of the cast. Some do regional theater or an occasional Broadway part and they're hard-working long-timers." I paused to tuck my hair behind one ear and continued, warming to my theme. "The second think they're either on their way somewhere or pretend they've been there and deign to grace us with their presence. They expect special treatment and can usually find someone willing to give it to them, but not me. Griff Kennedy belongs—belonged—to group number two."

"So you didn't like Mr. Kennedy?"

I shifted in my seat before answering. This guy was tricky. "I wasn't paid to like him. Yesterday I was paid to teach him how to act like he was having a heart attack."

O'Malley glanced at his watch. "It would appear he flowered under your tutelage, Miss Genova."

Borelli snorted but I was pleased to see O'Malley shut him up with a glance, even if the guy had quick wits. "I have to ask you about the victim's dying statement. Several witnesses have stated—"

"I know," I jumped in. "He pointed his finger at me and yelled "YOU!" but I've no idea why. I've been trying to think of a reason for that since it happened." I saw the look that passed between the two detectives. "What? You can't think *I* poisoned him." The anger won out. "Jeez, I'm the person who tried to save his life, and this is the thanks I get? Look, let me read you something." I picked up a paperback by W. J. Burley lying open on the coffee table and flipped a few pages back, searching for a passage I'd read earlier. " 'In a murder case the rules are clear: you look to the oracles, the Three Wise Monkeys of criminal investigation: Motive, Means and Opportunity, and the greatest of these is Motive . . . ' I happen to agree with W. J. Burley and his fictional detective, Wycliffe. I certainly did not have *any* motive to murder Griff Kennedy." That should hold them at bay.

"And that helps how?" Borelli asked.

"I just told you I have no motive, none at all." I looked at both men. "Mild dislike, even annoyance, is hardly grounds for poisoning someone. He touched me inappropriately a few times and made annoying comments but that was it. And then, what, I poisoned him yet jumped in to save his life?" I shook my head, and tried hard not to tell these two of New York's Finest what I really thought of them. Not quite the role models I wanted for my future book.

"That hardly clears you as a suspect," O'Malley pointed out. "Remorse, or covering for your crime, also fits those actions."

The guy was certainly tough to pin down—one minute sincere, the next throwing me off guard. I suppose it's a useful tactic in dealing with murderers, but I *wasn't* one. Borelli simply annoyed me with his smug attitude.

I took three deep calming breaths. I wasn't guilty. But somehow I would have to convince these detectives of that.

CHAPTER FIVE

I steeled myself for a grilling and thought of the phrase "on the hot seat." I tried to give O'Malley what I thought was a steely gaze.

"Say for a moment I believe you had nothing to do with Mr. Kennedy's poisoning. Why would he point his finger accusingly at you?" O'Malley folded one long leg over the other and watched me struggle to find an answer.

"I don't know, Detective, I've been thinking all night about that." I bit my lip and raised an eyebrow. "Only maybe he wasn't pointing to me at all." I inched to the edge of my chair, putting both feet on the floor. "There was an entire circle of people around me. I was near the front because of the computer, but what if he was really pointing at someone behind me?"

The detective had the grace to consider this. "So who was behind you?"

I slumped back into the rocker. "I have no clear idea. There were crew from each department, but people move around and talk off camera. My eyes were focused on the monitor and Griff."

I heard Borelli mutter "real helpful." O'Malley shot him

a silencing look. Borelli must be a newbie and O'Malley didn't need his new subordinate to antagonize the witness. Especially this witness.

I watched O'Malley look around the apartment as though taking it in for the first time and knew he'd decided to try another tack. "Nice place you've got here, Miss Genova. Consulting work must be lucrative."

I couldn't stop the color from rising in my face. Damn. He'd struck a nerve. But surely this was my business? "I've a low sublet from the owner," I admitted.

"And that would be?" Borelli asked, his pen poised over his page.

"Jake Forster." I knew my clipped speech and the way my face stiffened told them volumes. Some witness.

"An address for Mr. Forster?" Borelli persisted.

"It's Captain. He's Army, stationed in Germany at Spanghalem. I don't have a current APO address. I pay the co-op fee directly to the board."

"An unusual situation, Miss Genova . . . " O'Malley said.

This time I had my answer ready. My gaze was direct and unflinching. "One that has nothing at all to do with Griff Kennedy's death."

There was moment of silence that the detective let drag on. I'd learned witnesses often felt awkward and spoke to fill the gap. Two could play this game. The music changed again, Chris Botti's trumpet playing a stylized version of "My Romance." I remained silent and inspected my cuticles.

O'Malley caved first. "Perhaps you'd be good enough to think about who might have been behind you on set and compile a list for us."

I nodded, ever the helpful witness. He took me through routine background information: when I'd started working at the studio, where I'd worked and lived before. I knew he'd decided he'd gotten what he could out of this interview when O'Malley snapped his notebook shut and stowed it in his jacket pocket.

Borelli took his cue and straightened up, putting his own notebook away as O'Malley stood. "Thank you for your time, Miss Genova. We'll be in touch."

CHAPTER SIX

It took a great effort not to slam the door when the detectives left. "We'll be in touch," O'Malley had said. I bet he would. I hated the suspicion pointing squarely in my direction, just the way Griff had pointed at me.

I felt shocked and angry. How dare they think I'd had anything to do with Griff's death when I was the one who'd tried to save the sleaze's life? Despite my best efforts to explain, these guys obviously thought I had something to do with Griff's death. Having to bring up Jake hadn't improved my mood, and being linked to a murder brought back memories of my father that were too painful and too close to linger on. I pushed them away and fought the desire to crawl into bed and take a comforting nap. Instead I called Meg, only to get her voice mail.

"Hi, it's me. I just had a visit from two detectives. It seems Griff may have been poisoned and right now I'm their prime suspect. Weird, huh? Call me." I tried to keep the emotion from my voice and hoped I'd been successful.

The reality of my situation forced me to concentrate. I pulled on a pair of soft socks to warm my cold feet, then grabbed a bottle of flavored water, supposedly filled with vitamins and antioxidants, from the fridge. I drank it because

I liked the taste.

Grabbing a pen and pad from the desk, I snuggled into my rocker and closed my eyes, trying to picture the others on set when the taping of Griff's scene had started. I didn't believe in ghosts, but if Griff Kennedy's energy was still around, I telegraphed him a message: *All right Griff—in life you wanted my attention; in death you've finally got it.*

I closed my eyes and tried to separate out the blocking rehearsal from the taping, although many of the same people were present at both. Nikki Olivier had definitely arrived last when I was performing CPR. As the taping started there had been two cameramen; Frank the stage manager; Eva and Li, Hair and Makeup; Gary Knowles and two of his prop men; plus assorted stage crew I knew only by sight, including the grip who had helped me with CPR on Griff.

Ron Dowling had been in the console room offstage watching the scene unfold on a video monitor, but then I realized anyone could have given Griff poison before it took effect. Just how long would depend on which poison, information I wasn't privy to at the moment, if it was even known yet. However, it meant that all of the cast and crew, including the director and Nikki Olivier, had to be included as suspects.

This left entirely too many people to begin to narrow down for O'Malley's list. I didn't know what motives lurked behind the scenes, and there would be relationships I didn't know about since I wasn't on-set every day. How could I find out?

Detective Inspector Ned O'Malley entered the 20th Precinct on West 82nd Street, hoping to find news that something had broken on a series of recent beatings that had him puzzled. The usual smells mingled in the foyer: clandestine cigarettes, stale food and urine, and the morning's floor bleach all met his nose. He passed the bulletin board, mentally cataloging the date of the next Community Meeting. His progress was blocked by an unlikely trio: the desk sergeant, trying to keep an old woman with hair in a gray bun and a surprisingly strong left hook from using her purse to beat up a disheveled workman.

"He's the one!" she yelled. "He tried to steal my purse!" The purse in question was a cracked black plastic purse she wielded with great enthusiasm.

"Ma'am, I've been trying to tell you—this man's been here reporting a mugging. He couldn't be the same man who tried to take your purse." The sergeant's voice rang out. "Just CHILL OUT!"

The woman dropped her arm, stepping closer to scrutinize the man she was certain was her robber. "Well, I guess my guy smelled better than *him*," she reluctantly acknowledged.

Throughout the exchange, the man had cowered behind the sergeant. He had the beginnings of a black eye; dried blood from a nosebleed added to the many stains down the front of his denim shirt. He drew himself up taller. "Who are you calling smelly? This here is the scent of good hard work, and I've better things to do than try to steal your crummy handbag."

The sergeant caught Ned's eye and rolled his own.

"Having a good morning, Sarge?" Ned edged his way past the trio and made his way upstairs to the Detectives Offices. There was something to be said for leaving uniformed service behind.

He rifled through the pile of pink message slips on his desk, hoping for a break in the beatings case. Nothing. The worker downstairs seemed to have been the victim of a more routine mugging than this string of severe beatings.

The "Two-O" prided themselves on their low serious crime statistics, despite being a mixed residential and commercial area. His beat included major tourist destinations like Lincoln Center, The American Museum of Natural History and The Dakota Hotel. In the last two years, and with a population of over 96,000 culturally diverse people, the precinct had logged no murders and only two rapes, while their already-low numbers of assaults, robberies and burglaries continued to steadily drop. The largest number of complaints had been from senior citizens relating to reckless bicyclists.

All that had changed in March, with a rash of assaults on men in the area, unsolved rage beatings that ran across ethnic borders with no known connection between the victims. And now an apparent murder had been thrown into the mix, and Ned was unhappy.

It wasn't simply the matter of skewing those stats he was so proud of—he'd handled heavy crime and far too many murders when stationed in other areas of the city. By using poison, the murderer showed a cynical audacity, as though

Ned or any other detective wouldn't get to the bottom of it. Ned took this as a personal affront.

As if a murder case weren't bad enough, it had to happen in the middle of the day in front of a cluster of suspects, on a cold sound stage at a daytime soap opera. But then, would it have been better to have occurred on the hallowed stage of the Metropolitan Opera House, or at Avery Fisher Hall, where he'd once listened spellbound as Itzhak Perlman brought him close to tears? Of course not. God, what a snob he could be.

A murder was a murder, regardless of where it happened, and the victim deserved his sympathy and his attention, even if said victim was a womanizing alcoholic.

Ned loosened his tie, remembering the spare set of underwear and clean shirt he kept in his locker had been used this morning, and made a mental note to replace them. It had been a long night, going through initial statements, setting up a murder room after news had reached him that actor Griff Kennedy's death was a probable a homicide. They'd know more after today's autopsy. He'd had the studio cordoned off and today sent a forensic crew over. This morning he started his team on the background checks of the large staff and crew working on that ridiculous soap opera. He'd managed to catch a few hours rest on the leather couch in his captain's office. It was the director, Ron Dowling, who'd called his captain and insisted Trudy Genova be looked at as a suspect, mentioning the damning way Griff had pointed at her before collapsing. A copy of that tape was on its way to Ned's office.

Ned made notes for his report and thought back to Trudy Genova and how he'd sunk into the futon. He hated those flimsy excuses for a sofa. They were too low and didn't give the support a tall man needed; he'd had to try hard not to struggle getting out of it, thankful for strong quads. He'd always enjoyed his tall stature, except in instances like that, although he'd seen more than his share of dirty fridge tops and women needing touch-ups.

Ned had been surprised by the woman's apartment, expecting a modern, minimalist décor with leather sofas and sleek tables, or perhaps trendy Retro-style, all linear contempo lines from the Fifties. At the other end of the spectrum would have been a crash pad for three or more, vomiting piles of clothing and personal effects stacked in plastic bins and wash baskets, a shared situation to allow the rent in the nice building. Instead, the space was obviously Genova's alone and bore the imprint of her personality.

Her style was softer, with modern kitchen appliances, light oak and pine furniture, decorated in soft, faded colors on the walls but bright colorful splashes of color that kept it contemporary, like the quilt that covered the futon. It had a vintage bohemian feel about it. He'd scanned her Ikea bookshelves when they'd entered the room, noting the medical reference books and the preponderance of American mystery authors—Laura Lippman, Denise Lehane, Michael Connelly, Sue Grafton—with a sprinkling of UK police procedurals thrown in. A fan of crime fiction, he read many of the same authors. So she was a mystery fan who enjoyed a good puzzle. He'd heard Johnny Hartman softly singing "The Very Thought of You" when he'd arrived change to Jack Johnson's smooth vocals. A woman of eclectic tastes.

Ned liked to see his suspects in their homes. Where and how someone lived gave him clues about the owner's personality he might miss in a formal interview at the station. He was good at sizing people up and had learned to rely on his instincts, considering himself something of a problem solver, able to exercise restraint when others got carried away with their emotions. His gut told him the young woman he'd just interviewed was intelligent, if a bit scared of him.

That was natural; most people didn't have experience with the police. He had to admit he didn't see why she would need to murder someone who'd hit on her too hard and too often, and then try to save his life when she could just have taken her time and let him die. But as she'd pointed out herself, that might have been to deflect her motive, which he couldn't see right now. He'd have to learn more about Griff Kennedy to know who would have wanted him dead.

She'd definitely clammed up when she had to talk about the owner of that very nice apartment she rented. What was the real situation there, and could it have any bearing on the case? And there was that damning pronouncement from the victim at his dying moment that had to be explored.

Borelli interrupted his musing. "Jellyroll's ready for a briefing." Captain Jack Morton's nickname, derived from his fondness for doughnuts, had already been adopted by the new detective.

Ned watched Borelli suck down the first of today's many colas. He gathered his report and straightened his tie, mentally adding one more item to the list of things bothering him today. He would need to spoon-feed the new Third-Grade detective through this entire process. Mentoring a new detective meant explaining procedures he took for granted as he assessed Borelli's initiative and competence. He tapped

Borelli's soda can as he walked away. "That stuff'll rot your teeth."

I sat back and sighed. I knew for certain I was innocent and so was Meg. Big deal. There were far too many names on the list I was compiling for O'Malley.

I admit it made me anxious to be seen as a murder suspect, a new experience I wasn't enjoying one iota. I had to keep rubbing my palms on my yoga pants to dry off them off. I tamped down a rush of fear whenever I considered those two detectives looked at me as a serious suspect.

But to remove my name from that category I needed more information, and that meant getting creative. Maybe I could enlist Meg's help. There was always the chance that poking into a murder investigation might offend Meg's Puritan ethics, but I doubted it. Meg was adventurous, yet her soft demeanor meant others often bent to her wishes. If Meg would help me, I'd also have a sounding board for my thoughts as I tried to figure things out. Plus, I'd have access to the staff files if Meg were my accomplice. No, accomplice was the wrong word. I wasn't out to commit a crime; I was out to solve one and clear my name.

I tried Meg's cell phone again and this time she answered on the second ring.

"Where are you?"

"Just entering your building."

"See you in a few." How like Meg to drop by and check on me.

"I was on my way over when I got your message about the detectives," she said when I greeted her moments later. "Are they kidding? Or just interviewing everyone?"

I explained that news of Griff's pointing his finger at me, along with the pie incident, had reached their ears. This was coupled with the medical examiner's feeling Griff was poisoned.

"So what, they think because you dumped a piece of pie on the creep's head you murdered him? We need to hire you a lawyer, right now." Meg drew out her cell phone and started to scroll down, looking for a number.

My hand on Meg's stopped her. "Meg, I can't afford a lawyer, you know that. And right now I don't really need one." But I loved that my friend was upset for me. "I have to do something constructive to prove I had nothing to do with this. Otherwise, I might find myself on the wrong side of a jail cell."

Meg shuddered. "Please, don't even go there. I still say you need a good lawyer."

Instead I explained the plan I'd come up with for that afternoon and asked if she would play along, mentally crossing my fingers.

"Are you kidding? Of course, I'll do anything to help you clear yourself."

"Great! I knew I could count on you."

"But I have to think how to, without compromising my position at the studio."

I waited patiently while she tapped one tapered finger on my counter and made up her mind.

"I'll read the personnel files and then pass on anything pertinent I find. That way I can say I never let you have access to them when you shouldn't.'"

So much for forgetting the Pilgrims. "It's a deal." Now we just had to agree on what was pertinent and I had to hope Meg would recognize it when she saw it.

A subway ride later we stood at the hot dog stand on the busy corner up the block from the *Thornfield Place* studio. Wolfing down a chilidog each and sharing a diet soda, we agreed on our scheme.

Meg would go up to the office and, if questioned, say she was checking the day's mail for anything too important to be overlooked. She would glance at as many files as she could before she was stopped or had to leave, then wait for me on this same corner.

I would try to get past the guard and get downstairs to Griff's dressing room, depending on how much fast talking I could do. I needed to start there. I was still trying to decide exactly what approach to use when we reached the studio. In high school I'd always been able to get out of minor trouble with my gift of gab. Hopefully I hadn't lost my touch.

NEW YORK DAILY POST

Tuesday, May 5ᵗʰ 2008

NYC weather: Hi 63, Lo 48   Still only 50 cents!

LEGEND SLIPS FATALLY ON SOAP!

Attempts to resuscitate soap opera legend Griff Kennedy failed after he collapsed while taping an episode of *Thornfield Place*. Kennedy, whose exact age is unknown at this time, was filming a hospital scene when he dramatically fell to the floor, prompting one observer to think he was ad-libbing the planned scene.

A nurse and a grip initiated CPR before paramedics arrived. Kennedy was ultimately pronounced dead on arrival at St Luke's-Roosevelt Hospital Center.

Photos, story page 3
Obituary, pg. 56

Yanks-White Sox: pg. 23 ‖ Headless Body in Topless Club!

M.K. GRAFF

CHAPTER SEVEN

Borelli slapped a newspaper open on Ned's desk. "Check this out."

Ned scanned the front page and turned to page three, where a studio shot at least fifteen years old of Griff Kennedy took up a quarter of the page. The actor's smile was as artificial as his teeth, though at that time he had nary a hair plug in sight. An insert in the upper right corner showed Nikki Olivier, wearing dark glasses and a shawl, ducking into her limousine last night. The caption at the bottom read: *Nikki's Lost Love— End of an Era at Thornfield Place?*

Ned read aloud, "'Longtime paramour, sometime wife, *TP* star Nikki Olivier was visibly shaken as she was bundled into her limo after the sudden death of Griff Kennedy. The two had a steamy alliance that survived two marriages over the last eighteen years. One staff member called them 'the Liz Taylor and Richard Burton of soaps.'

"'Kennedy was a native New Yorker . . .'" Ned slapped the paper shut. "I've read enough—'exact age unknown.' Let's see what the CSI's have turned up in Kennedy's dressing room. Jellyroll said the chief's already had a pressure call from some PBJ exec about opening the studio to let taping continue."

"How can they keep taping with the male star dead?" Borelli

asked.

"I imagine they'll write his death into the script. Can you picture their ratings on the day that show airs, especially if they use real footage of him collapsing?" Ned shook his head disdainfully.

"Would they do that? Wouldn't his family object?" Borelli followed his boss from the squad room. "Can we stop at Starbuck's on the way?"

Ned paused on the front stoop to look at Borelli over the rim of his sunglasses. "Yes, don't know if he has any, and only if there's parking on the corner."

An eerie silence greeted us inside the brick studio. Yellow crime scene tape stretched across the sound stage door, bringing with it the reality of Griff's death. The desk was unmanned though, and I shrugged my shoulders as Meg pointed up and quietly mounted the stairs.

I couldn't believe my luck and started down the stairs, only to hear voices coming towards me. I tried to act as though I belonged there, and nodded briskly at two white-suited CSI's ripping off gloves as they passed me, both carrying battered equipment cases. They went upstairs without comment.

After exhaling my breath, I scurried across the U-5 waiting room and turned right. Dressing rooms lined both sides of the hall, which turned left and then left again, making a square around the central Hair and Makeup Room. Wardrobe stood off in one corner behind the rehearsal hall on the fourth wall. Torn crime scene tape dangled from Griff's doorknob.

I drew on the gloves I'd shoved in my jacket pocket and put them on. The knob turned easily, and with a hasty glance over my shoulder, I ducked inside, closing the door quietly behind me. Safe.

"Miss Genova, what a surprise." O'Malley's sarcasm was pointed. Borelli just looked startled.

I blushed furiously, something I'd never been able to control once it started, and let loose with a curse under my breath. Damn. So much for slipping in unseen.

Ned moved Trudy Genova to the U-5 lobby and stood towering over her while Borelli paced the small area.

"There wasn't anyone at the desk," she protested from the folding chair he'd insisted she occupy. She sat with her arms folded across her chest, her anger apparent in her scowl.

At Ned's nod, Borelli put his coffee cup down and ran up the stairs.

"This is absurd, you know that?" She sat forward and used her hands when she spoke. "I tried to save the man's life and you keep treating me like some kind of suspect."

O'Malley ignored her protests. "Do you mind telling me what you were looking for in Griff Kennedy's dressing room?"

Ned watched the color rise again in the woman's face as she looked down at the dirty Berber carpet, bringing his attention to a few freckles scattered across her nose.

"Do you think I was looking for an autographed photo? I was looking for clues to who might have wanted to poison Griff. " She'd opted for righteous indignation.

They heard voices from the main floor in discussion while Ned thought she might have muttered "idiot" under her breath. Let her fuss; he'd been called worse in his career.

Borelli jogged down. "The guard was in the john," he said, adding: "He said he heard noises upstairs so I went up. A secretary came in to go through the mail. I gave her five minutes to check it out and leave."

Ned nodded. Hearing a breath escape Genova, he turned his attention back to her with what he hoped was the same stern face his father made when he was a boy.

She burst out: "If you must know, Detectives, I was hoping to discover evidence as to who murdered him, since you seem to think I'm a likely suspect—and I don't appreciate it one bit. Arghh! This is so damn frustrating."

Borelli reached for his Starbucks cup, muttering "Freakin' Nancy Drew . . . "

Ned silenced him with a look. "Don't you think you should leave investigating to the professionals, Miss Genova?"

She slid to the edge of her seat and looked up at him. "Trudy—Miss Genova is my aunt. Stop being so smug. And can't you please sit down? You're giving me a crick in my neck."

Borelli choked on his coffee. Ned sat down next to her. Apparently his angry expression hadn't gotten the message through. He leaned forward, narrowing his eyes to his best felon-menacing glare. "All right, *Trudy,*" he said in a low, cold voice. "I would like to point out you're the one giving me a pain and it isn't in my neck." His voice rose significantly. "What exactly were you planning back there?"

"I *told* you, I was going to look for clues, maybe letters from someone who was blackmailing Griff, or had a grudge against him."

"Oh, Jeez-" Borelli said.

"Look, you need me," she insisted. "Let me help you. I've worked with these people for a few years. They'll talk to me in a way they won't talk to you, let their guard down—" She was cut off by the tone of Ned's cell phone.

It was the medical examiner's office. "Yes, we'll be there." Ned stood, snapped the phone shut and consulted his watch.

"We have to go," he told Borelli. He scowled and looked down again at the Genova woman, loosening his tie in frustration. "I advise you to stop playing amateur detective and leave this to us. We've seen the tape of Griff Kennedy using his dying breath to point his finger at you. You *are* under suspicion and I could arrest you for trespassing or compromising a crime scene." Ned pointed upstairs and she led the way.

He watched her leave the studio and saw her glance back over her shoulder when she hit the pavement. When she met his look, she flashed her fingers at him, turning what he thought started out as a middle finger salute into a wave.

Ned sighed as Borelli signed them out on the log. Genova was lucky her background check was totally clean or he would have taken her in already. He didn't think Trudy Genova realized how seriously he took his job, nor how bad things looked for her. He spoke to the desk guard.

"Did the secretary upstairs leave?" Ned asked.

"A minute ago." The guard consulted the log. "I had her sign in and out, a Miss Meg Pitman."

The detectives walked to their car, parked across the street in a loading zone for the Passion Broadcasting Junction building. Looking up the street toward Broadway, Ned saw Trudy Genova at the corner, waiting for the light to change, in heated discussion with a slender blonde. "Tony, do you recognize that woman with Genova?"

Borelli stuck his head out the car window. "Sure, I just met her. Cute, huh? That's the Pitman woman who works upstairs. She was there checking the mail—"

Ned slammed his door. "Checking the mail, my ass."

CHAPTER EIGHT

The distinctive bass of Pink Floyd's "Money" accompanied Byron Burknikoff, who sang the lyrics softly as he adjusted his mask and nodded to his morgue assistant, the diener, to remove Griff Kennedy's liver for weighing before taking slices for microscopic examination. Born in Russia, Byron carried traces of his native accent, which became exaggerated if someone tried to call him "Ronnie" or "Ron." His bulky frame was frightening to most people, but Ned O'Malley had worked with Byron for almost three years now and knew him to be a teddy bear with a practical joker streak. Ned had also become accustomed to the medical examiner's hearty demeanor when working, his appreciation for classic rock, and his ability to eat immediately before or after carving up a human body. But he knew Byron was respectful of the bodies he autopsied, especially children, handling them with a delicacy few seeing his large hands could imagine.

Byron's skills were lost on Borelli, who stood back from the table, sucking down Ned's mints, one after another, in what Ned knew was a futile attempt to stave off the acrid smells of the autopsy room, an unfortunate mix of antiseptic and rank bodily fluids. Ned preferred globs of Vick's Vaporub in each nostril to combat the odors, but Borelli had refused, saying it stung too much. Both men wore yellow paper gowns over their clothing.

"A bit fatty and swollen, with expected cirrhotic changes based on his alcohol intake," Byron told the detectives, pointing to the liver. "You said he was filming a medical scene—I don't suppose there's a rat's bum chance they did any real cardiac monitoring strips?"

"Ass," Ned corrected. "Rat's ass is the saying, Byron. I don't think so, I'll check with the nurse who was there."

A loud burp issued from Borelli. "Sorry."

Ned stood within the bright circle from the overhead light, peering down into the abdominal cavity of what had once been a breathing, thinking human. The interior of the body never ceased to fill him with awe, with its kaleidoscope of bright colors and fetid odors, organs crammed up against each other, laced with the network of blue veins and red arteries that fed and nourished each organ for its distinct function.

"When will you have those toxicology reports, Byron?" Ned asked.

The ME probed Griff's spleen before handing it to his diener, a quiet young man who seemed awed by Byron but worked competently. "Probably by tomorrow. I put on the priority rush. The heart failure could be consistent with aging and his heavy smoking, but no signs of recent infarction. I'm waiting on the serum cardiac glycoside levels, and of course, the ocular glycoside levels will tell us a good story."

"Ocular, as in eyes?" Borelli asked, cracking his mint and chewing furiously.

There was a clang and a muttered Russian oath as the

ME misjudged his size yet again, banging into a metal stand, setting his instruments rattling. His diener competently steadied the tray. "Good, young one, we teach you something yet. Yes, we take a needle and insert it into the eye—"

Ned saw Byron glance up over his mask to watch Borelli cringe and lose even more color in his face before he continued. "You remember I pointed out his thyroid was enlarged?"

"Oh yeah," Borelli said, popping in two mints at one time and sucking hard.

"And the bright red venous blood we see here is oxygenated, blocked in going to the cell tissues, all signs of glycoside poisoning. This man's medical history doesn't include prescribed digitalis, so unless he committed suicide by taking large doses of someone else's heart pills, he ingested a heavy amount of glycosides at his last meal, in this case, lunch. The contents are being analyzed but there were few solids, mostly liquids, which were largely dispersed."

"So I would be looking for someone in the studio who took or had access to digitalis?" Ned confirmed, jotting notes. "Could it be administered through eye drops?"

"Only if the quantity were large enough, but if there were plants, then of course through his drink," Byron said, probing the small intestine as though it were a length of sausage.

"Plants?" Borelli asked, followed quickly by Ned: "Which ones?"

"Let us think," Byron said, and Ned knew if not for the gloves, the big man would be thoughtfully pulling on his goatee, combing it with his fingers. "You have the digitalis plant, which is foxglove, of course, but these cardiac glycosides are also found in oleander, common and yellow, lily of the valley, and wallflower. Unless you have the venom gland of a cane toad, *Bufo marinus,* which contains it in a large quantity. I'm assuming there wasn't a cane toad at this studio?" He looked at the two detectives with raised eyebrows and the hint of a smile over his mask. "Were there any flowers around?"

"Hell yeah," said Borelli, cracking his mints and chewing vigorously.

"Too numerous to count, as you say, Byron," said Ned. He snapped his notebook shut, tucking it in his jacket pocket.

"Good!" The medical examiner beamed. "Of course, not so good for this gentleman, but good for you when you're looking for who murdered him. Now all you have to do is find out which of those flowers were there, and who had access to them."

"I saw pink oleander, not yellow, in a big bucket on that cottage set. I recognized it because my grandma used to grow it in her yard in Virginia," offered Borelli.

"I thought your grandmother was in Italy, Borelli," said Ned.

Borelli launched into an explanation. "That's my father's mother, but my mother's mother lived in Virginia and every summer—"

"Enough." Ned held up one hand. "I'm not really interested in your family's gardening habits." He tore off the paper gown he wore over his suit. "There were two vases of lily of the valley on the mantel in a living room set and another on a night-stand in the hospital room set."

"There you go," Bryon said. "All of its parts are toxic, especially the leaves, and even the water in which the cut flowers are kept. Now, who had access to these?"

O'Malley and Borelli said in unison: "Everyone."

When Ned and Borelli returned to the precinct, Ned handed Borelli a policy and procedure manual the new detective had to finish reading and sign off on. Ned busied himself reading reports and updating the murder room white board. When the phone rang, he instructed his younger partner to answer it on speakerphone in case it was for him.

"Oh, Detective Borelli—just who I was looking for. This is Meg Pitman. We met at the studio this afternoon when I came in for the mail—?"

"Of course. What can I do for you, Miss Pitman?" Borelli raised his eyebrows.

Ned made gathering motions, indicating Borelli should keep up his end of the conversation. What the hell was the Pitman woman doing calling Borelli?

"I was wondering if we could meet tomorrow, before work. I wanted to talk to you about Griff Kennedy. You said when you gave me your card to call if I thought of anything, but I don't really want to talk over the phone. I'd rather talk in private."

"Talk in private?" Ned nodded to urge Borelli on. "Sure . . . where did you have in mind?"

Pitman's voice echoed with a tinny sound. "There's a coffee shop on Columbus right around the corner from the studio that has great coffee and muffins. Next to the Folk Art Museum. Say 8:30?"

"I'll be there."

The phone disconnected. Ned had never seen an Italian blush, if that's what you would call the dusky flush that had spread over Borelli's face and neck.

"What do you suppose that's all about?" Borelli picked up the policy book and studied the first page.

"I don't know, Borelli, but that's what you're going to find out."

CHAPTER NINE

Thursday, May 6ᵗʰ

I watched Tony Borelli enter the EuroPan Bakery and Café and inhale the heady scents of just-baked danishes, muffins and pastries, along with freshly brewed coffees. He must be in heaven. I turned around quickly, making sure he didn't see me sitting in a corner, half hidden by a coat rack. With my hair tucked up under a baseball cap and my back to his, I doubted the detective would recognize me in the crowded shop. Meg would wave to him when she caught his eye. She was seated at the table behind me that she'd taken ten minutes earlier, a latte and orange muffin already in front of her.

From behind the hand over my face, I saw Borelli return the wave and wait in line at the bustling counter, crowded with businessmen and women and a few employees of the American Museum of Folk Art next door. With Meg getting her own meal, we'd resolved any question of Borelli buying her breakfast. I hoped the detective had spent his evening fantasizing about the pretty blonde after Meg's phone call.

"Good morning, Miss Pitman," he said, setting down his

coffee. It's scent reached me: mocha java, grande, no doubt. With our backs together I could hear him just fine. "I have no idea what this muffin is, but it's supposed to be healthy."

I pictured him beaming a generous smile to Meg.

"Please call me Meg—Miss Pitman's so formal. That muffin's called Morning Glory, filled with sunflower seeds. Your mother would be proud."

Way to go, Meg. I imagined her light brown eyes, large and trusting, twinkling at him.

"All right, Meg, what can I do for you?"

Meg's slight hesitation was spot on. "It's probably nothing important . . . but with a suspicious death like Griff's—"

"Who said it was suspicious?"

Uh-oh, Meggie, watch out.

"It was all over the studio gossip line," she hastened to assure him. "I had three calls last night about it. Soap operas are a closed community—the gossip mill works day and night."

Borelli slurped his coffee. "Let's say the ME is awaiting some test results."

"Oh, I understand you can't reveal information. I just thought you'd want to know the gossip about Griff's personal life. They say where there's smoke, there's fire, and Griff was stoking the embers an awful lot. You know he hit on Trudy, but that was the tip of his iceberg, so to speak."

Good girl. I could picture Meg smiling, her teeth even and white. The detective seemed to be chewing. I'd bet he was trying to decide what O'Malley would want him to do. Go for it, Borelli, I silently urged.

"OK, I'm listening. Let's hear what the goldfish bowl has to say about Griff Kennedy."

The crime scene tape had been removed from the sound stage when I arrived, but I imagined it still closed off Griff's dressing room. It was hushed and quiet when I entered and signed in. I nodded to the regular guard, who handed me a sticky ID badge. Clamping down on security was a good thing after what had happened, I guess. I stowed my backpack at the lockers outside the bathrooms, then went downstairs and walked a circuit around the dressing rooms to give Meg time to arrive.

When I crept up to the second floor open-plan office, the usual office pandemonium was absent. Staffers walked around quietly, as if Griff's ghost was watching them. Meg was at her desk, squirting a glob of cream into one hand. She waved me over and handed me the tube.

"He took the bait," I affirmed, sniffing appreciatively as I helped myself to the cream. Meg always smelled good and today's lavender stuff was no exception.

Meg nodded, shoving the tube in a drawer. "I had one bad moment when he wondered how I knew Griff's death was suspicious—"

"I know, I could hear pretty well, but I thought you recovered nicely."

"It's true this morning, too. You should hear the whispering going on. So I just feel a teensy bit guilty."

Those damn Puritans again. I waved to one of the associate producers passing by and picked up a script, pretending to be consulting it as I spoke to Meg.

"Yes, I know about that change." I dropped my voice as he walked away. "The point is, did you learn anything useful for us? I had to give up my table to a foursome."

"I saw you leave by the other door." Meg sighed as she worked the cream around her cuticles. "Afraid not. He was good at asking questions but not at answering them. I gave him the usual chat about Griff that everyone will tell them. However, all's not lost."

"Give." I returned the script to Meg.

"He told me in-depth interviews are today, and I convinced him to make mine over lunch at the cafeteria. His mother is a big fan of the King and Kiley show. I said we might score her an autograph." Meg sat back with a smug smile.

"King and Kiley usually hightail it out of their studio by ten-thirty after taping. It was a fluke we saw King on Monday."

"I know that, but Tony Borelli doesn't."

"ATTENTION PLEASE!" Frank Resnicks's piercing voice gave new meaning to his title of Stage Manager. The loudspeaker system, used to call crew and cast alike and piped into every office, workroom, and dressing room, had been turned up. Frank reminded me of Radar from M*A*S*H, which my brothers watched in reruns until they could recite the lines. "All cast and crew, be on the sound stage at 10 AM sharp for NYPD. Yes, this means you."

"Let's go," I said. "I need to hit the Ladies first and want to hear what's being said in the underground, and see how Ned-O handles Director Himself."

"Save me a seat, I have to finish sorting the mail first," Meg said. "And I wouldn't let O'Malley catch you calling him that," she cautioned. "I can handle Borelli; not sure I'd like to tackle his boss from what you said. This is serious, Trudy."

Taking off my cap, I loosened my hair. "Piece of cake, my dear." I just wished I felt as secure as I managed to sound.

Griff's hospital room set was still blocked with crime tape, a grim reminder of his death, so the largest open space was a restaurant set that was up for Friday's taping. Small dining tables had been pushed back into corners to fit in three rows of folding chairs, set in a semi-circle to accommodate the employees crowded in. By an unspoken hierarchy, Nikki Olivier, Misty Raines, Reece Hunter and Ron Dowling filled the front row, sitting alongside the production bosses and writers who were usually closeted on the third floor. The rest filled the next rows, where I headed to save a seat for Meg, and tried to tamp down my growing anxiety.

I'd been afraid I was the topic of discussion after Griff's pointing finger. A few people nodded but no one engaged me in the usual banter. Another thing to thank O'Malley for, putting me under the microscope, but I suppose while no one here would know he and Borelli had been to my apartment, they sure knew Griff was dead and they'd all seen him point at me. I'd just have to soldier on and hold my head high, as my mother had told me that day in second grade I'd forgotten my gym shorts but hadn't remembered until I'd taken my skirt

When I sat down, I realized the heated discussion in process was about abortion, avoiding the real reason we were here. Today's debate centered on one of the show's current story lines. A few weeks ago, Nikki's character, Vikki Starr, discovered one of her twin daughters had undergone an abortion, but neither girl would own up to it. This idea had provoked several discussions recently when there were lulls in the action.

"It's a woman's body and a woman's right to choose," Misty Raines declared. Hair Gal Eva nodded vigorously in agreement.

"It goes against the laws of nature," Prop Master Gary Knowles argued. Several older grips sided with him.

"I don't know if I could ever have one," Li, the makeup gal said, throwing in her two cents opinion. "But I would want to have that option available to me."

"If a baby isn't wanted why can't it be given away for adoption?" Frank asked. "There are many people out there who would love to raise a child as their own."

Edith in Wardrobe nodded in assent. The producers stayed out of the discussion entirely, consulting their phones and checking emails instead.

One of the production assistants timidly raised her hand, then quickly lowered it and spoke. "I think the mother should keep her nose out of her daughter's business. The twins are supposed to be almost eighteen." For this pronouncement the girl received a host of withering glances from the writers, all looking behind them to see who could possibly be questioning their storyline.

M.K. GRAFF

I heard a giggle I recognized and turned to see Borelli holding the door for Meg, who was certainly overdoing it. Just what had been said after I left the coffee shop? I patted the seat beside me and Meg sat down, smiling at Borelli as he walked past and up to the front of the assembly. O'Malley stayed by the door holding clipboards and I swear I could feel his eyes boring into my back. Frank Resnick stood up and the two men spoke quietly for a moment, then Frank nodded to the head producer, A. J. Egan, who rose and turned to the audience.

"Thank you all for meeting here. This is a tragic time for *Thornfield Place* and I know you are interested to learn how we are expected to carry on with the loss of one of our stars. Such loss affects us all, some more than others, but we'll never forget . . . "

Egan's listing of Griff Kennedy's attributes were drowned out by loud sobbing from Nikki, a bit too theatrical from my point of view. Ron Dowling comforted Nikki, arm around her shoulders, rubbing up and down soothingly. Misty Raines' quieter tears were muffled by tucking her head into Reece Hunter's side, but her grief seemed more genuine.

" . . . and will always remain in our hearts." Egan wrapped up. "Details of a memorial service have not been confirmed yet as the, um, remains have not been released, but I will certainly keep you all informed. Now Detective Anthony Borelli will speak to you about today's schedule."

Meg sat up straighter as Borelli took center stage. I dug my elbow into Meg's side. "You don't have to fall all over the guy, Meg. He'll get suspicious you're just pumping him for information."

DEATH UNSCRIPTED

"But I am, Trudy, remember? Your idea. Besides, he's cute and he has these great hazel eyes that shine when he smiles."

"No-o-o, Meg," I wailed under her breath. "He's supposed to fall for you, not the other way around. We need to pick his brain on the investigation."

Meg's eyes widened. "I see no problem there at all."

We were shushed to silence by Li, the makeup gal whose real first name was unpronounceable. O'Malley made his way to Borelli's side as the junior detective continued.

"Members of our team will be here and across the street all day. Everyone will be asked to give their fingerprints for elimination purposes. I've been told after the perpetrator is caught these will be destroyed. Please sign up for a session during your down time, and hopefully we'll blend our work in with yours with the least amount of disruption." Borelli ended with a boyish smile and Eva clapped for him. O'Malley frowned in annoyance. Meg managed to restrain herself after I shot her a glare.

Frank stood again. "Any questions?"

"How are you going to handle Griff's death in the script?" Nikki asked, her voice shaky. Frank turned to Egan for the answer.

"Our wonderful writing team is working on that today and will adjust the script to follow the tragic event. Of course, we'll add a funeral scene, but we don't expect to tape that until next Monday."

A collective groan rippled through the audience. Funeral and wedding scenes were long, tedious days for all, sorting out gowns and flowers, to say nothing of the entire cast being required for such scenes. The older child actors would be called in, and the director and writers would spend hours on who would sit where in the chapel set, and what kind of commotion would occur. I suspected that since Griff was actually dead, they might tone this down. Still, all of the hallmarks of a real funeral would be replicated without a body in the coffin, except in this case, a real one had caused it. A shudder ran through me at the thought.

Ron Dowling stood next and addressed his remarks to the first row. "My dears, this has been a terrible ordeal for us all, but we must remember we have an audience who welcomes us into their homes five days a week and they crave the next installment of life in *Thornfield Place*. We must hold our heads up high and call on our professionalism." He consulted his notes. "Today we will continue with the rest of the subplot scenes as slated while the writers do their magic. So wipe your tears, and we'll start blocking Scene 3, Savannah's bedroom and terrace, in fifteen minutes."

"I was waiting for him to say the show must go on," I whispered to Meg. We took our places in line as people shuffled to the door. O'Malley stood with Borelli, each holding clipboards and signing people up for interviews. I decided magnanimously that O'Malley had been doing his job yesterday and determined I wasn't going to hold his negative attitude against him.

"Who gets us?" I asked when it was our turn, trying to see O'Malley's clipboard.

"I have Miss Pitman down for lunch time today," Borelli answered, consulting his clipboard without looking up.

"That leaves me for you at some point, O'Malley," I told the detective. If I provoked him, he hid it well.

DEATH UNSCRIPTED

"What are your duties for today?" he asked, consulting his openings. "I'm very interested in having a more in-depth talk with you, Miss Genova." The look he gave me was steely and direct.

My insides clenched. "I have to talk to the writers, see what they decide so I know when I'm needed. I'm guessing they'll have a scene with everyone in the waiting room, and then have Nikki rushing in after she hears of Griff's death."

He nodded. "I'm seeing Nikki Olivier right now. Look for me when you're done upstairs before I go to Misty Raines or Reece Hunter."

"Or, I could go with you to help soften them up for you." I raised one eyebrow in question. I needed to get on this guy's good side, show him I was a team player.

For answer, O'Malley frowned and opened his jacket to display the badge he wore next to his gun. "Not until you earn one of these."

"Oh, that? I got one of those in my Cheerios box years ago." I shot him a flinty look and walked out the door without looking back.

CHAPTER TEN

After talking to the writers, I walked downstairs with Misty Raines. One current story line had her character, Savannah Dale, fighting to keep nude photographs out of the local tabloids, which would ruin her chances of marrying Reece's character, Bryce Kenyon, the wealthy heir to *Thornfield Place's* fortune. The next scene to be taped had her arguing with the "photographer," a swarthy U-5 named Pete. I suspected Pete had enjoyed a nice lunch with Misty before getting this minor role.

"Big scene coming up for you, Misty," I noted.

"Sugar, I can do these in my sleep."

I decided Misty pumped up the volume on her southern accent at will. We stopped outside her dressing room; I heard coughing coming from inside it. The U-5 waiting?

"See you, Trudy." Misty dismissed me, opening the door and slipping inside, leaving behind a whiff of heavy floral perfume.

I caught a glimpse of a man's arm and then the door was shut. It looked like Misty was going to have some help working up a head of steam for her big scene.

O'Malley was just down the hall, standing outside Nikki's

dressing room, looking back through his notebook.

"Done already in there?" I asked.

He started to look past me but then grimaced. "Haven't even started. She felt faint and had to lie down, but as soon as I'd gone down the hall I think she went into the shower. I thought you had to wait upstairs?"

"The head writer came out after only a few minutes and said they wouldn't need me today. But there is some good news." I smiled brightly.

"I can't wait to hear what you term good news, Miss Genova."

"*Trudy.*" This detective could sure get under my skin, but I plowed on. "They need me to baby wrangle tomorrow." I explained child actors required a nurse when they worked. "Parents have to wait in the dressing room; I take them up on set and make sure they get breaks, and that they don't get hurt in any way."

O'Malley nodded, glancing at his watch. I sensed his impatience; he had too much to do to wait on the hysterics of Nikki Olivier. "This is ridiculous."

An idea occurred to me to ingratiate myself to O'Malley. "I'll be right back. Wait here."

Ned watched Trudy Genova walk quickly back up the hall. He'd feel badly if he had to arrest the woman. Despite being a suspect, she worked hard at being engaging. He was surprised at how the cast had taken Griff's death in stride and seemed ready to plunge back into work. Maybe Griff Kennedy had more enemies than he'd first thought and the nurse was only one of many suspects. That remained to be seen.

He finished making a note and a minute later Genova returned, carrying a steaming mug in one hand. The other held an ammonia inhaler, which she showed to him, then pocketed. She knocked on Nikki's door.

"Miss Nikki? It's Trudy. I heard you were faint and brought you some herbal tea, just the way you like it." She whispered to Ned: "When she opens up follow me in."

The door opened and Trudy proffered the tea, stepping into the dressing room, talking the entire time. "Here you go, thought you might need this. Would you like me to stay while you talk to the detective, in case you get faint again?" Trudy rested her hand briefly on the woman's shoulder.

Ned opened his mouth to protest but shut it again when Nikki waved them in and shut the door. Her hair was wrapped in a towel, confirming Ned's suspicion that while she hadn't been ready to be interviewed she *had* managed to summon up the strength for a shower. He watched her slurp from the mug, then sink down onto a small leather couch. Trudy motioned him to the dressing table chair.

"Feeling better?" Trudy was the height of solicitation, sitting beside Nikki and patting her knee.

The room's scent was overpowering from a huge arrangement of white freesias and yellow roses standing on the floor. Without makeup, the lines on Nikki's face and its uneven coloring were apparent, the bags under her eyes swollen.

DEATH UNSCRIPTED

"A bit," Nikki said, making the most of sipping from the mug. Ned used the opportunity to look around the small room. Next to the loveseat sat a side table and a closet door. On the opposite wall hung five pictures of the actor holding her Daytime Emmys, hugging Griff Kennedy in three of them, speaking volumes to the wavering nature of their relationship. The dressing table ran against the back wall, its top littered with the contents of a huge makeup case, the area lit on three sides with garish globes. One small drawer stood open, a tangle of bright silk scarves on view. Actress camouflage, Ned thought, then corrected his thought. "Actress" was old school—women preferred to be called by the generic "actor" these days.

Trudy caught his eye and gestured for him to begin.

"We met yesterday. I'm Detective O'Malley, Miss Oliver," he began, only to be stopped immediately by the harsh intake of Nikki's breath.

She drew herself up to the edge of the sofa, threw her shoulders back and announced: "*Olivier*, Detective."

"As in the great Lawrence of the English Theater," Trudy explained. She widened her eyes and he translated her look to mean: "Don't screw up this opportunity I've handed you."

"Yes, of course, Miss Olivier," he said, trying hard not to stress all four syllables. "I understand you've known Mr. Kennedy for many years and were married at one time. How would you describe your relationship at this point?"

Even without makeup, the actor used body language to reveal expression. She arched her eyebrows and tilted her head in amusement.

"We were lovers, Detective O'Malley, after being married

in the 80's and divorced in the 90's—a few times. We had a need to be part of each other's lives, and so kept an open flow. Even when we occasionally saw other people, we remained close. We do—did—live separately. But we were considering reconciliation. Does that satisfy your question?" She lowered her chin demurely.

"Yes, fine. I need to know your movements Tuesday. Let's start with the morning."

Nikki took him through her morning at home and arrival at the studio by limousine, the rehearsal downstairs, then the blocking on set. She paused to sip her tea.

"And lunch that day, where did you eat?" Ned asked.

"Why, where I always do, Detective, right here in my dressing room. One gets so tired of trying to combat the autograph hounds and thrill seekers lurking outside the studio. I do that at public appearances and Emmy night, of course. Frank runs across and brings me a salad or something equally vulgar to keep my strength up."

Ned resisted pointing out these same fans gave her show the ratings that kept her employed. "And did you see Mr. Kennedy at lunch time?"

At the mention of his name, she handed Trudy her mug and groped for a tissue in her pocket, dabbing at dry eyes. "I stopped by his dressing room briefly to wish him luck on his big scene when he got back from the cafeteria. He could be very tense before a dramatic scene like that."

Ned read the subtext: *As opposed to me, used to being the focus of big scenes.* He noticed Trudy squirm and realized the woman hadn't mentioned the pie incident. Perhaps Griff had kept the news from Nikki that Trudy had dumped pie on his head.

It would hardly endear him to her if they were thinking of reconciling. He asked, "Was anyone with him then, or did you see anyone entering or leaving?"

"No, he was alone. We only spoke for a minute. I had to have my hair and makeup done for my own scenes."

Trudy spoke up. "Miss Nikki?" She ignored Ned shaking his head to warn her off. "Did you notice Griff's special cup?"

"What special cup?" he asked.

Now real tears spouted from Nikki's eyes. "His Emmy cup, one of those stupid plastic jugs with a long straw. He's used it since he hosted two years ago, kept it filled with fluids to hydrate, drank from it all day."

Ned hadn't seen any jug or cup in the actor's dressing room, but his interest had roused Nikki Olivier's own.

"Why are you asking about that ridiculous cup?"

"We're trying to establish what Mr. Kennedy had to eat and drink that day," Ned answered carefully.

"Do you think something he ate made him sick?" The actress appeared puzzled, then thoughtful, her reddened eyes meeting Ned's. "Oh, no! The gossip was right—you think Griff was poisoned!"

Nikki started to gasp for breath. Trudy reached immediately for the ammonia inhaler. Waving it front of the actor was enough to settle her down.

"Put that thing away—I hate it!" she announced, narrowing her eyes and looking critically at Ned. "I'm right, aren't I?" she challenged.

"I'm afraid we're still waiting for the toxicology test results, Miss Olivier, but all bases have to be covered." The ringing of his cell phone saved him from further questions. "Excuse me."

He took the call outside the door, aware that Trudy had stood up. While he waited to be connected, he heard her tell the actress: "I'll see what's up."

It was the ME. "It's what we thought, Ned."

After a brief discussion with Byron Burknikoff, Ned thrust his head back inside the dressing room as Trudy was stepping outside. "That's all for today, thank you ma'am." He hurried down the hall, Trudy two steps behind him.

"Wait up! What's happened?" She touched his shoulder.

Ned hesitated. She was a civilian, after all, and still a suspect.

"Look, I got you in there, and without me you wouldn't have known about Griff's cup, which I realized when we were talking to Nikki might be the way the poison was administered." Trudy persisted. "C'mon, O'Malley, we had a deal."

"No deals," he said. There was a beat of silence. He met Trudy's gaze, unwavering and open in expectation. Ned looked around, then hissed quietly: "Tox is positive for glycosides, but not in the eye drops," before heading up the stairs. No harm done; it would be common knowledge soon enough when their interviews took a harder turn. Trudy followed him up the stairs. He stopped to ask the guard where Borelli could be found.

"On the sound stage," the guard answered.

Ned ignored Trudy as they passed through the stage door, aware she kept a few paces behind him as he passed several unlit sets, nearing the living room set. He slowed as voices reached them, then motioned for Trudy to hang back. They stopped in the shadows and listened to Borelli wrap up his interview with the stage manager.

Borelli sat on a sofa, stage manager Frank Resnick opposite him in a brocaded wing chair, his feet propped up on an ottoman. The young man had broad cheekbones, his dark-rimmed Geek Squad glasses a contrast to his pale coloring and flaxen hair. Ned knew his trendy casual clothes were understated but expensive. He listened as Borelli interviewed the young man.

"These multiple women you say Griff was involved with, who would that mean in particular at the moment?" Borelli said.

"You mean besides his ex-wife and whomever he hadn't already gotten to in the extras? He had a thing for the nurse, Trudy Genova, but he really pissed her off. And Misty Raines seemed pretty close to him lately . . . "

"That sounds like speculation, Mr. Resnick. You've worked with Mr. Kennedy for how long?"

"Three years at *Thornfield Place*, but I've spent five total in soaps. I'm actually taking directing courses and one of these days you'll see me giving the orders instead of taking them."

Ned deemed the gist of the interview was over and walked onto the set, Trudy right behind him. On the mantel were two vases of lily of the valley on either side of an elaborate clock, their sweet scent permeating the space.

"Borelli!" he barked. "Stop what you're doing and get those vases collected into evidence, then go to the hospital set and do the same with the one there, water included. And then get a search organized for a cup Griff Kennedy carried around." He gave him a run down on Griff's Emmy cup.

Borelli left to get evidence bags and call the precinct. Ned scrutinized Resnick.

"You have no idea why I want those if anyone asks you," Ned said, the merest hint of threat in his voice. He was annoyed they hadn't been collected yesterday when he'd given that order. Was this Borelli's screw up or someone else's?

The stage manager stood, hands thrust into his pockets. "And I don't want to know," he said, sauntering off into the darkness.

"What do we do next?" Trudy asked.

In his annoyance he'd almost forgotten she was there. "*We* don't do anything next. You're done here for today, aren't you?"

Trudy looked crestfallen; Ned could feel her trying to manufacture a reason to stick around. "Sit," he said, pointing to the sofa. He sat in the chair, still warm from Frank Resnick. Better to have this out with her now than have her trailing him around.

Trudy sat. "You're almost as melodramatic as Nikki," she ventured. "Look, I know you think I shouldn't get involved, but you're missing the point. I *am* involved. Griff pointed to me with his dying breath, it's *me* who's a suspect to everyone around here and to you, even if you don't have evidence. And he was my patient, sort of. I have a right to be involved, if only to clear myself." She paused for breath, leaning forward with a pleading expression.

Ned ran his hand over his hair, shaking his head. "Now who's being melodramatic? I let you coerce me into staying with Oliver before—"

"*Olivier*," she interjected. "It matters to her. She's convinced she's an unacknowledged relation of Lawrence . . ."

DEATH UNSCRIPTED

"You see, that's what an amateur does. You're getting all hung up on names when evidence is what matters. I appreciate your help with her, but I can't condone you sticking your nose into—"

Trudy stood up abruptly, her neck reddening. "You don't get it, do you? This is a world you don't know. It's just a name to you, but to her it's who she is, or maybe who she needs to be." She pointed a finger at him. "You're going to antagonize these people and not get the evidence you want because you don't know this world or how these people function in it. *I do.* You need me and you're either too proud or too obtuse to acknowledge it. I think you're a snob."

Trudy turned on her heel and stomped away, narrowly missing a lighting cable running across the floor, but turning the stumble into a graceful leap across it. The heavy sound stage door slammed behind her back.

Ned stayed in his chair, musing over what Trudy had said. There might be a kernel of truth in her position, but he couldn't allow a civilian to get closely involved in a criminal investigation. As it was, he'd given away more than he should have. And what was that all about, letting her listen in to Borelli's interview? He was getting soft.

The stage door opened, and he wondered if Trudy had returned to argue her point again, but it was Borelli, returning with a stack of waterproof evidence bags.

"What'd you do to the Genova gal? She flew past me like a jet plane."

"Nothing," Ned said. "Absolutely nothing."

CHAPTER ELEVEN

Ned watched Borelli, sitting across from Meg Pitman in the huge PBJ cafeteria, wolfing down a sandwich and fries. Neither noticed Ned in the busy lunchroom. He slid into an empty seat at the next table and saw Tony's right foot steadily bouncing. The jury was still out on the novice detective, and Ned hoped he would prove to be more of an asset than a liability. He'd checked into the evidence collection and it had been the usual: a simple computer glitch that had put the request into the wrong inbox for the CSI. Sometimes he thought technology was highly overrated. Sometimes.

He bit into his chicken parmagiana sandwich and tried to make eye contact with Tony. Still nothing. He leaned in to listen to their conversation.

"Sorry about missing King and Kiley," Meg said, picking at her salad. "I'll try to get one next week for your mom. So, how's your investigation going?"

"Early days." Borelli stuffed a huge bite of his roast beef into his mouth. "This horseradish sauce is incredible."

"Trudy says the first forty-eight hours are the most important in a case."

"Sure, we'd like it to be that way, but it rarely happens in real life," Borelli said. "Evidence needs to be gathered quickly before it gets destroyed or contaminated."

"Like those bags you sent out with that policeman?" she asked. "They were huge."

Enough. "But not as huge as Detective Borelli's mouth." Borelli's head finally swiveled in his direction. Ned slid his chair over to their table with his tray. "Move over." He crammed himself next to Borelli, who scowled and made room for him. Meg Pitman looked surprised, then went back to her salad. Conversation ground to a halt.

"Lighten up Tony, have a coke or something." Ned continued to eat, chewing enthusiastically. "Mmmm, good sauce. Real cheese, too. You should've had this, Borelli."

Beside him, Borelli shifted in his seat, obviously annoyed at the intrusion into the conversation with the Pitman woman. Not a bad way to interview a witness, but Ned had the feeling from what he'd overheard that the woman was doing more of the interviewing. Borelli was losing himself in that sunny smile and those liquid eyes of hers. And to boot, this was Genova's friend.

"Too bad Trudy Genova couldn't join us, Miss Pitman," Ned said, just to shake things up and let her know he knew she was snooping for her friend.

"Um, Trudy left just before I came to lunch. She went home to work," Meg said.

"Good thing, too, because if she hadn't she'd have been in a peck of trouble with me." Ned swallowed the last bite of his sandwich with relish, wiping his hands on a paper napkin. "I'll tell you what I told your friend, Miss Pitman." He hardened his voice. "Stay out of a police investigation and let the professionals do their work."

He stood and took his tray. "Nice to see you both. Looks like you're done here, Borelli. You have more interviews to do. Ones that don't require lunch."

"He's on to us," Meg told me over the phone, proceeding to recount her cafeteria experience with O'Malley and his sudden appearance and warning. I had gone home and done research on my laptop for a while with Wilkie purring around my ankles under my desk.

"Of course he is," I reassured her. "He wouldn't be fusty O'Malley if he wasn't. I've been doing background checks of my own, and this guy is known for closing cases. Our head detective's a local boy; parents are frequent flyers at Lincoln Center. I'm surprised you haven't run into him before in your circle—check with your mom tonight, see what you can dig up on Lois and Patrick O'Malley, known affectionately as Paddy. Ned's full name's not Edward but Edmunde, don't know which they called him in high society." I heard Meg scribbling.

"Got it. What else?"

"Fordham grad, private New York prep before that. Get this—his 'sport' was fencing, can you believe it? There was an article about his great solve rate in the Times Square District back when Giuliani cleaned it up. His reward was a promotion to home turf, which he took after some hesitation. That's about it."

"Maybe he didn't want to ride on his family coat tails. I can empathize with that. Anything about Tony Borelli?"

I chose to ignore her. "Did you get anything useful out of him before Ned-O butted in?"

"Some large evidence bags went out. The head producers seem to be in the clear, none were on the premises that day at all unless they somehow prepared Griff's cup the day before. But then he'd have been sick the night before he died." Meg sighed. "This is hard. Tony's with the writers now. Have you noticed that cute fold on the top of his left ear?"

"You mean that flap that makes him look like an elf?" I couldn't believe they were on a first name basis.

"Isn't it adorable?"

That was one word for it. Meg was close to gushing. This was not the Meg I knew. "Just keep flirting with him, Meg."

"I plan to—but even though O'Malley knows what I'm doing?"

"Oh, yes, *especially* because he knows what you're doing. You do know Borelli's definitely a caffeine addict with all that jiggling."

"I know, he's sweet, isn't he?" Meg stifled a giggle.

"If you say so. Hey, so what does he wear under his Calvin Kleins?" We played this game often and Meg's swift answer let me know she'd already been thinking about just that.

"Knit boxers," Meg declared.

"Think so? I pictured tighty whities," I said to goad her.

"Maybe in high school, but not now," she insisted. "What about O'Malley?"

"Brooks Brothers, for sure—button-fly Egyptian cotton boxers."

"Monogrammed?"

"Definitely."

I clicked my phone off and sat back. Okay, so O'Malley knew I'd recruited Meg to work with me. It didn't take a rocket scientist to figure that one out. But Meg's growing attraction to Tony Borelli had not been part of my original plan. By rights she should be attracted to Ned O'Malley. He ran in her circles, had the same type of education and background. I would bet my granny's poker pennies that their parents knew each other.

At least I'd be back in the studio to baby wrangle tomorrow. That was light duty. I should have free time to do some questioning of my own. Who knew what would pop up? Just by being in the place where the crime had been committed and keeping my eyes and ears open, I was certain to find out something.

This afternoon's music was Tchaikovsky, the vibrant Andante from his "Serenade for Strings in C Major." I hummed the familiar tune as I turned back to my work, pages faxed from a movie studio for the Denzel Washington/ John Travolta remake of *The Taking of Pelham 123*. This was the other part of my job and I relished marking up a script and making suggestions, even if I didn't know if they would be used.

But I was distracted. Griff Kennedy's murder was totally foreign to my nursing ethos. Maybe I hadn't been able to control any patient's death from illness, but at least I'd understood the underlying process or disease at work. I thought of the many people I'd helped to recover, too, but I liked to think that in my nine-year nursing career I'd helped others go gently into that good night.

Never before had I lost a patient due to the deliberate actions of another human being. It violated everything I thought of when I examined why I'd become a nurse. I'd wanted to help people facing an illness they couldn't control alone, to assist them with their healing if that was possible, not watch them die right in front me by some nameless foe who'd taken an easy way out to remove a problem. Just erase Griff, rub him out, as the bad guys in Travolta's gang would say.

I'd been intimately involved in an unsolved murder once before. That was not going to happen again on my watch. It was enough to set my stubborn streak on edge. And being a suspect meant I had more than a vested interest in finding the real killer. It still made me angry to think these detectives could be so shortsighted to consider me a suspect just because of Griff's pointing finger.

With a sigh, I put Griff and murder out of my mind for a while and turned back to the faxed script pages, trying to breathe credible first aid into a major shoot-out scene.

Leaving Tony sulking at lunch with Meg Pitman, and having made his point clearly to the young woman, Ned arrived in the PBJ lobby in time to watch his afternoon interviews, Misty Raines and Reece Hunter, as the young stars signed autographs for the crowd gathered outside the studio. He wasn't surprised at the number of young men in the crowd, probably waiting for Misty, but was by the middle-aged women vying for Reece's attention.

This whole world of soaps was foreign to him. He enjoyed the end result of show business, the plays and musicals, the concerts and ballets. That smacked to him of hard work, rehearsing and working over and over to get it right. This was different. Quick takes, unbelievable story lines, high drama that bordered on melodrama. With a start, he thought that maybe Trudy Genova was right. Maybe he was a snob.

He moved past the autograph hounds and went downstairs to Hunter's dressing room and waited outside it, using the time to review his notes and wonder when the hell Griff Kennedy's cup would be found. This place was unreal. Ned's time in the 2-0 precinct had taught him he didn't enjoy dealing with white-collar crime. He preferred a tougher criminal, a drug dealer who thought a gun was the way to solve an argument, or a master burglar who just couldn't control his itchy fingers. He knew where he stood with them even if they'd lie to him in a heartbeat.

Celebrities could prevaricate far too easily and always seemed to sit next to the Mayor, the Police Commissioner, or even more ghastly, his own parents, at some Lincoln Center function. He had the feeling they assumed because they didn't look like the gang-bangers usually depicted on page A-6 of the *Post*, they couldn't possibly be mistaken for one, carrying an aura of presumed innocence. In their world the perpetrator would surely turn out to be a homeless man, a drug lord, or a mobster who had gotten into the studio and poisoned Griff Kennedy because he was a lousy actor. And with the studio's one-guard security, they could even be right.

No, O'Malley was no fan of celebrity unless he was sitting in a seat being entertained by their talent. Borelli appeared, walking down the stairs from the business wing, clipboard in hand.

"Everything's fine, boss. CSI's on their way to get those bags processed and a team is on its way to search the studio for Kennedy's cup."

"Good. Now go back upstairs and ask the Pitman woman if the victim had any issues with stalkers or crazy fans."

Borelli took off at a trot just as Hunter braved the gauntlet and ushered Ned into his dressing room, pumped up by being the center of attention to the autograph seekers. His dressing room had the same small space as the others and was littered with gym sneakers, used socks, and hand and ankle weights. Framed prominently on one wall was a 16 X 14 head shot of . . . Reece Hunter.

"Just a few questions, Mr. Hunter. How many years have you been working on this soap?"

Reece answered Ned's questions in monosyllables. "One."

"How would you describe your relationship with Griff Kennedy?"

"Fine."

Ned shifted in his seat and tried again. "Was there any friction between you? I mean, a young actor such as you must have been seen by Griff Kennedy as enormous competition—"

"Nope."

Dialogue must be tough for this guy, Ned thought. It didn't help his mental-giant image with Ned when the actor kept stealing glances of himself in his dressing room mirror, nor when the detective glimpsed a *Big Jugs* magazine jutting out of a carryall. Hunter's color did heighten when Misty Raines was mentioned; then he managed to vocalize a sentence.

"We work together," he said.

"I figured that," Ned answered. Irony was lost on Reece. Was the actor as mentally inept as he appeared, or was this a way to disguise an otherwise devious mind?

Hunter finally was provoked into his longest off camera speech. He denied more than a professional relationship with Misty, although he seemed to think it was in the cards they would eventually get together, if only because it said so in their scripts.

"You should've seen the way she kissed me Monday morning, and that was just rehearsal."

The kisser in question was a different interview entirely. Misty Raines was leaving Hair and Makeup, ready to dress for taping a scene, when Ned sought her out. Her appearance had a disjointed effect, sophistication from the neck up with her heavily made-up eyes and glossy lips, mousey from the neck down with a sheep-patterned fleece robe with matching fuzzy kid's slippers. Her left foot said "baa" with each step.

She invited Ned into her dressing room. He felt a feral quality emanate from the woman, and wondered briefly if he should leave the door ajar.

Her room was set up to mirror Nikki Olivier's. Pictures of Misty wearing her crown as Miss Okra and another as Miss Peach Tree hung on the wall. Diction classes had mellowed out her twang to a hint of southern comfort on camera. He watched her kick off her noisy slippers.

"My little brother sent me those, aren't they just so cute?" She favored him with a smile.

Ned avoided the question and consulted his notebook, taking her through the usual questions about her background and two years at the soap, before leading to her relationship with Griff Kennedy.

"He was a sweet man," she said, playing with the sash of her robe. "I was just devastated when I heard he might have been murdered. I liked him a lot."

"Just how much is a lot, Miss Raines?" Ned asked. He watched her large blue eyes open even wider as she understood his meaning. The blue was an artificial, brittle color.

"He was old enough to be my daddy," she drawled with a sudden infusion of twang.

"Several people have noted you were seen having private lunches in his dressing room in the past two weeks." Ned let the statement hang in the air for a moment, not attributing it to Borelli's interview with the stage manager, until it became obvious she wasn't going to add to her answer. "You know, murder is a funny issue, Miss Raines. Things that should by all rights remain private have to be scrutinized. I'm not digging for casual gossip here."

Misty dropped her sash and gave him her full attention, the soft voice hardening.

"I suppose you could say I encouraged Griff, flirted with him, hoping he'd push to get me a bigger storyline. That hadn't happened yet, but I want to make one thing clear: despite what those old nannies out there have told you, Misty Raines doesn't give it away without reason." She leaned forward during this speech, the robe gaping open, two-thirds of her firm breasts on view. "And I hadn't been given that reason yet."

Ned blinked and drew his eyes from the view on offer back to her face. He saw the tenacity hidden within her soft voice and curvy body.

"Do we understand each other, Detective?" she said, a steely edge in her voice.

"I think we do, Miss Raines."

Chapter Twelve

POLICE DEPARTMENT: CITY OF NEW YORK 20ᵀᴴ Precinct
120 West 82ⁿᵈ Street, New York, NY 10024
_____*Fidelis ad Mortem*_____

INTERNAL MEMO
TO: Capt. Jack Morton
FROM: Edmunde O'Malley, Det. 1st Gr.
RE: Kennedy, Griffon: homicide case # 08-215984
DATE: May 6, 2008

The victim's movements prior to his death have been investigated. Housekeeper Rita DelGado, 2113 East 109ᵗʰ St, Bronx, NY, states her employer was not ill recently, and had not been stalked. She worked from 7 am to 3 pm weekdays. There were occasionally evening visitors she cleaned up after the next morning but she did not know the identity of anyone specific. Photographs in the home are of the deceased's parents from Iowa, and of him with Nikki Olivier.

Victim's only medication was for hypertension, once daily, which DelGado doled out with orange

*juice before he left for the studio. A check with
his personal physician, Dr. Henry Schadel, confirmed
this. He was aware of the victim's high daily alcohol
intake and had been unsuccessfully trying to get
him to cut back. Dr. Schadel denied ever prescribing
any medicine containing cardiac glycosides, and had
been Kennedy's physician for the last seven years.*

*As usual, I will keep you informed of my team's
progress. E O'M*

Ned stood in front of the white board, studying the cumulative data on the timeline for Griff Kennedy's activities for the three days leading up to his murder. With lack of any evidence of a stalker, he'd turned his attention to phone interviews with Kennedy's lawyer and agent. Neither could think of anyone in his life who would have a reason to kill their client. Ned rubbed eyes that felt gritty and sore before he settled down to type up an overview of their progress—or lack thereof—and then head home for a well-deserved rest.

Borelli appeared in the doorway. "Anything else before I leave?" His cell phone rang and he looked at the number and grimaced, letting it go to voicemail.

"Your mother?" Ned guessed. He was rewarded with Tony's sheepish nod. "She's probably holding dinner for you. Nothing new on the beatings or from the writers?" He opened his desk drawer and took out a fresh roll of mints.

"Nada on the beatings, no new ones this week. On the writers, no motives that I can see. No close ties to Kennedy, unless someone's hiding something very well. It's like *Upstairs, Downstairs* at that place. The classes don't mingle and each one thinks they're the better one. Did you see my notes from the Resnick interview?" Borelli's foot was jiggling. He needed a fix.

Ned nodded and recited: "Griff was sleeping with at least Nikki, Misty Raines, possibly the hair and/or makeup gal, and he wasn't clear on the new receptionist. And who knows how many outside the studio? The guy must have had stock in Viagra."

"I can't see a motive for Resnick yet," Borelli said. "Not sure we can believe everything he says, though. 'Course, he may've been trying to deflect my interest."

"That's why they call it a soap opera, Borelli. Give your mother my regards." At least Borelli was keeping an open mind with his witnesses. With luck he'd turn into a good investigator. Before Borelli could leave, Ned's desk phone rang and he stayed his partner with a wave of his hand.

"Where? When?" Ned whispered to Borelli. "Did you know Damon found Kennedy's missing cup?" He turned his attention back to the phone, rifling through his stack of pink message slips, "We'll be right there." He hung up and pulled out a pink slip, crumpled it and threw it in the wastebasket. "Griff's cup was found and is covered in fingerprints. And the residue inside tested positive for glycosides."

I waited for the traffic signal to let me cross Amsterdam Avenue, my destination the deli nearest my building, situated midway between a yeshiva and a nail salon. I'd run out of Wilkie's food, and although the night was clear and cool, I didn't feel like walking to the West Side Market to stock up.

Most of the buildings in this neighborhood had yet to be renovated outside, and I enjoyed their architectural detailing, regardless of the nature of the business inside. Heavy corbels, decorated architraves (WOD), and carved lintels caught my eye. I'd been saving for a trip to Paris and London to see the historical buildings and was about halfway there.

The traffic stopped and I crossed toward the deli, deciding I didn't need much else to tide me over before a bigger shopping day. Two couples leaving an Italian restaurant in the middle of the block came towards me, discussing their meal and the fine quality of the wine, which they had clearly enjoyed. One couple had their arms entwined around each other, making it awkward to walk. The other couple moved as one person, the man's hand jammed down the pocket of his girlfriend's jeans as she leaned into him and matched his steps.

I entered the deli and grabbed a bottle of vitamin water and five cans of Healthy Cat, twisting off the cap of the water and taking a long slug after paying. Walking back outside, my eyes were irresistibly drawn to the two couples waiting at the corner for the light to change. They were talking animatedly to each other and laughing. I felt an unnerving stab at my core. I wanted someone outside my family to care for me, someone who would want me to be the center of his world.

The light changed and I strode across the broad avenue, chiding myself. Who was I kidding? I wasn't ready for that kind of relationship. Jake Forster had cured me of any serious entanglements for right now. While I'd had a few casual dates since our breakup, after a second date I wasn't prepared to see anyone a third time and pushed some very nice men away. Maybe I just didn't need a man in my life, not a steady one at least. I warmed to this theme as I strolled down the block. Maybe I was one of those women who would be happy with a superficial sexual fling now and then, one who kept a vibrator she named in a hidden drawer.

I reached my building and turned into the cobbled courtyard. Or maybe not. On reflection, that kind of existence seemed meaningless. That wasn't who I was, deep down.

But then a thought chilled me. Perhaps that was who I'd become. I wondered for perhaps the thousandth time what Jake Forster's German wife had offered him that I had not.

Sal rushed to open the door for me, looking flustered. "Trudy, I'm sorry—"

Ned O'Malley stepped forward, trailed by Borelli. "Miss Genova, I have to ask you to accompany me down to the precinct for questioning."

Sal raised his hands in a helpless gesture and went back behind the desk, averting his eyes.

My heart sped up. "What's happened?"

"We'll discuss that once we get to an interview room." Borelli's voice was firm.

I held up my bag. "Do I at least get to feed my cat?"

Seated in the back of the squad car, a metal grill separating me from the two detectives, I slid my cell phone from my pocket and turned the volume down, then texted Meg. Would they give me bail? Did they give suspected murderers bail? I looked out at the dark street and felt a sense of hollowness as the familiar streets slid past. My palms were sweaty and my racing heart seemed to have settled in my throat. I couldn't go to jail, I just couldn't.

The thought of being trapped inside a tiny jail cell with a bunch of thugs and drug addicts had my pulse pounding in my ears. A wave of nausea rolled over me. If I was sick in the car that wouldn't go down well with O'Malley, I could be sure of that. The only saving grace was that I hadn't been handcuffed but I noticed there weren't any handles on the doors in the back seat. A sense of claustrophobia hit me and I swallowed hard. This couldn't be happening.

The interview room I was led to had a peculiar odor, a mix of unwashed bodies, disinfectant and stale food odors. Someone had eaten popcorn in here recently and a few kernels littered the floor. The tabletop was old Formica, chipped and covered with graffiti and gouges. I could make out the words THIS SUCKS dug in with a sharp point.

I knew just how that writer felt.

I took a few deep breaths, trying to squash my nausea and remain calm. True to form, one wall had a large mirror I knew was a two-way mirror. I felt scrutinized as I tucked my hair behind my ear and resisted the urge to give the watcher the middle finger. Showing my temper wouldn't help me. I wondered who stood on the other side, watching my every movement. How long would they make me wait? What was the proper behavior of an innocent person? I was long past looking nonchalant or cool. I felt very alone.

After what seemed an interminable wait, the door opened and O'Malley entered with Borelli trailing behind like a big puppy. The senior detective slapped a folder on the table, and I tried not to jump in reaction.

I've always tried to hide fear with bravado. While Borelli fussed with a recorder, I looked O'Malley right in the eye and uttered with what I hoped was great disdain: "You know, in England the cops are called 'the filth.'"

He leaned toward me. "Only by the criminals."

I sat back, properly chastened. That didn't go over as I'd expected.

"Tell us about Kennedy's cup." O'Malley's lips were set in a hard line.

For a second I fancied I saw disappointment on O'Malley's face. His look bored into me as I hesitated. Answer or wait for a lawyer? I cleared my throat as I stalled. Would I appear guilty if I refused to answer their questions? But if I asked for one they couldn't question me until he arrived, right?

"Should I wait for my lawyer?" I finally croaked out.

"That's entirely up to you, Miss Genova. I didn't realize you had someone on retainer."

I looked at him in surprise. "Of course I don't. I thought I would get a public defender—"

"Are you asking for a public defender?" Borelli looked annoyed.

A sharp rap on the door prevented my answer; an officer poked his head inside. "Her lawyer's here."

I hid my surprise as the door opened wider to admit a

striking woman, dressed in a sleek burgundy power suit, her dark hair twisted into an efficient chignon. Although it was dinnertime, the woman looked as though she'd just stepped out of the shower.

"Marit Van Aken. I'm representing Miss Genova." The woman did a double take. "Neddy?"

I spun my head between the lawyer and O'Malley, who glowered. "Hello, Marit. It's Detective O'Malley in here, please."

The lawyer laughed with delight as she shook hands with me and sat down. She took her time as she opened her leather briefcase and took out a fresh legal pad and a silver pen. This was a public defender? Then it hit me: Meg. What was she thinking? I couldn't afford this pricey lawyer. And someone who ran in O'Malley's circles, to boot. Unbelieveable.

"All right, Neddy, we'll keep it formal. Allow me a moment to confer with my client, please." She waited for the detectives to leave the room before turning to me and introducing herself. "Meg Pitman has explained the situation, Miss Genova. This is a fishing expedition. Just relax. If I don't want you to answer a question, I'll let you know. And just answer a direct question without elaborating, all right?"

I nodded, grateful to have someone in my corner.

Marit waved one hand in the air and the men came back in. Of course, the two-way mirror. She consulted her notes. "Exactly why is my client even here?"

It was obvious O'Malley was unhappy. "I was just starting to ask Miss Genova a few questions when you interrupted."

"Protecting one's constitutional rights is never an interruption, Detective," Van Aken said lightly, but with just the right amount of steel in her voice.

I smiled at the woman who was unequivocally on my side. Maybe this was a good idea. I could yell at Meg later, if I ever got to go home.

"Miss Genova, could you tell us about Mr. Kennedy's cup, the one he carried around?"

Van Aken's presence gave me backbone. "You mean the one *I* told you about when you first questioned me at home? It was a souvenir of his hosting the Daytime Emmy's. He carried it around all day, every day, and from his actions, I'd say the majority of the time it contained some kind of adult beverage."

"And would you have had access to that cup?"

I thought about that. "I don't think so. I mean, I saw him carry it around, but access, no."

O'Malley withdrew a form he slid across the table to my lawyer. "Then perhaps you'd care to explain how your fingerprints were found on it?"

Van Aken leaned over to whisper to me. "Want to talk to me alone?"

"No." I racked my brains and then felt a huge jolt of relief. "Yes, I remember. The day he died, I took the cup from him in the rehearsal hall and put it on a shelf so he could go over his actions. Ron Dowling and Nikki Olivier were there. They'll confirm that." I blew out a breath and sat back.

"How convenient," O'Malley said. "And can you also account for the glycosides found in the mix of bourbon and Coke inside it?"

I frowned. "I told *you* I thought he was poisoned before you told me the Medical Examiner was thinking that." I turned to my new lawyer and briefly explained how Griff Kennedy had died and the symptoms I'd researched. "I told these two I thought he'd been poisoned. Would I have told them about the cup *and* that I thought he'd been poisoned if I were the one who'd done it?"

"My client has a point, Detective. And were hers the only fingerprints on this special cup?" Von Aken seemed to be playing with O'Malley, but I didn't care. All I knew was that this woman was here for me and that I needed to get away before I threw up.

"There were others," O'Malley admitted, "but too smeared to print well."

Borelli spoke up. "What about the pie?"

Van Aken looked puzzled. "Pie?"

I explained Griff's behavior after the knee incident, culminating in the pie dumped over his head.

Van Aken laughed. "I'd say you must have a whole stable of suspects for this guy, Neddy. Sorry—Detective."

"But not ones with their fingerprints on the murder weapon, Counselor."

"Which my client has explained and has witnesses to back up."

I watched the two battle back and forth. It made my head spin.

"Then there's the fact of Miss Genova's nursing history," Ned persisted. "How many people would know about poisons and how to obtain them?"

That brought a bark from Van Aken. "Anyone with a computer who knows how to Google, Detective." She stood up and threw her pad in her briefcase. "I think we're done here if that's the kind of evidence you have against my client."

CHAPTER THIRTEEN

Friday, May 7th

After Marit Von Aken had dropped me at my apartment, I'd had a tough time sleeping. Being dragged down to the precinct like a common criminal will do that to you. My fear had melted to annoyance at still being considered a suspect by the time dawn arrived, after I'd intervened to help O'Malley with the Olivier interivew, too. On top of that, I had to reach Meg first thing in the morning before she left for the studio.

"Meg, Marit was wonderful but I can't afford her, no matter how good she is." I explained the events at the precinct. "I appreciate that she got me out of there, but the cost of that one hour is probably more than I have in my checking account right now."

"Relax, Trudy. She's on retainer for one of my father's boards and came down as a favor to me." Meg laughed. "I only wish I'd seen O'Malley's face when she called him 'Neddy.' You shouldn't need her again. By the way, was Tony there, too?"

"Tony? You mean Borelli?" I sighed. Meg was far too concerned with Tony Borelli. "He was there all right, looking pleased as punch that they'd got their man, until Marit set them both straight."

"See, I told you she was good. It's fine, really. Now what did she say about work?"

"I'm coming in. She said I should hold my head up and treat everything as normal. But it's not normal, Meg . . . "

"Trudy Genova, you listen to me. You didn't have anything to do with Griff Kennedy's death. I know that and so does anyone who knows you. So you get your butt in gear and get in to work. No one there will even know you were brought in for questioning. It's like all those mysteries you read—you were simply helping them with their enquiries if anyone asks."

She hung up and I hit the shower, wondering how people at work would react to me today. Meg was right. I needed to pull on my big girl panties. Anyone who knew me wouldn't give Griff's pointing finger a second thought. And anyone who didn't and had the temerity to think otherwise had better get out of my way today.

"Hello—anybody home?" I knocked on the open Wardrobe Department door. Despite the rampant gossip that was a daily ritual on any soap set, actors and crew bustled around as before and left me alone. Except for the crime tape on Griff's dressing room and the hospital set, it was business as usual, and I suspected the network and its advertisers were enforcing the tone. Best of all, everyone seemed so caught up in their work that not one person had mentioned Griff's pointing finger—yet. Maybe their memories were short.

The Wardrobe Mistress, a petite woman with large glasses, emerged from the back room. "Who's on tap for me today, Edith?" I asked. Although Edith Carlisle stood barely five feet tall, she exuded a vigor and energy I'd always admired. Petite gals had to stick together.

With cropped silver hair and trademark oversized purple glasses, Edith's nickname was "The Silver Bullet," garnered from years of zipping around the actors she dressed. Her energy level never flagged, whether fitting a new cast member, choosing outfits for the week, or advising which wedding gown a prospective *Thornfield Place* bride should choose. Edith was on close terms with the buyers and personal shoppers at all of New York's flagship stores: Saks Fifth Avenue, Lord & Taylor, Barney's, and even Bergdorf Goodman, along with a host of designer boutiques and opulent jewelers.

I knew she'd started as a dresser and risen through talent and experience to become a costume designer for Broadway. Now in her early sixties, Edith preferred the regular hours and weekends off a soap opera usually allowed and I didn't blame her.

"You've got Allison Stewart; she's in Nine running lines with her mom." Edith rifled through costumes on a rack just inside the door that held today's costumes, searching for the outfit chosen for the young actor's scene. "And she's in her usual cheerful mood."

"I try pointedly to ignore those moods," I said with a smile. The hormonal twelve-year-old with the face of an angel had a

devilish personality until she hit the sound stage. Taking the
hanger Edith held out, I admired the plaid kilt, ruffled white
blouse, and black velvet vest. "Cute—knee socks?"

"And these kiltie loafers." Edith handed me the shoes with
white socks stuffed inside. "Try to get her to keep juice off
that blouse if you can. I don't have a backup that fits her."

"Will do—thanks." I turned to leave.

"Um, Trudy? Come in and close the door for a minute."

I returned as bidden and shut the door to the department,
my curiosity piqued. "What's up?"

"While I had a minute alone, I wanted you to know . . . "
her voice trailed off.

Here it comes, I thought. My first accusation. And I'd
thought I was home free. "What's wrong, Edith?" I steeled
myself for a host of questions about Griff's pointing finger.

"I just wanted to say I know you had nothing to do with
Griff's death."

"Why, Edith, thank you. Of course I didn't." I breathed
out the breath I'd been holding. "I'm still trying to figure
out what happened and why he pointed to me like that." I
looked at Edith closely, noting the deep circles under her eyes,
the puffy lids. "Are you all right?" To my surprise, the older
woman burst into tears.

"No, no I'm not all right. Not at all."

I grabbed a box of tissues from the worktable and guided
Edith to the back room, where I pushed her down into a chair
and sat beside her.

"Tell me all about it," I said—and Edith did.

While Borelli kept busy gathering information by drinking coffee with a group of grips and the gaffer, Ned squared his shoulders and entered the central room occupied by Hair and Makeup. Eva Hendricksen was spraying Reese Hunter's hair in place; Li Yung washed makeup brushes. The young star mumbled his thanks, nodded in the detective's direction and left without meeting his eye.

"Autograph session," the hair stylist explained, rinsing her sink.

"Then he can't get into trouble if he only has to smile and sign," Ned said to gauge their reaction. He was rewarded with knowing laughter from both women, especially Li, who giggled loudly. He pointed to the two empty makeup chairs, leaning against the counter. Li climbed into the elevated chair; the taller Eva sat down easily.

"I'm going to interview you together since you work in the same room and probably have seen the same things. Unless you have a problem with that?" Ned asked, offering his roll of mints around. He'd decided it would be interesting to play them off each other. After the sting of last night he needed more evidence and better information before he brought someone else down to the station. He still smarted at being bested by Marit Von Aken, and a small part of him felt bad he'd brought Trudy Genova down instead of asking her those questions at her apartment. She would have explained about the fingerprints, he would have checked out the witnesses, and last night didn't have to have happened at all.

"Is fine with me," Li said, looking to her partner, who nodded.

The women went out of their way to assure him neither had a close personal relationship with Kennedy, despite studio gossip that he'd bedded them both at some time.

"We've seen too many of his conquests end in tears," Eva explained.

"I'm engaged to an engineering student," Li told him, flashing a substantial rock.

Ned took them through the day of the murder. "Griff was here just after taking his lunch hour," Eva said.

"His 'sick' makeup had to be in place, to see the effect under the lights before taping," Li explained. "He was in a good mood, told me he was going to take me out, buy me steak dinner to fatten me up." She laughed, then immediately sobered. "He was big teaser."

"He thanked me for washing the pie out of his hair," Eva said. "I guess you heard about that? He really did have a thing for Trudy, poor kid. I'm surprised no one had dumped pie on him before this."

"At the time of the taping, both of you were up on the sound stage?" Ned confirmed, checking his notes.

"We always go up for taping; Li takes a small kit with powder and blush for touch ups. I take a comb and spray." Eva gestured to Li, who nodded.

"And you would wait where?" he asked.

"My feet hurt; I sat on the next set, on a couch," Li said.

"I was near Frank, behind Camera Two. That would be to the left side of the set as you face it," Eva explained. "I suppose you've already heard Frank and I date sometimes, nothing serious."

Ned nodded, jotting a note, expertly concealing his surprise, since not one person he and Borelli had spoken with had even hinted at this relationship.

So much for the open cooperation he'd been promised.

When I approached Dressing Room Nine I could easily hear the raised voices inside.

"Mom, you don't know jack sh—" Allison was yelling as I knocked.

Allison's mother, a thin, anxious woman with frosted blonde hair, opened the door. "Look dear, here's Trudy." Clearly relieved at the interruption, Monica Stewart ushered me into the small dressing room where the sullen girl lay sprawled across the love seat. "And I may not know your friend Jack, but he does not have the right to decide if you need highlights in your hair or not. They'd make you look too hard. What do you think, Trudy?"

Allison's wavy dark hair and creamy skin recalled a young Elizabeth Taylor. "I don't know too many eleven-year-olds who highlight their hair, Ally, and that's the age of the character you play. Besides, I'm pretty certain any hairstyle changes have to be approved by the studio first."

Monica Stewart beamed. "Of course, I'd forgotten that. I'll

pull your contract tonight, sweetheart, and we can check it out together. You wouldn't want to endanger your role."

Allison glared at me for providing the insight. "Swell." Then she noticed the outfit I held and curled her lip. "I hope you know I'm not wearing *that*."

It was going to be one of those days. I frowned and pointed to Allison's chin. "Oh, is that a pimple?"

Allison shrieked as she ran to the mirror. I smiled at Monica. "Between us we'll hold her down and she *will* wear it."

It was obvious Edith Carlisle was distraught. Her reddened eyes and distracted manner as she answered Ned's questions kept him off base as he tried to get somewhere in the interview. He was frustrated.

"I saw Griff in the morning after rehearsals. He asked me to find a pair of gym shorts to wear under his hospital gown for taping," she said. She refused to make eye contact.

"How did he appear to you?" Ned asked.

"Just fine. We chatted briefly. His mood was high—I think he was looking forward to his big scene." Edith blinked back tears.

"So you found him the shorts—" Ned prompted. He was tired of having to draw these supposedly helpful accounts out of his witnesses.

"During lunch I brought them to his dressing room. I didn't

even stay a minute."

Ned consulted his notes, deciding to bring up the cup in an innocent manner. "I've heard he had a special cup, from when he hosted the Emmys—did you notice that there?"

"I didn't know I was supposed to look for it." She narrowed her eyes as she finally met his. "I simply wished him luck on his big scene and left. It was the last time I saw him," she added, trying not to break down.

Ned thanked her, left her wiping her eyes, and sat in the empty rehearsal room for a minute to gather his thoughts. He had the distinct feeling there was more to that story.

He paged back to the list he'd started of people who'd visited Griff Kennedy in his dressing room, adding Edith Carlisle's name under Misty Raines, Nikki Olivier, and Frank Resnick. Climbing the stairs, he went onto the sound stage in search of his next quarry, the Prop Master. Ned reflected on the tendrils of a murder investigation, creeping into innocent people's lives, exposing their secrets, all in the name of justice for the victim. Everyone had secrets they carried around. Even him.

After ascertaining a zit wasn't about to pop out on her chin, Allison Stewart resumed arguing with me and her mother about her costume.

"It's silly and childish. I wouldn't be caught dead wearing

that."

"Now, Allison. It's not that bad . . ." Monica Stewart's main discipline tactic consisted of trailing statements.

I had a distinctly different approach in mind. "It might appear childish to your sophisticated tastes, but your character is only eleven. It's called acting," I told the girl, helping her into the clothes. "And you have this part because you're good at it. Anyone watching knows this isn't at all what you wear outside your work."

Allison looked at herself in the mirror and straightened her blouse under the vest.

"Slip those shoes on and let's get you to Edith. Maybe she'll let you leave the socks off." I doubted this would happen, but it would get us out of the tiny dressing room so I could scout out what was going on in the rest of the studio.

We started down the hall together, Allison dragging the toes of her shoes in bad temper against the carpeting at each step. Frank Resnick appeared at the end of the hallway.

"Hey, Trudy—do me a favor and knock on Misty's door. She's missed her call and they're waiting for her up on set." The stage manager made a note on his shooting script and rushed away.

We stopped at Misty Raines' dressing room. "Misty, Frank said they're ready for you upstairs." I knocked as I spoke while Allison danced from foot to foot. I stopped her with the same stern glance my mother had perfected in dealing with my two older brothers.

"Misty? You in there?" I tried the knob and the door opened a few inches, only to stop. I shoved harder; the door opened six inches, revealing the obstacle.

M.K. GRAFF

Misty Raines lay against the door, her face swollen and suffused with purple, her eyes wide open in panic. Allison squealed loudly.

"Get help!" I said, but the girl stared back at me, rooted to the spot, mouth wide open and howling loudly. Allison's caterwauling increased, bringing her mother running down the hall from one direction and Li and Eva from the other.

People expect a nurse to face death calmly, and I had eventually learned how to do just that. Still, my stomach tightened as I knelt down and reached my hand through the half-opened door to feel Misty's carotid artery, noting tiny bits of orange around the dead woman's mouth. Her hands were outstretched as though she'd been scrabbling at the door. I stood, pulling the door closed, and sent Li to call an ambulance and Eva to find O'Malley, just as Allison Stewart vomited all over her ruffled white blouse and black vest.

Upstairs in the Prop Room, Ned was finishing up his interview with Gary Knowles. As the department head, Gary spent most of his time in his "domain," as he called the long rectangular room off the sound stage door. The room was lined with shelves holding a plethora of labeled lamps, vases, centerpieces, and statues. Ned had to walk around a stack of heavily framed paintings leaning against one wall to face the head of the Properties Department.

DEATH UNSCRIPTED

Gary Knowles could have stepped out of a monastery his with gray hair closely cropped against his scalp in short, irregular bangs. The effect was enhanced by a large silver cross that hung suspended from a heavy chain around his neck. Its elaborate design reminded Ned of his mother's dated collection, only hers hung on the annual Christmas tree. Wearing gloves, Knowles polished an elaborate silver candelabrum at the worktop that spread down the middle of the room.

"I rarely venture downstairs, Detective," he told Ned in answer to his question about visiting Griff Kennedy in his dressing room. "Of course I've seen that ridiculous cup—he carried it all over the studio, reeking of the alcohol of the day, usually scotch. And I'm not even certain he had the sense to make it single-malt." He scowled in distaste.

"Were you friendly outside the studio?" Ned asked.

The very idea seemed to shock the prop man. "Oh, no, no. We revolved in different circles. Quite frankly, I loathed the man."

Ned's interest piqued. "And what would be the reasons for that?"

Knowles used his gloved fingers to polish his cross, caressing the heavy filigree. "The man had no conscience and little taste. One day he drank scotch, the next gin. I disliked his leering looks at women, the way he felt he deserved special attention, and especially the way he thought he was a great actor, when it was his association with Nikki Olivier that kept his job. Enough reasons?"

"Nothing specific then?" Ned's dryness elicited a smile from Knowles, suddenly animating his ascetic face.

"A cop with a sense of humor? Let's just say I'd known him way too long to be taken in by his tricks—" Knowles was cut off by the sound of muffled screams from downstairs. Ned ran out, meeting Eva Hendrickson at the top of the stairs.

"Trudy said to come quickly—something's happened to Misty."

He followed her down the stairs. Around Misty's door a small crowd had gathered, drawn by loud wailing. They parted to allow Ned access. Trudy Genova guarded the door while a sobbing young girl was bundled off down the hall by an older woman.

"What's happened?" He stepped over a pool of vomit on the floor. "Whose is this?"

"Allison's, my charge for the day." Trudy bit her lip. She opened the door carefully.

Ned glanced inside. "Is she—?"

"Very."

Chapter Fourteen

This time most of the cast and crew were kept in the lobby. After leaving contact information, they were sent home to be interviewed by Ned's team later. Those downstairs were kept there, and Borelli took a statement from Allison Stewart, who sniveled in shock. Ned gave permission for the girl and her mother to leave after Trudy explained how Frank's request led to her chancing upon Misty's body.

"Chance? I love your word choice, Genova." Ned grunted. He wondered if he should be having second thoughts about Trudy Genova, pricey lawyer or not. But he knew Marit Von Aken would point out there were plenty of witnesses who had heard and seen Frank ask Trudy to knock on Misty's door. For that matter, they already had Allison's statement that corroborated that sequence of events.

Still, he felt the need to keep an eye on Trudy as they stood in the doorway to Misty's dressing room, watching the crime scene techs work the disturbed room. The actress had been formally pronounced dead and her body removed to the Medical Examiner's Office.

The dead woman's purse had been turned out on the counter, its contents in a pile. Her dressing table drawers lay pulled onto the floor, the accumulation strewn about in a muddle of makeup, scarves, hairbrushes and fan letters.

"Someone was searching for something," Borelli said over Trudy's shoulder.

"Brilliant deduction." Ned shook his head.

Trudy snapped her fingers. "Nuts!"

Ned glared at her.

"Anaphylactic shock," she explained. "Misty had a severe peanut allergy, couldn't get near them without breaking out in hives. She was looking for her EpiPen to counteract the anaphylaxis."

"It would seem she didn't find it," Borelli added.

"You think, Borelli? A master of understatement." Ned wasn't certain Borelli understood his point from the blank look his partner gave him. Ned sighed in frustration. "Go call Byron and let him know to look for peanut ingestion." He rubbed his temples. "I'm getting a headache." He turned to Trudy. "Who knew about this allergy?"

Trudy answered in a small voice: "Everyone."

I sat between Borelli and O'Malley in the rehearsal hall, nervously picking at the sandwich Meg had brought before leaving to help upstairs with the massive rescheduling that Misty's death necessitated. I didn't miss the sly looks Borelli and Meg exchanged when she brought the food. My God, I'd created a monster. Make that two.

I couldn't figure out if O'Malley was ready to accept my help or was just keeping an eye on me as he and Borelli wolfed down their own sandwiches. I was still upset over last night's little trek to the police station and understood that the reason I was sequestered with the detectives could have ominous overtones. Yet again I was on the spot when someone lost their life. It was enough to bring out the truck driver in me. I could feel a curse hovering, just waiting to be let out if O'Malley so much as suggested I had anything to do with Misty's death.

The small room steadily filled with the scent of cheeses, meat, and hot coffees all around. It seems being exposed to sudden death again had given them an appetite and I watched them eat with gusto. Or maybe they just had to consume calories on the fly when they could.

"It was common knowledge in the studio about Misty's peanut allergy," I expounded. "She refused home-baked cookies or cakes in case they were tainted. Besides keeping her weight down, it was a major reason she kept herself supplied with carrots and celery." I nibbled my ham and cheese on whole wheat with mustard. Disgusting to be hungry at all if I gave it too much thought. Maybe something to do with that nursing background I'd had to learn, keeping my emotions in check, or just plain human survival instincts coupled with a secret celebration I was not the victim. With Griff's death I'd had no appetite. Maybe I was already becoming inured to violent death. My heart was definitely hardening.

"Frank confirmed he intercepted you in the hall and asked you to call Misty for him," Borelli said, interrupting my thoughts, munching his own sandwich piled high with salami and cheeses, oil and vinegar dripping between his fingers.

"Why, Borelli, I think you're disappointed," I said. "You fancy me for a murderer when I've introduced you to my best friend?" My look challenged him to dispute the point. Did this mean I'd finally been cleared?

"Enough, children," O'Malley said, balling up his sandwich paper and chucking it neatly into a wastebasket. "The CSIs said there are scratches on the back of the door where Misty tried to open it. And they couldn't find an EpiPen anywhere."

I shuddered, picturing Misty struggling for breath as her airways swelled, trying desperately to open the door for help as her throat closed. Misty knew the symptoms and would have known she was dying. "She'd been eating a carrot; there were bits of it in her mouth. One pen she carried in her purse so she'd always have it with her, and I thought she kept another in the drawer in her dressing room. If they're both gone, that means someone deliberately removed them and we definitely have another murder."

O'Malley sighed, rather dramatically, I thought.

"*We* don't have anything, Trudy. And when *you're* done, *you'll* have to leave, too. We've got your statement."

Uh-oh, back to square one. When was O'Malley going to learn he needed me in this investigation? I bit back a snarky retort and into a cookie instead. At least he'd called me by my first name. Small steps.

O'Malley took out his notebook, flipping back through pages, addressing his comments to his partner. "We'll have to organize a search of the studio for the EpiPen. By the way, partner, your gossipy pal Frank neglected to tell you he dates Eva, the hair gal. And Edith Carlisle, Wardrobe—she's holding back something but I couldn't get it out of her."

Oops. I struggled with my conscience. Should I offer up the knowledge I'd gleaned, or see how long it took the distinguished detective to ferret it out? I swung my feet under my chair while contemplating how I could turn this to my advantage.

"O'Malley, what if I happened to have information from a witness you'd interviewed, stuff they didn't volunteer to you?" I began. "Would that endear me to you, get you to cut me a little slack?" I gave him my best smile.

"Hm, let's see." O'Malley tilted his head to one side. "What if *I* told *you* I could arrest you for withholding evidence in an investigation?" He looked away.

I considered this. Women are masters of the white lie. They have far better training, years of assuring their best friend that the new haircut does NOT make her look like her mother, or that the new jeans really ARE slimming. When men tried to get away with telling lies, something about their shifting eyes and halting speech usually gave them away. That's how I knew immediately that O'Malley was lying his ass off. "You wouldn't," I stated.

"I would—" Borelli interjected.

"Tony, go upstairs and find out what the producers have decided," O'Malley said. "and call in backup to do a search for the EpiPen."

Tension filled the room after Borelli left. I wondered if he'd find an excuse to run upstairs and see Meg.

O'Malley paced. I inspected my cuticles, watching him from the corner of my eye as he stopped to scrutinize a framed cast photo that had appeared in an issue of *Soap Opera Digest*. I decided his look of pained concentration meant he was gathering his thoughts. I closed my eyes, wondering if Ned O'Malley ever followed his emotions, ever allowed himself to do anything spontaneously.

He kept his back to me while he spoke. "Do you understand you've already been allowed unusual access to a murder investigation, especially after being a suspect? Besides being totally contrary to protocol, which I suspect doesn't matter to you at all, it's not safe if this is a murder. It's quite likely the same person has killed twice in just a few days. You must know that indicates a high degree of instability at work."

My chin rested in one hand while I scrutinized him. When he turned to face me, I was surprised by his intense look. Had I shifted from suspect to damsel in distress? Was O'Malley seriously worried about me?

His brow furrowed. "Are you even listening to me?"

"I think you gave me your headache. Look—" I sat up straighter. "Do *you* understand I'm sincerely trying to help find that murderer? I know this isn't a lark. I was under suspicion and while I hope that idea's finally been put to bed, I want to prove to you I can be useful in this investigation. Now do you want my information or not?"

"Of course I need to know anything pertinent to this investigation-"

My frustration level boiled over. I threw up my hands and shot out of my chair. "Jeez, O'Malley, put the bloody Thesaurus away. Just say yes."

"Yes."

"Edith Carlisle was married to Griff Kennedy."

CHAPTER FIFTEEN

"What? When?" Ned looked down at Trudy standing defiantly in front of him, head craned up. This close, he noticed she only came up to his mid-chest. "You're really very short," he blurted before he could cram the words back.

"Petite, O'Malley, short women like to be called petite." She sat down as if holding court, motioning him into the chair beside her. "They were married in the Sixties, when he was doing bit parts Off Broadway and she was a dresser, way before Nikki Olivier came on the scene. After their divorce they stayed out of each other's way and haven't been close—no Christmas cards there. When Edith applied here, Griff agreed they shouldn't mention it, afraid it might affect both of their jobs and just ratchet up the gossip."

Ned whipped out his notebook. "Anything else?"

Trudy shook her head. "I gave you the peanuts, I gave you Griff's cup and his marriage to Edith, what more do you want?"

Ned thought long and hard before answering. "I want you to keep your eyes and ears open, just like you did today, but not get actively involved in this mess. It's dangerous." He hoped he wasn't opening Pandora's box. Ned had the feeling if he gave Trudy Genova the barest inch she would manage to turn it into a hundred yards and feel justified doing it. At some point he had to go with his gut, and his gut told him Trudy Genova was innocent of involvement in these murders.

She saluted him with her left hand. "Got it."

Ned decided Trudy had the fingers on her right crossed.

I started up the stairs to find Meg and saw Tony Borelli, fresh Coke in hand, a few steps above me, beating me to Meg's desk. Flattening myself against the curved wall, I halted near the top and listened to their conversation, praying no one would choose that moment to come up or down. I was not above a bit of eavesdropping, especially in the interests of a murder investigation. Hadn't O'Malley just told me to keep my eyes and ears open?

The Xerox machine whirred; I heard Meg's voice.

"If it isn't New York's finest, how was that sandwich?"

"Still licking oil off my fingers."

I pictured Borelli holding up one hand.

"Let me see," Meg said.

I slid forward on my stomach on the stairs, hoping no one tripped over me, pushing myself so that just the top of my head could peer at them. Meg was holding Borelli's hand, and as I watched, my friend flicked her pink tongue out between two of Borelli's fingers. Great, just great.

Borelli grabbed his hand back as though burned. "You, missy, are a tease. Tell me what's happening before I ravish you on top of the copy machine."

"Promises, promises." Meg winked and the witch handed him one of the sheets she was copying.

I couldn't believe Meg was really into this guy so much, or else she'd really taken her role to heart. And as for Borelli, was this kind of behavior allowed in a murder investigation? I think not. Note to self: do not allow your fictional detective to become so chummy with a witness he's only known a few days. Shows he's a newbie.

"The whole unit has to work all weekend to catch up," Meg explained. "The producers are having a fit at the overtime, too."

"As long as they know our crime scenes are off limits," Borelli said. He leaned over the copy machine toward her. "Does that mean you have to come in, too?"

Meg nodded. "I will, to keep things running up here. Trudy, too."

Borelli grimaced. "Your friend is getting an earful from my boss. She likes to stick her nose in where it doesn't belong."

"That's not fair." Meg twisted her gold signet ring around. "Trudy was right there when Griff pointed his finger at her, and today she happened to be the one to find Misty. It could just as easily have been—"

He put a hand over Meg's mouth to briefly silence her. "Take it easy. I'm just saying O'Malley needs her to back off. And you shouldn't get involved, either. This is serious."

"You don't know Trudy like I do. She's very stubborn when

she makes up her mind, that's how she got herself into trouble with Ja—" Meg cut herself off, pushing her hair behind one ear.

Good thing, too, because I was just getting ready to stand up and interrupt this little heart-to-heart.

"I'll let her know," Meg said, and changed the subject by asking where Borelli lived.

I slid down a few stairs and turned around, going back into the main lobby, where O'Malley paced the small space, talking animatedly on his cell phone. He lowered his voice when he noticed me approach.

I walked to the main door and looked out. The wind had picked up, tossing garbage and leaves down the sidewalk. A noisy garbage truck passed slowly, and I knew if I went outside I would smell rotten food and vegetables wafting behind it. Inside I was in an artificial cocoon, but this was certainly not any type of safe haven. The reality of Misty's death was sinking in, and those bits of hastily-downed sandwich churned in my stomach.

A van zoomed up the street, looking for a place to park, and I noted the satellite antenna. It hadn't taken long for the news channels to learn of the death of Misty Raines. Touching O'Malley on his arm as he passed me, I pointed it out.

Ned tapped his phone off. He'd called into the office to check

DEATH UNSCRIPTED

on the progress of the uniformed team he'd ordered to search the entire studio, and followed up on an earlier order he'd issued. Next, he directed squad member Damon to dig out the marriage certificate on Edith Carlisle and Griffin Kennedy and bring him a copy. He felt Trudy touch his arm and knew she'd overheard that last request. She pointed to a news van parking outside.

"I'll use the marriage certificate to question the Carlisle woman without bringing you into it," he told her.

"You mean without compromising your snitch?" She arched an eyebrow.

"You read too many mysteries." His cell phone rang. "O'Malley . . . yeah, okay. Thanks, Byron." He made a note and saw Trudy hovering, watching him intently.

"You're like a puppy waiting for a treat."

She couldn't stop her blush. "I'm just interested," she insisted, growing pensive. "It wasn't fun finding Misty like that."

Ned conceded the point. "The ME agrees with anaphylactic shock, considering her peanut allergy. He's sent carrot residue from her mouth for testing. Is that enough for you? Because some of us have work to do." He smiled politely and went back downstairs.

I took a few sips of water from the fountain by the rest rooms off the lobby. What was the connection between Griff Kennedy and Misty Raines that had led someone to kill them? Or *was* there a connection? Could there be a crazed fan or a sociopath who just got off on murdering people who worked on soaps? I hoped O'Malley was looking into that angle.

I digested this thought. What was to stop the murderer from going to the crew next? And what was his motive? For that matter, poison is usually a woman's weapon. It could easily be a woman I should fear.

I tabled these preposterous thoughts, gave myself an imaginary smack upside the head and ran upstairs to tell Meg the latest.

To my chagrin, Borelli was still there, helping Meg staple pages together. Just which one of them was pumping the other for information, I couldn't tell, but maybe they'd moved on to heating up their relationship and forgotten there were two murders right on these very premises that needed solving. "I can see you're hot on the trail of the murderer, Borelli."

Didn't faze him a bit. He just smiled at Meg. "I'm getting background information on the fan base for the actors."

Oh. So O'Malley *had* thought of that angle.

One of the writers emerged from the conference room long enough to thrust a sheaf of pages at Meg. His shirt collar was open, tie off. "We can't use the Savannah Dale nude photo storyline now. What a mess. We've sent Savannah home suddenly to tend to her dying mother while Casting finds a replacement. Copies to the usual to be expressed to their homes." He rolled up his shirtsleeves, casting a harried glance at the three of us. "Please," he added, before rushing back and slamming the door.

"I guess I've got work to do," Meg said.

"Me, too. See you tomorrow." Borelli threw his empty soda can in the trash, and left, whistling his way down the stairs.

"Tomorrow?" I squawked. "Don't tell me you have a date, Meg." I hoped both hands on my hips relayed my displeasure.

"Tomorrow we all have to work, Trudy, including you." Meg handed me the weekend shooting schedule.

"Oh . . . " I said, properly chastened, until I remembered the little intimate scene Meg didn't know I'd witnessed. Still, it was her business if she wanted to ruin her life getting mixed up with a detective.

Ned had confirmation his plans were in progress and set to go. He watched the crime scene squad gather evidence in Misty's dressing room. The contents of the drawers and her purse had been bagged and tagged after the video and photographing of the interior. Now two specialists were dusting the surfaces for fingerprints.

There was a silence down here that was unlike the usual bustle of voices and ringing cell phones. All telephone calls to the studio were temporarily being forwarded across the street, and Ned still had to walk across to talk with the producers. He could only imagine the pressure that would be put on his superiors now that a second murder had occurred, literally right under his nose.

This case confused him. It had been one thing to seek a murderer for the womanizing Griff Kennedy, but now a second murder at the soap opera pointed directly at this closed community. Or did it? It should be easy to connect the two, as not everyone in Griff's life would have known Misty. But, if their relationship had been more than Misty had admitted, that wasn't necessarily true. There might be people outside the studio who had known them both together, and he would have no way to track them down. A stalker would have been seen following the actors, or the victims would have mentioned a crazy follower to one of their friends or acquaintances. That kind of thing became known fairly quickly.

He was lost in his thoughts when Borelli found him. "Get over to Kennedy's building, Tony, and show Misty's photo to the doorman. See if you can find out if she ever visited him there and check if there were any crazed fans hanging out."

Out on the street, I felt like walking. There was a light breeze I hoped would blow away the thoughts of death that lingered in my brain, at least temporarily. It was too nice a day to be squished on the subway. I walked up the block and called Meg on her cell phone.

"Busy?"

"Just finished the FedEx packets."

"Good, because seeing you with Borelli made me forget what I'd come upstairs to tell you." I recited Edith Carlisle's admission.

"I had no idea Edith and Griff were married," Meg said. "And in all the mess after Misty's death, I never told you I asked my mom about O'Malley's parents. She does know them, from charity events for the museums and The New School. His grandmother was a good friend of Vera List, who started the art poster program at Lincoln Center. Mom said the money comes from his mother's Jewish side of the family." Meg laughed. "Can you imagine her parents' faces when she brought home an Irishman named O'Malley?"

"Not unlike my Zimmer grandparents when their Hilda brought home Mario Genova," I said. "They had to elope and move upstate to get away. Hilda should have listened to her parents."

"Trudy—" Meg said with a warning tone. "This father was more of a charmer, eventually won them over. He's done very well for himself in banking, was even Grand Marshall of the St. Patty's Day Parade last year."

"As opposed to my father . . . " I mumbled.

"Don't go there, Trudy. Let it go."

"I'm going, all right—home to relax and try to get thoughts of murder out of my mind. See you tomorrow." I slipped my phone in my jeans pocket.

Shifting the backpack as I walked along, I stepped aside for a group of Japanese tourists, then wound my way around the outdoor tables and chairs of a café. I was determined not to let thoughts of my father emerge from the deepest recesses of my mind, trying instead to concentrate on the lovely bits of the day. There, that gingko tree with its unusually-shaped leaves had bloomed. I had never seen those before moving to New York and falling in love with my adopted city.

Despite the ridiculous cost of living, I'd embraced the variety of faces I saw every day, the squash of people on the sidewalks, even the traffic clogging the streets. Sure, there were times in the middle of the hot summer when the smell of too many bus fumes got to me and the heat rose and shimmered on the asphalt, but I still had my family upstate and could escape to the tall trees and the cool evenings when I felt oppressed. I never doubted the warmth of the welcome of my mother and the rest of my small family.

An odd feeling came over me, as though I was being watched. I looked behind me. An au pair pushed a stroller; a young teen bopped to his iPod; two businessmen with sleeves rolled and ties askew earnestly argued a point. I shrugged and turned onto Broadway, heading uptown, and the same feeling came over me a few blocks later.

I stopped to look in the window of an upscale stationary store, quickly scanning the opposite street in its reflection. A man among the string of walkers also stopped, turning to look at a children's shoe display.

My pulse beat faster. Was I being followed? I surged forward again another half block and halted suddenly to browse inside a clothing shop filled with racks of clothes I couldn't afford and couldn't fit into if I could. Glancing across the street I picked out the same man, his back to me, perusing the sales in a liquor store window. He had short hair, wore jeans and a windbreaker, and had 'cop' written all over him.

DEATH UNSCRIPTED

Was O'Malley having me tailed because he still thought I was in some way responsible for these two deaths?

Maybe the man wasn't a cop at all, but someone the murderer had sent to follow me. It could even *be* the murderer. My skin prickled with anxiety.

I couldn't see his face in the wavy window reflection, and didn't recognize the shape of his head or his stance. Maybe the fact of Griff pointing his finger at me, and then me finding Misty, had led the murderer to think I knew something I didn't. Did I?

I surged on, threading my way through clumps of school kids hefting backpacks, until I reached Zabar's delicatessen and broke into a sweat of indecision. At any time of day the popular store was packed, the narrow aisles jammed with shoppers waiting on lines at the different counters for fresh sliced meats or whitefish, baked goods or bagels. From inside the door, I watched the stranger wait at the light to cross the street, heading in my direction. I swallowed nervously and summoned up my courage. Two could play this game.

I made a beeline past cookies shaped like taxi cabs and pricey tins of caviar, and hooked a right into the back storeroom, pushing open the swinging door, coming face to face with a husky man carrying a huge wheel of Pecorino Romano cheese.

"Back door?" I asked, flashing a cheery smile. The man gestured behind him and walked out, leaving me to pick my way through stacks of goods and cartons to a side fire door.

I strode briskly up 81st Street toward West End Avenue, stopping once to slip off my sweater and stuff it inside my backpack. I twisted my hair into a high ponytail, securing it with a scrunchie from my pack, then wrapped the tail around and tucked the ends in under the elastic, capturing my long hair in a bun. This was the only means I had of changing my appearance and I hoped it would be enough.

When I reached West End Avenue I took a right and hesitated. Should I duck into another shop and wait to see if my pursuer found me? No, time would be on my side now as the man worked the aisles at Zabar's, searching for me. I picked up my pace, looking for a cab. Sixteen long city blocks stood between me and the safety of my apartment.

At the corner of 82nd a cab paused to let off a stout man carrying a Tattersall umbrella, and I slid inside before he'd finished paying. With great relief I gave my address, noting the driver's name, a habit I'd developed since moving to the Big Apple: Jesus DiAngelo. A smile flicked the corners of my mouth. A guardian angel just when I needed one.

Chapter Sixteen

Through the open window and above the usual city noises, Ned could hear the strains of the Fabbri Concert in progress across East 95ᵗʰ Street at the House of the Redeemer. He'd stopped home after the studio search to retrieve files he'd left in his apartment this morning. It was a fine night, a light breeze bringing in the scent of the shrubs and trees that flowered at the corner of Central Park, next to the stretch of Fifth Avenue known as "Museum Mile."

Ruth and Paddie O'Malley started their married life in this apartment, and brought baby Edmunde here from the hospital. Its high coffered ceilings and book-lined main room were the nexus of Ned's memories. His knowledge of his early years came from his mother's extensive photograph albums. It was Ruth's hobby, documenting her only child's every advancement and achievement.

Ned's hobby was going to the movies, something he hadn't done recently. He loved the cinema, sitting in the dark as he delved into the story unfolding up on the big screen. His parents preferred live entertainment, which he also enjoyed, but there was anticipation in the anonymity of a darkened theater as he lost himself in the story, an unexpected delight he'd never been able to properly explain.

Still, he was grateful for the easy relationship he shared with his parents, once Ned learned to let his father believe he was right about almost everything. His biggest failing in his mother's eyes had been choosing to become a policeman, but she'd made her peace with it once he made detective. Ned suspected Ruth Small O'Malley viewed her son as slumming in the world of murder and crime because it stimulated his intelligence, not really in any danger because he wore a suit and tie now instead of a uniform.

He hummed bits of the piece he could hear, Mozart, the piece they used in "Out of Africa." He sat down in his reading chair, the leather creaking, sorting out accumulated mail from these last hectic days.

A thorough search of the studio had taken the rest of the afternoon, its cavernous ceiling and depths revealing several dead mice and one live sparrow they'd released to freedom outside, but no EpiPens. After visiting the producers across the street, he'd returned to the precinct to set up the murder room for Misty Raines. He'd scanned his team's reports, pleased to see Borelli's in particular had been succinct. The young detective had gleaned what he could from the crew who worked the sound stage main floor.

Ned closed his eyes, trying to pull the pieces of these crimes together. What linked Griff Kennedy and Misty Raines? The obvious answer would be jealousy from either one of his wives, and both would have to be interviewed again. Jotting notes, setting up tomorrow's agenda, Ned scrutinized the yellow shooting schedule he'd received:

Scene I: TP Health Spa: Mindy and Cindy, 2 U-5 masseuses
Scene II: Town Board Mtg: Mayor Riggs, All Councilmen
Scene III: Hospital Waiting Rm: Vikki, children, 1 U-5 MD, 2
U-5 RN's

Ned flipped to the front of his notebook, consulted a list of phone numbers and dialed, then hung up before it could ring. Across the street the music had stopped. He knew the audience inside the wood-paneled library would be meeting the artists at a reception. Ned wondered if Trudy Genova would enjoy this kind of evening. His stomach growled. Shaking his head, he hit redial.

I was almost finished working at the kitchen table on pages I found on my fax machine when I'd gratefully arrived home. By that time I'd calmed down and decided I'd imagined the whole episode. The poor man was probably just on his way home from work, enjoying window-shopping, and I'd blown the entire episode out of proportion.

These pages were from a Thanksgiving special Jimmy Kimmel was planning, and I had to check a scene where he was playing a surgeon getting ready to dissect the family turkey. I had researched scalpel names on my laptop to see if I could add to the humor. My stomach growled, and when the phone rang, I was very aware my lunch sandwich was long gone.

"Hello?"

"Trudy, Ned O'Malley here. I had a few questions to ask you about the shooting schedule, and I wanted to know if you'd finished that list for me."

"Did you order the pizza?"

"The what?"

I smirked, pleased I'd caught the great detective off guard. "Up on the corner, Vinces', best pizza around. I'm ravenous and I'll bet you haven't had anything since those sandwiches at lunch. Bring the pizza and I'll give you that list and answer any questions you have."

"Well . . . "

I could feel him weighing his decision. Don't be a dud, Ned-O. Finally I heard a small sigh over the line, then:

"What do you like on yours?"

"Anything but anchovies. Surprise me."

I pushed my papers and laptop to one end of the table, figuring it would take O'Malley a while to catch a cab and pick up the pizza and I could accomplish more before he arrived. But first I set the table at the opposite end by the window seat with two places. My placemats and napkins were clean, but when had they gotten so washed out? I put out two wineglasses and took a bottle of Chianti Classico from the wine rack and opened it to breathe, then added water glasses, a shaker of crushed red pepper and a tub of grated cheese.

I debated for all of two seconds about putting on makeup but did brush my teeth and used a spritz of cologne to combat the garlic I knew Vince's used liberally. I twisted my hair up and off my neck, securing it with a clip, added lip-gloss and was back in the kitchen hard at work when the intercom buzzed twenty-five minutes later.

"Pizza by very special delivery," my doorman said. Sal was definitely amused. The same guy who'd carted me away was now bringing me pizza. It was the stuff of the movies I worked on.

"Send him up and no delivery-man jokes, Sal," I begged. Sal liked to think he was a stand-up comedian of sorts and had a joke stored up for every occasion.

Watching out my peephole, I saw a distorted detective carrying two pizza boxes coming down the hall toward my door. Overkill, just like a man—although I did like cold pizza for breakfast.

"Smells delicious," I told O'Malley as he entered. I pointed to the counter. "You can put them there." I realized I should have asked him about the wine. "I opened wine, I hope that's all right."

"No, it's fine. I'm off duty." He busied himself opening the boxes. "This one's chicken and pesto and that one's regular with pepperoni." O'Malley pointed to the appropriate boxes. "I got two so you could freeze the leftovers."

Spoken like a true bachelor, but then, I was a singleton, too. "Actually, I eat cold pizza for breakfast sometimes."

"Me, too!" O'Malley quickly tempered his burst of enthusiasm. "Technically I shouldn't be here, not in a social situation."

"But you said you had some questions for me and we both have to eat," I pointed out, getting out my pizza cutter. "So relax. It's sort of business. You can pour for us."

"You always have an angle, don't you?" He filled their

glasses.

"Does that smile mean you've crossed me off your suspect list?" I opened the boxes and inhaling appreciatively.

"Let's say I believe you wouldn't be caught under Griff Kennedy's spell." He held out his plate. "One of each, please."

I filled his plate. "Not likely." I was pleased he believed me now about Griff, and wondered if I should tell him I thought I'd been followed today. But then I didn't want him to think I was a wimp. I served myself and sat next to him on the bench, careful not to let my thigh touch his. "Let's have a truce." I raised my glass.

O'Malley raised his and we clinked. "Truce. As long as you report to me and keep your nose out of my investigation."

An hour later most of the wine was gone as well as a surprising amount of pizza. Talk turned to their families, and Ned learned Trudy's two brothers ran the family orchard business, and her mother and sister-in-law managed their roadside shop. Ned looked at the pages of the skit on the end of the table and asked her about them.

"My home work." Trudy explained the work she did on scripts and showed him some of the corrections she'd made. "And I get to do it in my jammies."

"Sounds really interesting," he said, picturing her sitting there in said jammies. Way too much wine.

"It is." Trudy rose. "I think we need coffee. I've got decaf if you don't want to be up all night." She took their plates to the dishwasher.

"Sounds good. I don't need the caffeine Borelli does."

Trudy nodded. "He definitely jitters a lot." She brought out a grinder; the rich smell of freshly ground beans rose in the tiny kitchen. "I've always thought coffee smells better than it tastes. Before we forget, I've made a copy of that list of anyone I could think of who was behind me when Griff died, but I'm not sure what good it will do. What were the other questions you had?"

"Oh, yeah." Ned reached for his jacket and pulled the yellow pages from his pocket. "There are names on tomorrow's schedule I haven't seen before."

"Sure, other story lines. They have to catch up on taping. You didn't think you'd met the entire cast?" She filled the coffee maker with water and turned it on. A tapping at the window behind Ned caught her attention. "Would you mind letting Wilkie in?"

Ned slid the window up and a large ginger cat sauntered in over the sill, dropped gracefully to the bench and down to the floor. The cat sniffed the detective's shoes. Apparently finding Ned acceptable, Wilkie wound his way around his legs, purring louder with each pass. "I think I've passed inspection. I'm more of a dog person, myself."

The brewing coffee gurgled as the carafe filled. "Me, too," Trudy said, "only he was a gift. And don't be too impressed. He's a food slut, hoping you'll feed him." She snapped open the lid of a can of cat food.

At the sound the cat immediately abandoned Ned's legs

and ran to his bowl. "Traitor. But back to the cast . . . "

"Let's see, Vikki has twin daughters you haven't met, Mindy and Cindy; there's Mayor Briggs and the city council who fight the town's progress, oh, and the district attorney who's having an affair with the mayor's wife. Then there's Wanda Wallace, the diner waitress, who everyone confides in, and Griff's stepson from his third marriage—"

Ned interrupted her recitation. "Where have these people been?"

"Most of them were in Monday and would have been back today, but we were behind due to Griff's death. If we fall too far behind, the entire show is off down the road, remember?" Trudy brought two full mugs to the table. "What do you take in it?"

She plunked a carton of skim milk on the table and added a small crock filled with pink, yellow and blue packets.

"Black is fine. Can't make up your mind?" he asked, gesturing to her crock.

"Purloined from restaurants. Guess I've always had a hankering to be on the wrong side of the law." Trudy's smile lit up the small kitchen.

Ned breathed in the clean scent of her, green and grassy with a hint of apple, maybe her shampoo or cologne, and became acutely aware he didn't belong there.

On his way to pick up the pizzas he'd rationalized that Trudy's background check was clean, she had no motive, and no relationship with her outside work had turned up for either victim. Putting her lawyer's objections aside, Trudy had readily pointed out the poisoning side effects before he'd told her of the ME's suspicions. All of those things had led him to trust his instincts on her innocence. Despite those feelings it hit him that having a meal socially with someone who was part of his investigation was the last thing he should be doing.

He drained his coffee mug. "I should be going." He slid off the bench seat and stood.

Trudy stood, too. "Thanks again. Dinner was really good and it was nice not to eat alone." She stayed by the table, pointing to the laptop and pages at the other end of the table. "I thought these were my companions for the night."

"It's really fascinating work you do," Ned told her.

"Not as fascinating as catching a murderer, though . . . " Her voice trailed off.

After refusing to take home leftover pizza, Ned left her apartment, wondering if Trudy Genova was lonely.

Ned O'Malley knew his strengths as a detective, but tonight he was puzzled by his own behavior. He decided to think of this evening's pizza dinner as a spontaneous meeting over food for two hungry people, just as Trudy had phrased it. Yes, it would be all right to think of it that way; gathering background information to help with his investigation was a good thing.

Trudy was an interesting person, very different from Lucilla, the dark-haired beauty his mother had tried to set him up with. Ruth O'Malley had sat them next to each other at a fundraiser a few months ago, and while the young woman was certainly attractive, there had been no spark between them. He'd been polite toward her, but he hadn't planned to see her again.

A few weeks later Ruth insisted his father had a terrible headache and she just couldn't attend the ballet on her own. He'd had the night off and let himself be talked into accompanying his mother, whose company he'd enjoyed—until they took their seats. He remembered his father hardly ever had headaches when he found Lucilla and her mother sitting next to them. Surprise, surprise.

He'd had to be stern with Ruth on their way home.

"Please stop matchmaking, Mother. I know you mean well, but I can find my own dates."

His mother pouted. "We could have had dessert with them. You told me you didn't have a big case on and suddenly you have an early meeting?"

"I have a job, Mom, and I'm a big boy now. Stop interfering, please."

His mother had sat back with a sigh but taken his hand and he knew on some level she understood. "It's the call of grandchildren I'm worried I'll never have spurring me on. But I'll try to leave you alone."

"Thank you." He kissed her hand and since then she'd kept her word.

He drew a sheaf of reports toward him, rubbing his eyes, wondering what Ruth O'Malley would make of Trudy Genova. The fact was that he'd crossed Trudy off his list of suspects before tonight. And he'd needed that list from her, although

DEATH UNSCRIPTED

she was correct when she said it wasn't as meaningful as when he'd first asked for it. Anyone at the studio could have put the poison in Griff's cup earlier in the day. Still, it was a reasonable meeting, and he'd learned about the cast members he still had to interview. Misty's death upped the stakes and he had to find the tie between the two deaths.

So why was he feeling guilty? One thing was certain, he needed to put some space between himself and the nurse whose damned cat had left hair all over his pants.

I scrubbed my face and brushed my teeth vigorously while I dissected the evening. There was no question O'Malley and I had gotten off to a shaky start at first. If I were being honest, which I could be in the privacy of my own bathroom, I enjoyed provoking his look of consternation when I refused to let him intimidate me.

Still, there was undeniable a shift tonight, something hanging in the air between us. After a glass of wine, Ned had let down his guard and become almost human. He'd asked a lot of questions about my family and growing up in the country, and I'd managed to deflect talking about my father with stories of life on a working apple farm. There were the seasonal workers who became part of the family for a few months of the year, and the many animals I'd had over the years. The family always had a dog or two, most who slept

M.K. GRAFF

on my bed, and numerous cats to keep the mice population at bay. There had been goats at one point, and ducks and chickens, too.

Ned seemed to enjoy the stories of my brothers bullying and teasing me when I was young. He admitted he was an only child, and at that moment had looked vulnerable. As I turned out my light, I decided he'd been lonely growing up. From the little I knew of this man, the insight was something he'd probably be horrified to learn I'd picked up on.

CHAPTER SEVENTEEN

Saturday, May 8th

Email Subject: WORRIED
From: GenovaOrchard@hotmail.com
Date: Fri, 8 May 2008 19:28:49
To: "Trudy" trudegen@gmail.net

Hello Trudy dear,

I know you'll check this before you would return a phone message. Whatever is going on down there? Are you safe? The news up here is full of the murders at that soap opera you work on. All of the neighbors have been calling to ask me if you know anything about it. Of course I've assured them you wouldn't be anywhere near that kind of thing. Ben and Gail and probably Rick and his friend are taking me to dinner in Albany, so don't worry about not getting home for my birthday. But don't forget the summer trip you promised. You may be surprised at some changes around here by then. Gail and Ben are trying for a baby, but please, keep that under your hat, you know how Ben can be. Stay safe, liebchen.

Love,
Mom

I'd fallen asleep pretty quickly for the first time all week—I might have to start drinking wine on a nightly basis—and was glad I'd checked my email when I rose. I dashed off a reassuring note back to my mother, warding off a stab of guilt, glad Hilda Genova wouldn't have to know the truth of my closeness to both murders.

Walking briskly down Columbus Avenue, I wove in and out of tourists, couples, mothers or nannies with strollers, and a man handing out flyers for a special rate on hair extensions. I felt as glad for the exercise as for the chance to brush the cobwebs from my brain. Although I'd slept better, I had still had one of those awful dreams just before waking.

This time I was in Central Park, tied to a tree. I watched helplessly, filled with remorse, as Misty Raines wolfed down a peanut butter and jelly sandwich, while the man who I imagined had followed me yesterday watched from behind a towering wisteria in full flower, its hanging purple flowers like bunches of grapes dangling in the breeze. Of course in the dream I couldn't see his face any more than I'd seen it yesterday.

An ambulance sprinted past, siren screeching, lights swirling. I hoped the paramedics would be of more help to their passenger than I'd been to Griff Kennedy or Misty Raines. As much as I wanted to insinuate myself into this investigation, I hadn't forgotten they were human beings who'd been murdered. One thing had been brought home to me this last week, something I'd forgotten since leaving clinical practice to work in the artificial world of soaps: life could end in a nanosecond, despite medical efforts and precautions.

DEATH UNSCRIPTED

My mother's birthday next week gave me the perfect excuse for a little retail therapy. I had to get her present in the mail by Monday to reach upstate in time. And although I would call Hilda on the day, I felt badly about not taking time off to get home to see her. I'd told my mother I was swamped with work and reaffirmed my summer visit when I answered her email. That was mostly true. But my mother wouldn't be particularly happy to know the work I was wrapped up with concerned two murders. Thank goodness my name hadn't been in the papers.

Going home is usually a mixed bag for me, something I looked forward to but could only take in small doses. I always left before the memories could crowd in, something that didn't seem to bother my brothers, who had made their peace with the ghosts of the past.

Stopping to cross at the light on West 83rd Street, I looked around. The architecture here wasn't as interesting, and I hadn't noticed anyone following me today. I also didn't see anyone remotely resembling the man from yesterday. An assortment of high-end vehicles, SUV's, and the ubiquitous taxis streamed past, then a woman in a black BMW M-3, wearing a black hijab. The woman slid her bright blue phone under the edge of the hijab, using it to clamp the phone in place. That was a new way to do hands-free calling, so New York. I would have to get my mom to visit the Big Apple for a change so I could show her the sights. Maybe after harvest.

I had the light and ran across the street, passing Lenny's Deli, where I'd grab lunch before heading to the studio. But first things first. I had a gift to find, and I turned into the April Cornell store. The shop's distinctively colored prints were some of Mom's favorites, and I browsed through the linens to check out tablecloths. Flipping through the bright nature-inspired patterns of flowers, leaves and birds, I found one that would look well in Mom's cheery country kitchen. A set of blue and green place mats on the next shelf caught my eye. These were my two favorite colors together, and they'd look great on my bleached pine table.

You hardly ever have company, my practical side argued. But then my rowdy side answered: "Who knows when someone might show up with pizza?"

"Can I help you?" A tall saleswoman with an armful of wooden bangles, wearing a deep rose Cornell-designed jumper, appeared by my side.

I handed over the tablecloth I'd chosen for Mom, hesitating over the place mats. A police car went past just then, its squealing siren and flashing lights ratcheting up the cacophony of the city's noises. I remembered Griff's pointing finger, Misty's frightened eyes, too much yellow crime scene tape.

"What the hell," I said, handing over the place mats and adding the matching napkins. "Maybe they'll force me to invite someone over for a real meal."

The morning had been busy for Ned's team, collecting information and statements from the cast members who had previously escaped their scrutiny. After a team meeting it was established that everyone took their days off seriously; none of the actors from Monday's cast had been to the studio on either of the pertinent days. Only the twins who played Nikki Olivier's daughters had been to PBJ headquarters across the street on the day Griff had died, for an appearance on the King and Kiley show. Taping finished at ten o'clock, and they had been getting a manicure together while Griff Kennedy was still in rehearsal.

Once the rest of the team had gone back to the precinct house, Ned and Tony sat in the rehearsal hall they'd commandeered, comparing notes. Tony had evidently enjoyed interviewing the curvaceous twins.

"They finish each other's sentences," he told Ned, draining his coffee cup.

"At least they're twins who play twins. The guy who plays Griff's stepson is supposed to have Dissociative Identity Disorder. One day—"

"Dis what?" Tony interrupted.

"What used to be called schizophrenia. Anyway, one day he's a good guy and the next he's a blackmailer. The viewers apparently eat that stuff up." Ned flipped through his notebook.

Tony nodded. "My mother was glued to *Bright and Beautiful* in the 80's and my father swears she wanted to name me after her hero. Instead of Anthony I could have been Nigel."

"Nigel? Nigel Borelli?" Ned had a good laugh at that one. "What changed her mind?"

"My father convinced her there wasn't a Saint Nigel."

A quick door knock was followed by Trudy sticking her

head around the doorway. "Hi there, what's new in the world of detecting?"

"We're just breaking for a late lunch. You go ahead and eat, Borelli. I've got two re-interviews here. Then go back and oversee the data loading at the precinct, and check with Byron in case any tests have come through. And don't forget any updates on those beatings." Ned was deep into his notebook, avoiding any hint that last night left a residual awkwardness. Business as usual.

Borelli shot out of his chair. "See ya, boss," he called.

Trudy entered the room but stayed by the door. Ned waited for her to ask about the beatings he'd mentioned, but instead she said: "Want me to get you something to eat?"

"No thanks, I'm still full from a late bagel sandwich this morning. Who are you here for today?" Ned kept his tone light.

Trudy advanced into the room. "The death scene when they get to it. I don't want to refuse the . . . work."

Ned stood, towering over her. "You mean you don't want to refuse the chance to snoop around," he chided. "Be careful. I can't watch over you."

"You don't need to," she protested, jutting her chin out. "I can take care of myself."

Ned briefly rested a hand on her shoulder. "I suspect Misty Raines had the same thought."

I poured a cup of coffee from the urn and took it with me, making a slow circuit of the sound stage, avoiding the end set where a scene with Nikki's twins and Griff's stepson was taping. They were staged in a cutaway, supposedly the back of a limousine, on their way to the hospital for a visit, arguing about petty things while Griff's life supposedly lay in limbo. One of the things I enjoyed learning when I'd first come to the soap was how the sets managed to convey things like the inside of cars and look so real on television. Yet anyone seeing this set now would marvel at the missing side of the car, lit from within to show the actor's faces to their best advantage, and the microphones hanging on a high boom just over the roof of the car, out of camera sight. More magic.

When I'd looked for Meg, I found a note on her desk: "Across the street." Probably sharing lunch with Borelli, this time without the added benefit of O'Malley's company. Humph.

I waved to a few crew members, then saw Frank Resnick arguing with Ron Dowling behind a health spa set. What would that be about? I tried to edge closer but they saw me and moved deeper into the shadows. I could try to get Frank alone later and ask him indirectly about it if time allowed. Eavesdropping was my specialty as the cast and crew were used to me wandering around the sets, staying in the background.

My slow circuit took me around to the Prop Room. Gary Knowles berated one of his helpers, a burly man carrying a large oil painting by the hanging wire.

"Hold it by the frame, Emilio," Knowles directed, pulling off his polishing gloves. He shook his head when he saw me; Emilio smiled on his way out. "The proverbial bull in a china shop," Knowles said.

"Where's that headed, Gary?" I perched on a stool facing his worktable.

"Over Vikki's mantel. Dowling decided the one we have there is too bright for the mood he wanted. As if now he's an interior decorator." Another shake of his head.

"I just saw him in a pretty heated discussion with Frank," I prodded. Maybe I could get the goods from Gary.

"This place will be lucky if they still have a stage manager by tomorrow. Dowling was bashing Griff Kennedy and Frank overheard him—" Knowles leaned over the table toward me, lowering his voice. "—telling a grip he was certain Griff had bedded Eva. You don't mess with Frank when it comes to Eva."

This was news to me but explained what I'd just seen. "I thought Frank and Eva's relationship was pretty casual."

"So does Eva."

Ned's mood was glum after taking a call from his captain. Jack Morton berated Ned about the lack of progress on the assaults on three men whose backgrounds didn't contain any criminal history.

"One of these men has permanent nerve damage to his back, O'Malley," Jellyroll said. "Another almost died when his broken ribs punctured a lung, and the third had his leg stomped to pieces."

"I'm aware of the injuries, sir."

His boss grunted. "Nothing from the streets?"

"None of the gangs are taking credit, and we can't find anything linking the three men. I've had a good researcher spending hours on it."

"Push harder, Ned. We need a result. And I hope there's one soon on these soap opera murders or the mayor may have both our heads." Jellyroll cut the connection and Ned sighed. He understood the man's frustration and shared it. They couldn't find an avenue to explore in the assault cases and had run out of places to look.

Ned pushed his hair back off his forehead and stretched his long legs. Right now the last thing he wanted to do was approach either of the women he'd assigned himself today. He'd checked the call schedule. Nikki wasn't involved in the scene taping upstairs at the moment. He reluctantly headed to her dressing room, hoping the latest tragedy would not encourage an encore performance of her crying jag.

To his surprise the door was ajar, and after knocking, the actress imperiously waved him in.

"Come in, Detective. Frank said you wanted to see me before taping." Nikki sat opening mail at her dressing table, composed and regal in full hair and makeup, and motioned him to the love seat.

"Thank you, Miss Olivier." Trudy would be proud of his pronunciation. He opened his notebook and sat across from her. "How are you managing after Misty's death?"

"Poor, dear girl. She was so young and so pretty, such a shame."

Ned was certain she didn't mean a word of it. "I'll start by asking if you were in her dressing room yesterday."

"I've never been in her dressing room, Detective. It wasn't a place I wanted to visit." Nikki rifled through a large stack of sympathy cards on her lap.

Ned shifted his legs on the low sofa. "Did you see anyone entering or leaving it after, say, eleven o'clock?"

She turned away from him, peering into the lighted magnifying mirror before her, inspecting her eyebrows for a stray hair. "I could hardly keep up with a revolving door, Detective. You'll have to ask someone else. I came in late, so distraught about Griff the night before, and kept to myself, right here."

So you could triumph over tragedy yet again. The lines between her acting life and her real life seemed to blur. So much for witness cooperation. "So if I were to tell you she and Griff Kennedy were rumored to be having an affair, you wouldn't have any personal knowledge of that?"

The actor arched an eyebrow and turned back to him. "I certainly do have personal knowledge. It's preposterous." Anger bathed her entire being, flooding her face with a rosy color. "This place is a haven for gossip. You shouldn't rely on *anything* anyone tells you to be the truth."

"If you never went in there, and you and Griff were divorced, how can you be so certain of his actions?" Ned pushed her, interested in her reaction.

She jumped to her feet. "Because he loved me, Detective O'Malley. Griff Kennedy liked people to think he slept around, but deep down, he was still in love with *me!*" Her body trembled, and she sat back down heavily. "Now please go. I have to be composed for my scene."

DEATH UNSCRIPTED

I watched the taping of the waiting room scene, pleased with my morning shopping on all counts, and intrigued by the information Gary Knowles had given me. Frank Resnick's jealousy over Eva made a compelling motive for murder and fit both victims: Griff for trying to bed her, and here I had to ask myself if he had succeeded; and Misty for spreading the rumor in the first place. Or perhaps Misty had teased Frank about it, or appeared to know something he didn't and he'd snapped. I'd have to tell Ned-O to look into Frank a bit deeper. Maybe I needed to get a notebook like the one he carried.

My musings were interrupted by a heated discussion between Edith Carlisle and Nikki Olivier. Nikki had just arrived on set, and although the two women stood well out of camera range and were attempting to keep their voices low, it was obvious they were in disagreement about something. A wardrobe choice or Griff Kennedy? Had Edith decided to tell Nikki about her youthful marriage to Griff?

Edith turned on her heel and left the sound stage. I watched Nikki compose herself and transform to Vikki just before her cue, reminding me that Nikki was an Emmy-winning actor. She could be stringing all of us along with her protestations of undying love for Griff, or for that matter, her supposed lack of jealousy of Misty.

As Vikki, she strode into the mock waiting room urgently, easily bursting into tears when the "doctor" came out of the hospital room to tell her and the waiting family that her husband had suffered a "major setback." I suppose that was one way of explaining things, death being a pretty major setback.

The twins rallied around Vikki, comforting her as she dabbed at her eyes with a tissue Mindy or Cindy handed her.

"How bad is it?" Vikki asked.

The doctor explained that Griff had suffered a cardiac arrest and had not survived resuscitation attempts.

"You mean—he's dead?" Vikki shrieked.

I could imagine the dramatic soundtrack that would accompany the question. Camera Two moved in for a few reaction close-ups of the family and Vikki, then Frank yelled "CUT!"

The crew started setting up to tape a scene of Nikki crying over Griff's body and reminiscing. Footage of past scenes of Nikki and Griff from previous shows would be spliced in later. This had turned out to be my challenge of the day, since of course, Griff Kennedy was not going to be in that hospital bed.

A U-5 resembling him in height and coloring lay in the hospital bed in his stead. I used Polaroids from Continuity, taken after I'd hooked Griff up previously, to approximate the same positions of the monitor leads and intravenous lines on the actor. He was a pleasant young man named Bill, disappointed when I explained his face wouldn't be in the camera's view, just his body.

My problem would be to keep Bill's chest from rising when he was supposed to be dead. Camera One would be trained on Nikki's face as she reminisced, but Camera Two would be a wide shot across the body as she cried or put her head down. Any rise or fall of his chest at that angle would be seen on camera and thus by the viewers at home, spoiling the illusion of Nikki crying over a dead Griff.

I pondered how to nail this when Ron Dowling minced over. "This is a tricky one without the real Griff Kennedy," I pointed out. Dead or alive, I mentally added.

"Nothing could be worse than working with that lush," Dowling muttered. "It was like trying to get emotion from a log."

Phew, there was real enmity here. "Doesn't sound like you cared for him too much," I whispered back, hoping to provoke a slip of something incriminating.

"What I care about is you, Nancy, figuring out a way to make this scene work." He consulted his watch. "And you've got nine minutes to do it." He flounced away to the Control Room, leaving me to wonder just how deep his hatred ran for Griff Kennedy, while I tried to sort out how to keep an actor from breathing, and on cue to boot.

CHAPTER EIGHTEEN

Ned sought out Edith Carlisle and found the woman downstairs in Wardrobe, a room filled with racks of recently worn clothing, organized by the dates of the shows they'd been worn in. Other racks held outfits by size to be chosen for future shows.

"Do you have a minute, Miss Carlisle?"

Edith pursed her lips. "Everyone's picked up their wardrobe. I was getting ready to turn everything off. We don't usually work on Saturday, you know."

"I'm aware of that," he said, advancing to the front of the room, "but this is a murder investigation." Tact was needed here. "I'm afraid allowances must be made on many levels."

"Very well." She took off her enormous glasses, searched a worktable until she found a cotton cloth, then breathed on the large lenses and wiped them carefully before putting them back in place. "You might as well come back here and be comfortable." She walked through the room, turning off switches on the sewing machines she passed.

Ned followed her into the small room that bridged the workroom and a huge wardrobe storage area. They settled into chairs beside a bank of storage closets, but the Wardrobe Mistress kept her sweater on and continued to clutch her oversized purse, a message she wasn't planning to be detained for long.

He withdrew his notebook and a copy of Griff and Edith's marriage certificate, leaving the paper folded on his lap. "You were less than frank with me when we spoke before, Miss Carlisle, and I'm wondering what prompted that."

She met his eyes. "I don't know what you mean. I answered your questions honestly."

Ned handed her the certificate and watched her eyes widen with recognition as she read it.

With a sigh, she folded it and handed it back. "You never asked me about that. It was a long time ago."

Ned was firm. "I hardly think you would forget you were once married to the victim, information that might have bearing on these murders."

Her look of surprise seemed real. "Murders? You mean Misty was murdered? I thought she died from her peanut allergy, a foolish mistake."

"More likely deliberate action. Did you go into her dressing room yesterday at all?"

"No—no, she picked up her costume from me before lunch." Edith pushed her glasses back up her nose. "I'm truly stunned. Why would someone kill Misty?"

Ned ignored the question and shifted his legs on the small chair. Nothing was sized for his height. "Tell me about the cup Griff carried all the time."

"That stupid the Emmy cup with the dirty straw? He did carry it around but he never left it in here. I told you that."

Ned changed his tack. "Were you and Griff still close?"

She shook her head. "Polite in public, never close. I didn't want anyone here to know of what I considered to be my youthful mistake. Unlike Nikki, I want people to respect me as a professional—something a relationship with Griff never inspired." She peered up at him through her glasses, her pupils enlarged. "I trust you don't have to make that information general knowledge? It was years ago and has no bearing on what's been happening."

"I certainly won't broadcast it, but in a murder investigation it's impossible to keep some things secret. Surely it wouldn't have any impact on your position here now?"

The woman slumped back against her chair. "No, I suppose not. I just hate to give *her* anything to crow about."

Ned raised his eyebrows in question and waited.

Edith complied. "Nikki Olivier—who do you think took Griff away from me? They were playing opposite each other in *Bell, Book and Candle* when I was dressing Katherine Hepburn in *Coco*, a truly marvelous woman you know. Kate saw some of my sketches and remembered me years later when she came back to Broadway in that play with Christopher Reeve, now what was the name?" Edith shook her head and looked down. "*A Matter of Gravity*, that's it. I swear my memory gets worse every day. Anyway, that break was my start in costume design. I was always grateful to her." Edith's dreamy look had her lost in memory.

Ned tried to guide her back to the topic at hand. "So Nikki and Griff met during that play and had an affair?"

"To be fair, we never advertised our marriage in the theater, and I used my maiden name, so only a few close friends knew we were married. It was as much Griff's fault as hers, with his wandering eye. I wouldn't put up with him once I knew he'd never be faithful." The tiny woman drew herself up and lifted her chin. "Still, if I ever wanted to murder anyone it would've been *her*, not him, or that poor deluded child."

"Why do you call Misty deluded?" Ned asked.

"Because of her mistaken belief Griff could help her career. It was all Griff could do to get himself to the set on the right days."

"So it wouldn't have mattered to you if Misty Raines had been having an affair with Griff? No lingering jealousy?"

"He'd ceased to be my problem years ago, Detective. And as for loving him, I detested him. Griff Kennedy is the only human being I can honestly say I grew to hate."

It took me all of my nine minutes, but I finally had a solution that would work. When I described it to the U-5 in bed, he gratefully agreed.

First, I asked Gary Knowles for a long length of string, which the Prop Master readily had at hand. I tied one end around the actor's big toe, threaded the string under the sheet and blanket down to the floor and ran it out to the edge of the set. Then I sat on the floor out of camera range, but where I had a good view of Camera Two's light, and wrapped the end of the string around my hand. I couldn't afford to let go of it if this was going to work.

"All set on the floor?" Ron Dowling's voice rumbled from

the Control Room.

"Quiet on the set," Frank called out. He picked up the clapperboard, held it in front of Camera One, and with its loud snap, called out "Action!"

The light on Camera One came on, tracking the door to the room as it opened. With her eyes already reddened from the previous scene and helped along with a few sniffs of Vicks Vaporub, Nikki rushed in.

"Oh, my darling," she cried, sinking down to the chair conveniently placed at her side of the bed. The light on Camera Two went on and I tugged hard on the string. The actor in bed held his breath through the shot of Nikki sobbing. When Camera One lit again for Nikki's close-up, I tugged the string again and the actor gulped a breath of air. I kept it up throughout the entire scene, a smile lighting my face. It was a success even Ron Dowling would have to admire.

Ned was going to enter the sound stage but the lit "Taping" sign over the door halted him. A crewman eased the door open on his way out and, one finger to his lips, held the door for Ned. As they passed each other, the man whispered: "Just walk quietly and don't let this door slam." Ned thanked him and closed the heavy door carefully behind him, standing inside the dark studio until his eyes adjusted.

It was clear from the lights where the action was, and Ned

carefully picked his way over the maze of lighting and camera cables as he approached the hospital set. Nikki Olivier had her head down on the bed, filled with a Griff Kennedy look-alike thirty years younger. Trudy sat on the floor holding a piece of string. She gave the string a sharp tug and the actor inhaled deeply.

"CUT! Nice work people." Dowling's voice boomed over the loudspeaker. Nikki and most of the crew moved off and left. Ned saw Trudy carefully loosen the tape on the leads and phony IV lines from the actor on the bed, chatting easily with him as she untied a string from his foot. The bright set lights picked up the fiery highlights in her hair. Eva and Li nodded to Ned as they gathered their gear and moved off set; the cameramen abandoned their posts, leaving their machines where they were. With a loud thump, the lights suddenly shut down, softer dim lighting from above showing the way out.

The actor thanked Trudy and got out of bed with her help. When she glimpsed Ned, she joined him.

"What was the string about?"

Trudy explained how the tugs allowed the actor to hold his breath during the shots across his chest. "Corpses don't usually breathe," she said poker-faced, then with concern, added, "You look exhausted. Let's sit down."

He followed her to the next set, the living room where he'd found Tony interviewing Frank Resnick the other day. Overcome with tiredness, Ned sank gratefully into a leather wing chair, while Trudy perched on the ottoman in front of him. She launched into a description of the argument she'd seen between Frank Resnick and Ron Dowling, and how Gary Knowles explained it concerned gossip about Eva that

Frank felt Ron had been spreading.

She looked happy to have contributed an avenue for him to explore. "Anything new on your end?"

Trudy's energy was contagious. He looked around before answering her; they seemed alone for the moment and she *had* been the one to let him know about Edith and Griff's marriage. "I confronted Edith Carlisle with her marriage license. Your name never came up, by the way. She said if it had been Nikki murdered, she could see she'd be a suspect, but as for Griff, she merely hated him."

"Not worth the effort to get rid of, huh?"

"Something like that." He shook his head. "As though hate isn't a strong enough emotion to provide a motive for murder. Misty Raines had the most motive so far, but she's not around to interrogate."

"I think it's highly unlikely Misty would choose that horrible death for a remorseful suicide." Trudy shifted around on the seat. "Ned, I have an idea."

Oh, joy. He groaned inwardly and braced himself even as the thought flitted through his mind that she'd called him by his first name. "I thought I heard the wheels turning."

"Don't be a smart-ass. Isn't it true people can't be somewhere without leaving trace evidence of themselves? A loose hair, a clothing fiber, a fingerprint?"

"*Locard's principle*—you've been reading again."

"Always. But the point is, did you find any fibers or hairs in Misty's dressing room?"

Ned nodded. "You're thinking of that man's arm you saw in there. We found a few, but who knows whom they belong to? The fibers could be from anyone's clothing, even Misty's.

DEATH UNSCRIPTED

Until we have something to try to match them against, we just hold them. Borelli called before and said our ME did find a cotton fiber in the peanut-laced carrot."

Trudy narrowed her eyes. "What about hair?"

"We'd need a warrant to get a DNA sample from a suspect— and we don't have enough probable cause to ask for one from anyone."

"Yet." Trudy's smile was infectious.

"Always the optimist."

"I'm trying to be a cup half-full person," she said, examining the scuffmarks on her suede boots. "Say O'Malley, want to come for dinner tonight? I owe you for that pizza. And we could talk the case through."

She was incorrigible when it came to getting involved in his case. He sighed. "Sorry, I'd really like to, but I already have a date with a pile of garbage."

Trudy snickered. "That's not a nice way to describe your girlfriend." She stood up.

He hesitated. "No, really, I have to see what the team has found, sorting through the garbage we picked up from the studio. Can I take a rain check though?"

"Sure. I'll just get my things."

She turned to leave and he followed her out, pausing at the staircase before she ran down for her backpack, casting around for something to say that wouldn't sound inane. God, he was out of practice at this, whatever this was.

"What's on your agenda tonight, Trudy?"

She shrugged. "Stay home and work, I suppose. And I always have a book going."

He nodded. "Coming in tomorrow?"

She shook her head. "I'm off until the big funeral Monday."

"I'll probably see you then." Ned watched her run downstairs. He pushed open the glass doors to the building, breathing in the fresh evening air, wishing he could follow Trudy to her apartment to have that dinner, instead of returning to the precinct house and the garbage trawl results that awaited him.

CHAPTER NINETEEN

I retrieved my backpack, annoyed I hadn't brought up with O'Malley the possibility I'd been followed. The more I thought about it, the more confused I became. If Ned had truly crossed me off his list of suspects, then why would he send someone to tail me? He hadn't flinched when I'd slipped and called him Ned—thank goodness I'd plugged my mouth before the 'O' came out. "Ned-O" was one nickname I had to stop using and soon. The last thing I wanted to do was to alienate him, just when it seemed he was finally including me in his investigation, however reluctantly.

I mounted the office stairs to show Meg the tablecloth I'd bought my mother.

"Your mom will love it, Trudy," Meg agreed.

Meg's color was high, a pretty natural pink glow on her cheeks. It must have been quite a lunch. "Anything from Borelli today?" I asked, re-wrapping the cloth carefully.

Meg frowned. "Nothing we didn't know before. He's really conscientious when it comes to his job. We did have a nice lunch, though. He lives in an apartment in Brooklyn and his father taught high school Biology before he retired."

"His apartment is probably over his parent's garage, Meg.

And I can say that, I'm half Italian, remember? I thought you were supposed to be pumping him for case information, not his personal history."

"I am, but he's not giving much away," Meg protested. "We just seem to have this . . . chemistry. Anyway, what're you doing tonight? Want to finally see a movie?"

I contrasted staying home alone feeling sorry for myself against watching a silly romantic comedy. After the increased menace around, the security of a good friend and a darkened theater seemed very attractive. "You're on."

I rode the elevator up to the fifth floor, humming one of the tunes from the movie. It had proved to be pure brain candy, and I'd enjoyed putting murder out of my mind for a few hours. We stopped afterward for dessert and paid way too much for teeny cups of gelato—amaretto for me and hazelnut for Meg—which we still gleefully wolfed down.

The elevator reached my floor with a jolt, and I walked to the door at the end of the hall. I inserted my key, but the door was unlocked and it pushed open easily. Hairs prickled on the back of my neck. I never went out without locking it. Could I have been in such a rush to meet Meg that I'd run out without locking the door?

Or else someone had been in the apartment. I hesitated in the doorway and thought I could feel the sense of a lingering presence. I stood rooted to the spot and suddenly felt a wave of understanding for Allison's shock, then stifled a scream when Wilkie tapped on the window.

There was no one in sight but the cat and the window was firmly closed. With its safety bars it only opened about five inches, so unless an intruder was an infant, they could hardly get in this way. Only minimally reassured, I threw my backpack down on the table and opened the window. The cat slipped inside and I grabbed him in the football hold I'd been taught to use on infants. He started purring, assuming a belly rub was on offer.

Silently, I lifted the biggest knife from the wooden block standing on the counter. Kicking my shoes off, I tiptoed into the living room.

The small light I left lit on my desk glowed and I could see around the entire room. Wilkie purred loudly. The room was empty.

My heart pulsed in my ears as I slipped down the hall to my bedroom, wondering why I'd grabbed the cat. My thoughts were wild. Was I planning to throw Wilkie at the intruder and lock myself in the bathroom and call 911? Could I even do that to the poor cat? Possibly.

But my cell phone was in my backpack on the kitchen table. I cursed myself for not bringing it with me.

My bedroom door was open, as I'd left it. I reached my hand tentatively inside, expecting at any moment for it to be grabbed, and flipped the light switch. The overhead fixture cleared the shadows. Empty.

That left the bathroom. The door stood ajar, the shower curtain pulled across the tub. I could see through the crack by the hinges that no one lurked inside the small room or behind the door. My hands were clammy as I swiftly pulled the curtain aside, holding Wilkie up threateningly. No one hunched at the bottom of tub; no one sprang out at me. Wilkie squirmed and I unceremoniously let him jump down.

"Some protector you are," I said aloud, just to hear my voice. I followed him back down the hall to the kitchen where he ran to his empty dish and meowed. My pulse slowed as I fed him. I felt strongly that someone had been in my apartment, and I usually listened to my inner voice. Past experience when evaluating a patient's condition had taught me that when an alarm bell rang, it should be heeded. But there was no one here.

I put the knife back in its place, deliberating what my reaction would have been if I'd come upon an intruder. I liked to think I wouldn't have screamed or fainted, but I also didn't know if I had the nerve to stab someone. And the knife could have been wrestled away from me, used on me as a weapon. Not a smart choice. Now that I thought about it, I hadn't handled this well at all. I should never have entered the apartment but stayed outside and called 911.

Gathering my courage, I made a closer circuit of the living room, looking for anything out of order. My glance fell to the desktop and on the notes I'd been making about Griff's symptoms, the cast members with motives, and the original list I'd made for Ned of who had been standing behind me when Griff died.

I frowned. Something was off. I remembered slapping the pages down after pulling out and copying the list for Ned the other night. Now they lay perfectly aligned.

DEATH UNSCRIPTED

I looked carefully at my desk as my heart beat climbed again. Everything else looked to be as I'd left it until I opened the top drawer where I kept letters from my mother. They looked out of order. Or were they? Maybe I was letting my imagination run away with itself.

Heading back down the hall, I went into my bedroom and stood in its center, making a slow circle as I searched the room for anything that looked disturbed. Nothing. Then I saw the drawer in the table next to my bed was not fully shut. The drawer stuck and unless you knew that and rammed it in just so, it slid in on an angle and didn't line up, just as it was now.

My heart started thumping again, the sour taste rising in my mouth a combination of buttered popcorn, amaretto gelato and stomach acids. I backed out of the room, although there was no immediate threat, on my way to my phone to call the police. My instincts had been right. Someone had been in my apartment.

Ned was tired and ready to call it a night. The garbage trawl had turned up one useful item that he'd sent off to be analyzed and he'd sent his team home. He had done tomorrow's assignments: one team member would Google celebrity sites, looking for common threads or gossip about Griff Kennedy and Misty Raines, and to see if there were any hints of a stalker for either of them. Another would check with paparazzi, a tougher job, cold-calling the celebrity photographers to see if they could offer any insights or had seen a person repeatedly hanging around the *Thornfield Place* studio.

On his way out of the studio tonight he'd run into PBJ producer AJ Eagen. The man insisted neither actor had complained of being stalked, but did mention something that had Ned's antennae twitching. There was a closed circuit camera mounted over the soap's front door. It allowed actors inside the building to see how heavy the autograph crowds were when they were planning to leave the studio, or to check if their limos were waiting outside. Every week the tape was reset, but Eagen promised to have the studio send the tape of the past week to the precinct tomorrow to be reviewed. That task he'd hand to Borelli. Be good practice and a bit of penance for enjoying Meg Pitman's company too much.

He'd then spent time going over his team's re-interviews with the beating victims. None could give more than a vague description of their assailant since they'd all been attacked from behind. He shuffled the case reports, looking for connections he might have missed before. The men were different ages, didn't live near each other, and didn't frequent the same bars or gyms. All had been taken off guard and jumped from behind, hit on the head, then beaten.

Only the method of the beatings was the same, convincing Ned they were committed by the same person, although the department chief was inclined to dismiss them as unrelated incidents. The thought of a serial attacker would send shivers through the city, not to mention affect the tourist season, which was just starting. Stowing his notebook, his thoughts turned to the tail he'd put on Trudy, and he reached for the phone to straighten things out with her. Time to come clean.

"Yes?" Trudy's voice was abrupt.

Ned hesitated. He realized with a jolt he didn't know if she had a current relationship, hoped he hadn't interrupted a romantic evening. "Trudy, it's-"

"Ned, someone was in my apartment." Her voice quavered.

"Grab your keys and cell phone and wait for me outside your door." Damn. He knew he shouldn't have called the tail off.

"I've searched—no one's here. But some things are out of order, and when I got home I felt this presence . . . "

"Did you check the closets?"

The silence lasted a single beat. "I'll be outside my door."

Ned grabbed a car from the precinct. Traffic was light, but the ride still seemed to take too long. Trudy was pacing the hall outside her apartment, Wilkie prowling the stairwell, when Ned arrived fifteen minutes later.

Trudy looked grateful, then embarrassed. "I'm afraid I might have over-reacted."

"We'll see. Wait here. I'll check all the closets." Wilkie ran in when Ned closed the door behind him. He quickly but thoroughly searched the large closets that lined the hall to her bedroom and bathroom, not wanting Trudy to see his drawn gun. Linens, blankets, out of season coats, clothes in garment bags and labeled plastic storage bins stood with crates of books stored on the floor. At one end were a stacked front-loading washer and dryer. Nice apartment, unusual storage. No wonder Trudy liked living here. Wilkie curled around his legs and he made certain he didn't close the animal inside one of the long sliding doors.

Black and white close-ups of architectural bits of city buildings were hung down the hall. When he entered her bedroom, he was struck by the intimacy of being in her personal space.

An elaborate iron bed was dressed with a crazy quilt in shades of blue and white. Piles of books occupied one whitewashed night table. Another stack next to the bed, waiting to be read, had toppled over. Several Impressionist prints hung on the walls. He recognized a Long Island scene by William Merritt Chase. A large blow-up of Sargent's "Carnation, Lily, Lily, Rose" hung on the wall between two sets of tall windows.

When he opened the set of closet sliders, Trudy's perfume wafted around him. Ned breathed in the light scent of citrus with apples and flowers, and something spicier he couldn't identify. He noted the stacked boxes of shoes on the high shelf, labeled on the outside in Trudy's scrawl. More shoes lay tossed in the bottom of the space, an interesting mixture of order and clutter.

He checked that the window latches were secure before he went back to open the door and motioned her inside. "All clear. What was out of order?"

Trudy showed him the drawer in her bedroom, then back

in the living room, pointed to the note pages, explaining how they were lined up after she knew she'd tossed them down, and the pile of her mother's letters jumbled and out of order. She bit her lip. "I know it's not a lot, but it wasn't how I'd left them. I'm feeling kind of foolish now."

"Get me a large ziplock bag." Ned took the pages from her desk by one corner and slid them into the bag.

He went back to her apartment door and scrutinized it from outside. The metal door displayed a profusion of scratches and nicks. It would be impossible to tell if any were fresh. "Did you have the dead bolt locked?" he asked.

Trudy shook her head. "At night I use it to lock myself in, but I admit with the doorman, I thought this building was safe. I only use the knob lock when I go out. Until now."

Ned nodded. "Get in the habit of locking everything. I checked with the doorman on the way in and he didn't see anyone go up, but he walks a few tenants' dogs around eight. You weren't home then?"

"I went to a movie with Meg."

"At least she wasn't out with Borelli." They shared a smile.

There were a few beats of silence until Trudy asked him to come back inside. "I was just going to have some tea," she said.

Ned knew he shouldn't stay, but hesitated when he considered Trudy's pale face and expectant look. She couldn't be happy going back in there alone. "Maybe just for a few minutes."

Over spiked tea for me and a shot of Jagermeister for Ned, I started to relax. This time we sat across the table from each other and he explained his team's garbage trawl find: a baggie with celery and carrot sticks inside.

I admit I was flattered he was willing to share these details. Wilkie jumped up on Ned's lap, throatily purring as his big belly got stroked.

"It's been sent for fingerprinting. Now we wait and see."

I wrinkled my nose. "That can't have been a pleasant chore for the team."

"Unfortunately, not a lot of detective work is," he said. "That CSI team needed long, hot showers tonight. I just had to look at their findings." Ned finished his shot. "Trudy, can you think of anyone who might have a problem with you? Or what they might have been looking for?"

She shook her head, her hair falling over her face as she thought. When she raised her eyes to his, he saw her frown.

"I can't think of anyone I've offended or what they could think I have here."

"All right. Let me know if anything occurs to you." Ned got to his feet. "Now I really am going. Go ahead and lock up and I'll try the door from the outside."

"Thanks again for coming over."

As he got to the door, he turned to me. "Don't apologize for following your instincts. You should change your locks. See you Monday."

I locked up, firmly turning the dead bolt. Ned tried the door and it stayed solidly closed. "Goodnight," I called through the door, eye to the peephole. Ned waved as he walked to the elevator.

DEATH UNSCRIPTED

Facing the empty apartment, I turned on my music. Eva Cassidy's sweet voice comforted me, singing Sting's "Fields of Gold." I washed the few dishes in the sink by hand, glad the lingering feeling here was Ned's presence, and not the unnamed person who had violated my home, bringing fear and reminding me of the two recent deaths.

I had almost successfully lifted my mood, thinking of Ned complimenting me on following my instincts, when I remembered the owner of that high, lilting voice I was listening to had died tragically in her thirties from melanoma. I couldn't escape thoughts of death tonight.

CHAPTER TWENTY

Sunday, May 9ᵗʰ

Ned brought his canteen coffee upstairs to the *Thornfield Place* office, hoping to find Meg Pitman. Although this investigation revolved around the sets and sound stage of the actors and the lower floor with their dressing rooms, he preferred this upstairs space, with its direct lighting and organized feel. He found Meg sitting at her desk, Borelli across from her. They had their own coffee and their bagels looked awfully good.

He pulled up a chair to the desk and helped himself to half of Tony's bagel. "Thanks, partner." Tony's look of chagrin was mollified when Meg pushed her uneaten half toward him.

"Sorry to interrupt, but I need to talk to you both. Meg, have you spoken to Trudy today?"

Meg shook her head. "She's not due in until tomorrow but I'll call her later."

Ned briefly described the 'incident,' as he called it, at Trudy's apartment last night. "I wanted you to know so you'll keep an eye on her when she's here. Her questions and snooping have aroused someone's interest." He didn't miss Meg's look of alarm. He hadn't told Borelli he'd put a tail on Trudy and decided not to mention it now.

"Who would want to search Trudy's place?" she asked.

"That's what I was hoping you could tell me. Trudy couldn't think of anyone but you're close to her. I need you to think of anyone who might have a problem with her outside the studio. For all we know, this may be an isolated incident and not related to the murders here at all." Ned gave Borelli a nod, which his partner correctly interpreted, then settled back to let the younger detective advance the discussion.

"Meg, remember when you started to talk to me about Trudy's problems and stopped? We already know from her background check her father died under suspicious circumstances when she was a teen. Ned didn't want to ask her last night but we need to know to see if there's any connection. What happened?"

"That was long before we met," Meg explained. "Her dad left home to pick up supplies and was found dead in town, an apparent accident. Trudy was just sixteen at the time. There are some circumstances she's angry about, with the manner of his death and the lack of a police investigation, but she doesn't like to talk about it. There are a lot of unresolved things from that event and she doesn't know if her father is to blame or not."

"It must have been tough for her," Borelli said, unusually sympathetic, Ned thought.

Meg agreed and gave him a grateful smile. "Trudy went to nursing school in Albany on a scholarship. Afterwards she worked at the med center there before moving to the city.

Her brothers manage the family business—I visited them when she went up last fall. It's lovely up there and they're all very sweet, her mom and two brothers, one married."

"How did you meet?" Ned interjected. He wanted to hear this story from Meg's perspective.

"Trudy was my roommate. She answered an ad I'd put out on Craig's list and we met when she interviewed at St. Vincent's and just clicked. A year later I told her about the opening at the studio."

Borelli drained his cup and took out his notebook. "And this Forster character, any chance he's come back and is stalking her?"

"He's still in Germany, as far as I know. I can't imagine he'd be stalking her. She met him at the ER after he'd sprained an ankle in a softball game while on leave. He turned out to be a real slick talker. I begged her not to move in with him after only a few months, but once Trudy makes up her mind . . . "

"Believe me, we've both seen her stubborn streak firsthand," Borelli said. "I'll run a check on his whereabouts. What's the deal there? We know he still owns her apartment and she pays a low rent."

Meg shifted in her seat. She seemed uncomfortable talking about Trudy.

"We can find out anyway," Ned pointed out. "Meg, it's easier this way."

"That's pure guilt on his part," she admitted. "He went to Iraq and Trudy had us all sending care packages to his unit. She wrote to him every night and worried about him every day—she's very loyal. Even I was relieved when he was sent to Germany—the louse. Do you know what he did?" Her voice shook with irritation.

"Tell us," Ned encouraged.

"After twenty months of worrying and writing, the creep sends her a letter—a letter! Tells her he's married a German girl. Add that to her father's sudden death and you can see why she feels disappointed with men."

"What do you think?" Borelli asked Ned.

"I think if Forster's married to someone else and still in Germany, he's not an option, but you still need to check." Ned brushed his hair off his forehead. "No, if someone really was in Trudy's apartment last night, chances are it's connected with this place."

I finished my second cup of coffee after changing my sheets and remaking the bed. Who knew if my visitor had sat on it? I threw in a second load of wash and put my sheets in the dryer. Wilkie hated the sound of any machine. He'd run to the window to be let out as soon as he saw me load the washer. Now the apartment was empty and the walls seemed to echo.

Last night had been frightening. Ned's call had come as I was hesitating to dial 911. Because what would I have said? Please come because I *feel* someone was in my apartment? Because a few pieces of paper are out of order and a drawer stuck? I know it's their job and all, but I didn't want to be labeled as one more hysterical female. At least after Ned's search I'd fallen into an exhausted sleep.

The day loomed in front of me. Usually I enjoyed Sundays, choosing a museum or exhibit to visit, hitting the Highline, or taking a long walk to window-shop. Today all I wanted was an excuse to go to the studio, to forge ahead asking questions. But after last night I felt a menace around me, and ultimately decided it was best if I stayed in to wait for the 24-hour locksmith to arrive.

With a sigh I put my tea mug in the sink. It was the perfect day to switch over my warmer weather clothes, take stock of what was definitely cold weather wear and could be stored in the hall closet. I looked carefully at my shoeboxes, afraid to see something else out of order, but they appeared untouched.

It was unsettling, the feeling that some stranger had been in my home, searching through my things for who-knew-what. Nothing of value had been taken so it was obviously not a thief. This was more personal, and while I couldn't think of what I might have that someone else could want, the feeling alone was downright ugly.

Two hours later the locksmith left and I hauled a stuffed bag outside my apartment door to take to the women's shelter before heading into the studio tomorrow. It was amazing how my style and taste had changed since moving to Manhattan. JC Penny sweaters had been exchanged for a soft leather jacket; sneakers had been replaced by leather boots; corduroy slacks by yoga pants.

Besides, I rationalized, firmly locking my door and shooting the shiny new dead bolt home, most of the stuff reminded me of Jake Forster and the time I'd wasted mooning over him. I was turning over a new leaf. Waiting for the kettle to boil for a much-deserved tea break, I remembered how Meg had cautioned me about moving in with Jake. The two had maintained a frosty politeness in my presence, their dislike of each other barely disguised. Meg had clearly seen through Jake's allure when I had announced I was moving in with him.

"It's not that I don't want you to leave here—I'll miss you but I can get another roommate. But Trudy, he's a born womanizer. He can't help himself, he's wired that way. He looks at every woman when he thinks you don't notice and sometimes even when you do. I don't trust him at all. I'm so afraid he's going to break your heart."

She'd been right, of course, but I'd been convinced Jake's roaming eye was nothing more than a healthy appetite for women. Meg's a good friend, I decided, pouring hot water over the Earl Grey tea into my mug. It couldn't have been easy for her to be so brutally honest for my benefit.

Not that I'd listened. I'd cleaned and cooked for him, performed all of the wifely duties he could want while still working full time, and in the end he'd left me his cat and his flat and, indeed, a broken heart.

I sipped my tea, debating whether I absolutely needed a few cookies to dunk in it, when I realized whom Jake Forster reminded me of—a younger Griff Kennedy. Suddenly I could see how someone might be hurt enough to feel compelled to murder him.

The studio was filled with people but to Ned it felt lonely. Byron's preliminary autopsy report on Griff Kennedy ruled out suicide; the official cause of death was "homicide secondary to poison ingestion."

Ned re-interviewed Reece Hunter and Frank Resnick as planned about Misty Raines. Frank denied holding Misty responsible for spreading rumors about his relationship with Eva. Both men denied seeing her after rehearsal or being in her dressing room. He felt uneasy. If they were telling the truth, the man Trudy glimpsed in Misty's dressing room was someone else entirely.

He tracked down the janitor, who couldn't determine the origin of the garbage bag that had contained Misty's carrot bag.

"I don't pick through the stuff, ya know, I just close 'em up and get 'em outta here," the man told Ned by phone from his apartment in the Bronx. He explained that script paper and empty cans were recycled from containers on all three floors and emptied into larger recycling bins. Refuse gathered daily was thrown in the Dumpster. The one bright note was that the Dumpster was emptied on Mondays, or the evidence they'd found might have been lost.

Ned returned to the precinct house. He needed to get Trudy's pages from last night to Fingerprint, and was pulling them out of his briefcase when Borelli returned, waving a stack of printouts.

"No surprises I can see. The surveillance tapes were a bust, except for one woman who was aggressive about grabbing Reece Hunter's crotch as he passed by." Borelli flipped through the pages of more background checks. "Li Yung was born in

San Francisco, no immigration problem there. Reece Hunter had one possession of marijuana in drama school, probation. Frank Resnick, born in Poland but emigrated as an infant and is a citizen. One arrest for demonstrating outside The Plaza against women wearing fur, back in '92 . . . "

"The follies of youth," Ned said, handing Borelli a plastic bag. "These need to get to Fingerprint; they're the pages from Trudy's apartment."

"You think someone was really there?" Borelli asked.

"I think someone picked up on her snooping and was trying to find out what she knows."

"But she doesn't know anything we don't know, probably less."

Ned wiped a hand over his face. "Let's hope this obscure 'someone' figures that out."

CHAPTER TWENTY ONE

Looking back later that night, I remembered I almost hadn't answered the phone.

"I thought I was going to get your voicemail. What are your plans for tonight?" Meg asked.

"Watching the new *Inspector Lewis* on *Masterpiece*," I answered.

"DVR it and come out with me. Mom paid for two tickets to a gallery sale that's a fundraiser for St. Vincent's and they're not going."

"I got that flyer a few weeks ago," I remembered. "No thanks." As a former employee I still received the hospital's fundraiser mailings. No way would I ever pay two hundred and fifty dollars to look at art I wouldn't like and food I wouldn't eat.

"Come on," Meg wheedled. "There's free champagne and the goodies are from *Provence*, you love that place."

"Even if the food is good the evening will be boring, watching all of those glitterati amusing themselves with artspeak."

"That's the whole point," Meg insisted. "We eat and drink for free and watch the others go on as though they know what they're talking about. And leave when we want."

"Meg, it's hardly free if your parents paid five hundred dollars for the tickets."

"Which they consider a donation to the hospital and have no intention of using."

A thought sprang to mind. "You haven't set this up to run into Borelli by any chance, have you?"

"I hardly think a policeman's salary runs to this kind of event. Just meet me there for a few hours, okay? If I have to spend another Sunday night listening to my mother expound one more time on why I shouldn't return to the studio, I think I'll explode."

At last I had the real reason for Meg's insistence. Certainly I could do my friend this favor. "Fine. If you promise we can stop for cheesecake on the way home, and leave at the first sighting of fecal matter on a canvas."

"You're on. I'll meet you in Soho outside the Fitzpatrick Gallery at eight."

By seven-thirty I was on the "C" train. The DVR was set at home, my hair was freshly washed and I'd anchored the curls on top of my head. I'd even shaved my legs, applied a tinge of makeup, and felt decidedly sexy this evening, a far cry from my recent mood. It felt good to primp.

I'd left the backpack home and switched to a regular purse

for the event, but there was room for a small notebook I pulled out and used the travel time to make a list of suspects in the *Thornfield Place* murders. With Misty's death I had to rule her out for Griff's poisoning, I supposed, but that was only if the same person had committed both murders. It felt like that to me, though, and I suspected it felt like that to O'Malley, too.

That still left a wide field to choose from: two ex-wives, Frank, Reece, Ron, any number of crew and who knew about people from outside the studio? The car swayed on the curve just before Washington Square, and momentarily I rubbed shoulders with the older man sitting next to me, reading *The Financial Times.* I stowed my notes and stood for my stop.

I exited at Spring Street and walked down a block to Broome and over one to Thompson. The Fitzpatrick Gallery occupied a large commercial space just off the corner; the beat of music from inside reached the street. A huge banner outside the building snapped in the breeze, proclaiming this the site of "St. Vincent's FitzArt for Heart Sale." Smaller print underneath noted that fifteen percent of all monies taken in would be donated by the artists to St. Vincent's Cardiology wing. Fat chance of them getting any out of me. I was here for the food and the wine and, afterwards, that piece of cheesecake Meg had promised.

A skinny artsy male at the door collected tickets, wearing a black turtleneck and slim pants, a clone of Audrey Hepburn except for his equipment. He stared at me as I waited for Meg, looking at me with undisguised distaste. I shifted my attention to the next wave of people entering the gallery. I scrutinized them, looked down at my clothes, then back at the waiting line. I knew by now that at any New York evening event, black would be evident, and tons of it. But this group wore it like a uniform, and my own outfit, which I'd felt so secure in only moments ago, now seemed obtrusive. My WOD was working; my outfit clearly wasn't.

I was so taken up with noticing this that I failed to see Meg alight from her taxi, turning when she tapped me on the shoulder.

"Don't you look nice," Meg said warmly.

"You're my friend, you don't count," I answered a tad waspishly, looking down at my cream silk empire dress with a floral scarf I'd thought brought out the green in my eyes. It had been trendy last year but now I felt like something out of another era, or perhaps country-come-to-town.

"What's the matter?" Meg asked, moving up the line.

I took in Meg's gray dress with its shiny black patent belt and matching heels. A glob of amber surrounded by jet beads on a chain brought out the golden hue in her eyes. "Ask him," I said, nodding to the ticket taker and entering the gallery.

"You're not making sense," Meg said, grabbing two flutes off the first passing waiter's tray and handing me one.

I expected the music inside to be quiet and classical, but instead Leona Lewis was *Bleeding Love.* "My clothes are all wrong," I whispered. "Everyone's in black." And then I immediately felt ridiculous to be so insecure. When had that happened?

"Don't be absurd," Meg said, propelling me in a circle by the elbow. "There's a floral scarf . . . okay it's on a black dress, but over there's a dark blue suit . . . that woman has a white blouse with her black suit . . . um, well, there *is* a lot of black, but these people wear it like a safety net. Even I pulled out an easy outfit tonight. Don't sweat it. You look fine, very springy. And original, which these people could use." She dismissed my worries and rubbed her hands. "Let's find something to eat."

Thirty minutes and two glasses of champagne later I managed to relax and forget my clothes. The hors d'oeuvres were delicious, tiny pinwheels of delicate pastry lined with pate` and herbed olives, broiled dates wrapped in bacon, shrimp glossy with a citrus-coriander glaze.

The best part was eavesdropping on the commentary as we circled the gallery. L-shaped walls sprinkled throughout the showroom added hanging space and allowed for groupings by the same artist. I had to admit most of the art left me cold. I had trouble warming up to the splashes and drips of oils on canvas, but then I was the one here in a cream dress, so what did I know?

"Hey, Meg, see that gal over there with the long angular face? Doesn't she look like that actress from *Four Weddings and a Funeral*? The one the Hugh Grant character finds out his friends call 'Duckface'?"

"I've seen her before, at the opera, I think. And she's more of a 'Horseface' than a 'Duckface,' don't you think?"

We giggled. "I think we should lay off the champagne. We're being seriously rude."

The music had become reggae, Gregory Isaacs smoothly proclaiming he needed his "Night Nurse." This had been a favorite of mine in nursing school, and I hummed along as we moved to inspect an item placed on an ornate marble stand that garnered a huge circle of admirers. "Such an imagination!"

"It's the definition of mankind." The definition in question was encapsulated in a clear Plexiglas dome. Underneath sat a plain brown china plate. Opened and on its side, an unlabeled jar of spaghetti sauce poured its contents onto the plate. The pint's red filling had coagulated and solidified into a gooey mass, sprouting green moldy spots.

"Puh-leeze," I muttered to Meg "This is some kind of joke, right? Tell me there's a Candid Camera crew here tonight."

Meg bit her lip, suppressing laughter. "It's not exactly a Rembrandt, is it?"

"What's it called?" I asked. "Wait, don't tell me—" I put one hand up to my forehead in my best imitation of a seer. "Hoax for the Masses," I pronounced.

Meg checked the label on the column. "Untitled."

Now we both had to suppress roars of laughter.

Ned O'Malley checked his watch for the third time. He'd forgotten his weeks-old promise to escort his cousin to this gallery opening. The last time Ned had seen Meredith, she'd been a lanky teenager, moping shyly at her parents' twenty-fifth anniversary party. Moving to the city a few months ago from Boston, Meredith was still meeting people and feeling her way in her new surroundings. Ned's mother had made it a personal campaign to have her niece settle in, helping her find an apartment in the East Village near her graduate classes in Film at NYU. Part of that included getting her "out in public,"

as Ruth O'Malley phrased it, taking Meredith to the opera and ballet, and corralling Ned into agreeing to escort her to this event.

Ned thought Meredith was adjusting just fine, greeting other students she'd met and generally ignoring him when she dove into their conversations. He wandered away, the proverbial bump on a log, wondering how long he had to stay. He should be at the precinct reading reports, or at the very least going over team interviews at home, sitting in his worn leather chair, feet up and a single-malt on ice at his side.

Instead, he'd spent the last hour bored to tears, surrounded by a sea of people dressed for a funeral looking at art he couldn't picture hanging on his apartment walls. There was one bright spot of color. One woman had the temerity to wear a creamy dress, and even as he admired her hair piled on top of her head, the tilt of her neck and the color of that hair seemed familiar. And then she turned around.

Meg and I have a running battle about artists who called their work "Untitled."

"They don't have the imagination to come up with a title that conveys their meaning," I always argue. "It's like they don't care enough about their viewer to share their inspiration."

"It's their way of letting the viewer decide what the art is about," Meg insists.

DEATH UNSCRIPTED

We strolled into the next room of the gallery, still squabbling good-naturedly, stopping in front of a huge canvas of black spots dripped on a white background. I resisted commenting while Meg checked out the title. Turning around to look for a place to throw away my napkin, the hairs on the back of my neck rose. I had the same feeling as the other day, that I was being watched.

"This one's called 'Black on White'—Trudy, what's the matter?"

My eyes had roamed the crowd and locked on a face I knew. "Ned-O's here."

We watched as his attention was diverted to a tall brunette dressed in an expensive black sheath, who sidled up to him and hooked her arm over his elbow. I lost my appetite for cheesecake just then, but it was Meg who whispered: "Horseface!"

Ned started across the gallery floor with Meredith in tow. "There's someone here I'd like you to meet."

When he got to where Meg stood, he saw Trudy's back disappearing into the crowd.

"Hi, Meg. This is Meredith Bauman. Merry, this is Meg Pitman." The two women nodded, appraising each other. "Where's Trudy going?"

"She had to take an important call, " Meg stammered,

clearly uncomfortable.

This was one of those occasions it paid to be one of the tallest people in the room. Ned searched the gallery for Trudy and saw her heading for the door. That figured; she could hardly hear between the music and the talking.

"Merry's from Boston, studying film at NYU," Ned explained.

"How do you like Greenwich Village?" Meg asked, her good manners to the rescue.

While the two women chatted about coffee shops and boutiques, Ned scanned the doorway, watching for Trudy to return. He couldn't see her outside the doorway and suddenly running into her seemed clumsy. Then he had another idea as he thought back to her intruder last night.

He waited for a moment to interject into the conversation. "Meg, do you know who called Trudy?"

By the inquisitive look Meg gave him, he realized the question was none of his business. "She didn't say . . . "

"I'm just concerned about, you know, the *case*," he stressed, hoping Meg would understand he didn't want to talk about the murder case in front of Meredith.

"I'm sure she's fine," Meg insisted.

"I'll be right back." Ned excused himself and went to the door of the gallery and stepped out. He scanned the immediate area, noting the tail he had on Trudy across the street. The officer wore a baseball cap and scanned the rows of used books set outside a secondhand bookstore. When their eyes met, the officer scratched his left ear.

Ned looked to his right. Trudy slouched against a light pole, reading something on her cell phone. When he approached her and she noticed him, Trudy stood up quickly and put her phone in her purse.

"Hi. Everything all right? Only you left so quickly and I wanted you to meet someone."

"Phone call." Trudy touched her purse.

"Not anyone harassing you? I mean, after last night I just wanted to be sure—"

"No! No, just a regular old call. Um, too noisy in there for me to hear."

"Sure." They stood there awkwardly for a second. A taxi pulled up to the curb but Ned waved him on. "Are you going back inside?"

"Uh, no, think I'll wait for Meg out here. I only came tonight because Meg insisted. Warm in there and not really my scene, you know . . . " Her voice petered out.

"I certainly do know. Not my idea to be here tonight, either." He looked at her in the feminine dress with her hair up and had a sudden desire to kiss the nape of her neck.

"Ah." Trudy nodded and bit her lip.

Ned the distinct feeling they were talking at cross purposes.

"There you are!" Meg came rushing up. "I've had enough of that. Ready to go?"

"Oh, yes." Was it his imagination or did Trudy seem relieved?

Meg turned to Ned. "Your friend said she's ready to go, too."

"Taxi!" Trudy hailed the next cab and waved to Ned as she bundled inside.

"See you." Meg followed her and in a flash the two women were gone.

Now what was that all about, Ned wondered as he went back to find Merry. Women. He'd never understand them. Or himself for that matter.

Chapter Twenty Two

Monday, May 10th

From Ned's perspective, the *Thornfield Place* studio was in a state of controlled pandemonium. It seemed the entire cast roamed between the soundstage and dressing rooms in varied states of dress, gathered for the taping of Griff Kennedy's funeral scene.

He'd left Borelli at the precinct house to placate Jellyroll with a dozen doughnuts and to comb back through their mounds of compiled data for any pattern they'd missed. Any link mattered if it would make sense of two apparently unconnected murders, whether it was an old relationship between the two victims that had been missed, a new much-gossiped-about one, or perhaps a tie to someone the victims both knew outside the studio.

Ned had dismissed the writers and producers from his suspect list, along with Meg and the rest of the upstairs clerical staff. He was close to deleting Reece Hunter, too—his gut told him the actor wasn't capable of the cunning needed to commit these two murders. And as for Griff's pointing finger, he'd concluded Griff either thought the eye drops Trudy had administered were tainted, or he really was pointing to someone behind her. He wasn't going to closely examine why he'd dismissed Trudy as a suspect, although he told himself that W. J. Burley would approve—she had opportunity and means but no motive he'd unearthed.

The situation was eerily reminiscent of the assault cases that haunted him. There, the three male victims appeared unconnected, the method of their beatings the only thing they had in common. In all three cases, the beatings were severe enough to cause major damage but not death. Ned suspected the rage behind the acts was the key to the motive. But what had prompted that rage? And what had prompted a person to take two other lives?

Today Ned had come to the studio because it seemed obvious to him that, until he had other concrete evidence, this setting was the heart of the murder cases. Even if an outside perpetrator was involved, the studio held a key. He was determined to figure out why the studio linked the murders of Griff Kennedy and Misty Raines.

He sent team members armed with photographs of both victims to canvass the shops along Columbus Avenue, looking for descriptions of anyone seen with either of the victims in the last two weeks. Across the street in the PBJ building, others interviewed employees whose windows looked down on the *TP* studio in the slim hope that someone had seen something.

Ned felt frustrated and grouchy, reduced to dealing in "someone" and "something," nebulous ideas instead of hard facts he could digest and firm evidence he could see. He finally snapped at Damon, the youngest member of his squad, when she hung back and shyly asked exactly what the PBJ employees might have seen that would prove to be useful.

"How would I know? Use your brain, Damon," he barked, then watched the woman's face fall and immediately apologized.

"Sorry, Damon." Ned knew she was interested in taking the detective exam; great role model he was providing.

"I understand, sir," she answered, not meeting his eyes.

"No excuse on my part. Look, we don't know what's germane. Jot everything down and we'll sort through it later, all right?"

She smiled, but he still felt like a complete shit for yelling. There were too many leads to nowhere, too many suspects, and not enough concrete evidence in this investigation. His intuition told him something bad was going to happen soon and he wanted to be on the spot when it did.

Thoughts of Trudy brought him back to the gallery last night. He hadn't had a chance to introduce her to his cousin after she and Meg had run out. He still hadn't been able to figure Trudy's odd behavior out, either, any more than he could understand why he'd suddenly been drawn to the back of her neck.

Allison Stewart had been excused from the funeral scene, still "under sedation" at home. I felt the teeniest thread of empathy for her as I combed my hair in the ladies' room, pulling it back neatly with a clip, and straightening the collar of my blouse. The cynic in me pictured the cranky teen surrounded by stuffed animals, iPods and hormonal girlfriends, retelling her story and enjoying the attention while avoiding both school and work.

Then I felt a pang of guilt. At her age, Ally might not have seen a dead body before, certainly no one *in extremis* as Misty had been.

I'd been raised in a rural area, where the life cycle became apparent early on to any child observing nature. Witnessing numerous deaths during my career had left little mystery for me. I wasn't cavalier about the end of a life by any means. In fact, my exposure to death had included a stint on the terminal cancer unit in Albany. I had sat with dying patients on my night shift rotations—when truly ill people tend to let go of their earthly surroundings—feeling that no one should leave this life alone. I had watched the light ebb from their eyes as the person they had been ceased to *be*. With my father's death and the way he'd died, death was different for me, whether I liked it or not.

No, I had gained a healthy respect for life, knowing full well how each day was to be savored, which was why these murders had gotten my dander up. I was desperate to find the person or persons who had the audacity to choose when to end two lives. I shied from this thought. Could there be a duo at work here? What could be the motive behind that? And if I was having trouble discerning one murderer, how could I possibly find two?

My day's workload was light, and that was a good thing.

DEATH UNSCRIPTED

I was mortified to have had that run-in with O'Malley and Horseface, and had ducked out of the gallery and left immediately with Meg after that stilted conversation with O'Malley on the sidewalk. Why had I acted like that? She was just the sort of young woman who ran in his circle.

"His mother had probably set them up," I'd told Meg in the taxi we took home.

"She was actually nice when we talked, which you would have found out if you'd stayed around to meet her instead of chickening out," Meg insisted. "She's studying film at NYU."

"So is half the East Coast," I replied.

I'd accomplished my goal, getting Meg out of her apartment and away from her mother's persistent phone calls for a few hours. Meg was free to go back to her own place and it was with great relief that I went to mine. I'd lost my craving for cheesecake, yet my reaction bewildered me as much as it annoyed me.

Today I would only have to be on set for taping in case someone took ill or had histrionics, or one of the youngsters needed a bathroom break or first aid, a sort of damage control person. I had ammonia capsules in my pocket and a first aid kit on set for any emergency, but I was hoping for a quiet day to allow me to continue my own investigation. I wanted to find out who had had the audacity to break into my apartment and what they'd hoped to find there, now that I knew it was more secure.

I knew full well I was poking my nose into other people's business, asking impertinent questions sometimes, and generally making a pest of myself without any authority to do so. Even my huddled discussion with Edith might have been seen. The frequent times I was with O'Malley and Borelli were certainly noticed. But my meddling had taken on the stamp of a mission, especially after the break-in at my apartment when the threat had become even more personal.

Sliding my comb into my backpack to leave, I pushed open the ladies room door, directly across the hall from the bank of pay phones. Gary Knowles was using the phone, arguing, and I stopped to root around in my backpack so I could eavesdrop, hoping I looked nonchalant .

"Just take the pills, Willy, I don't care how they taste. You need them. Yes, I'll bring dinner home tonight . . . just rest . . . Okay, then fold the clothes in the dryer. Bye." He slammed the phone down as I triumphantly pulled out my lip-gloss, smiling a greeting.

"Trouble at home?" I kept my tone light as I applied the gloss liberally.

"Just my brother. Nothing important." Gary brushed past me and hurried away.

I filed that information away to ask Meg about later. That was an area I should have her look into, I realized, family members of staff whom Griff had known. But then how did Misty fit into that picture? For that matter, maybe I needed to take a closer look at both of Griff's ex-wives. Many a murder has been committed for love. Despite both of their protestations, either woman might have had enough of Griff's shenanigans and been convinced Misty was her next competitor. Edith might have secretly been pining away for Griff to come back to her. Nikki could've felt threatened on both a personal and professional basis.

I checked my watch. Plenty of time to mail the package to

my mom and then try to question the ex-wives. With no lines for the youngsters, I wouldn't be needed until it was time to bring them up to the sound stage.

I had wrapped the tablecloth in printed tissue paper tied with a ribbon. Together with the kind of sappy card my mom saved, I'd shoved them both into a pre-paid Priority Mail carton and slapped a label on it. I ran upstairs to retrieve the carton from under Meg's desk. Meg was fielding a phone call and waved.

Running back down the stairs, I made the halfway turn and ran smack into O'Malley on his way up.

"Whoa, there. Where's the fire?"

Today he was wearing a glen plaid suit with a classy burgundy tie and pale pink shirt. I didn't think I'd ever seen a man wearing a pink shirt, except in an ad for Bermuda vacations, but it looked just fine on O'Malley. The outfit had him looking like a British inspector, and I wondered if my original assessment during The Underwear Game should be changed to silk underwear. Horseface would probably know.

"Just heading to the corner to mail my mom's birthday gift," I said, trying to stifle the blush that accompanied my thoughts.

"I'll walk with you, if that's all right. I had a question."

I wondered if he would bring up last night and decided not to mention it unless he did, although now I was dying to work in a reference to Horseface. He had a right to go out with anyone he wanted, to go to art galleries, too. "Sure, I told you I'm at your service." Finally he was using me as a resource. He fell in step beside me and we exited the studio together.

Traffic had slowed to a steady crawl after the frenetic

craziness of rush hour. Yellow cabs roamed up 66th toward Columbus, searching for fares around Lincoln Center. The air was cool and clean, without bus fumes at the moment, and I drew in a deep breath, pleased to be walking in this vibrant city, pleased to be alive. It gave me the unreasonable feeling I was getting close to unearthing the truth about the murders and could begin to leave this episode behind me. The clip on my hair suddenly felt too constricting and I pulled it off.

O'Malley pulled a yellow taping schedule from his pocket. He ran his finger down the cast listing. "Who's this Phyllis James, with an asterisk next to her name?"

We reached the corner and I mailed my box. "I've got some time. Let's go check out the Lincoln Center fountain."

While we waited on the corner for the crosswalk light, I answered Ned's question. "Phyllis is Nikki's nemesis on the show. The asterisk means she's on vacation; they've written her out for two weeks."

"How do they do that, write someone out?" he asked.

"On the show she's supposed to be away visiting her second husband in prison. He murdered her first one."

O'Malley came to a sudden stop on the pavement. "Wait. You mean this woman supposedly married the man who killed her first husband?"

I nodded. "She figured he loved her enough to murder for her and she couldn't resist that kind of devotion."

He grimaced. "These people are crazy."

I laughed at his dismay. "O'Malley," I reminded him, "it's a *soap opera*."

Ned played with the roll of mints in his pocket. Just now he felt decidedly dull, despite his education and polish, as though by toeing some imaginary line he'd allowed his life to be sanded down. Watching Trudy running her fingers through Lincoln Center's fountain to alternate the light and stream display, oblivious to the mist settling on her hair, he coveted her exuberance.

Sunlight picked out sparkling webs of spray around her head. The word "halo" came to mind, and Ned quickly dismissed it. There was nothing angelic about Trudy Genova. She was stubborn and fiercely independent and opinionated. And still he felt that twinge of envy.

"Any results from your garbage pickings?"

Trudy's question startled him back into the case.

"No fingerprints except Misty's, but none of the carrots in the plastic bag were poisoned," he admitted.

Trudy considered this information. "That must be the bag Misty brought in with her, since the one in the dressing room had the tainted carrot." She pulled Ned to a bench at the foot of the fountain. "The murderer switched bags at some point and then waited for her to eat the right carrot or, in this case, the wrong one."

Ned agreed. "It could have happened at any time during the day. The murderer didn't even have to be on the premises when she actually took ill. It's a diabolical plan."

"It makes finding the culprit harder," Trudy agreed.

One of Trudy's earlier comments stirred his thoughts: "He loved her enough to murder for her" might be a soap opera story line, but in reality, it was a potent motive for murder.

Once the children were settled on the set, I decided to look for Frank Resnick first. Those geek glasses gave him an air of innocence, but when I thought about the cases, he also had a strong motive to want both victims out of the way: Griff, for either attempting to seduce Eva or accomplishing it; or Misty, for spreading rumors about it. Or had she? I only knew for certain that Ron Dowling had spread that rumor, and he remained unscathed, for the moment, although he'd blamed Misty.

But then I was brought right back to the ex-wives. Wouldn't Nikki have the better motive, seeing as how she was still so entangled emotionally with Griff? What if she knew Griff was planning an affair with Misty? That would be motive to murder both of them, right there.

And then there was Edith, sweet woman that she was. She might protest that she didn't care what Griff did at this date, but she admitted she hated him. Hate was a strong motive for murder. But then why kill Misty?

My head spun with all the possibilities and threads, and still I saw no clear answer. I plunked down on a folding chair on the outskirts of the lit chapel set. Frank was inaccessible to me at the moment, conferring with Ron Dowling and Lighting and Sound, taking final checks before taping. Edith Carlisle, Eva and Li were already seated in a back pew together, filling in as unknown townspeople to plump out the chapel setting and be on-set if they were needed.

Everyone I wanted to pump for information was here, leaving me few options. The cast lounged together in the front pews, quietly dishing gossip. My youthful charges were all accounted for, sitting with their stage parents and behaving nicely for once. A video monitor downstairs where their mothers waited covered their actions even before the cameras rolled. Dressed precociously, the youngest was a very self-sufficient eight-year-old boy who looked like he was accustomed to wearing a blazer and tie. He sat playing Angry Birds without fidgeting.

The group surrounding Nikki Olivier was the most subdued. The actress had her face hidden by the veiled hat she wore. I was certain that at a dramatic moment in the faux service, Nikki would throw the veil up to reveal her tear-stained face. Let's hear one for the Emmy nominations.

I had forgotten my sweater today and was rubbing my arms when I felt a touch on my shoulder. Was it O'Malley rescuing me from boredom? Turning around, I saw Reece Hunter leaning over. I'd neglected to notice he wasn't sitting with the others. Some detective I'd make.

"Delivery for you at the door." Reece was handsome, I had to give him that, especially in the dark dress suit, bolo tie and snakeskin boots Edith had chosen for him.

"Thanks." I left my chair and made my way over cables to the door. How had I forgotten Reece when lining up my suspects today? He could've been jealous of Griff's attention to Misty. As for Misty, maybe she'd found out he'd murdered Griff and threatened to go to the police. Or maybe she'd laughed at him, which would have been even worse.

The front door guard was browsing through a *People Magazine* at his desk.

"Reece said there was a delivery for me?"

"Outside—you have an admirer." He pointed to the glass doors, where a small Hispanic youth waited on the top step, holding a huge bouquet of mixed spring flowers. The young boy peered through the doors into the lobby.

I opened the door. "I'm Trudy Genova." I smiled at him. The boy looked over his shoulder, then thrust the flowers at me.

"They're for you," he said, relinquishing his sweaty hold on the bouquet. He jumped off the stoop, running to the right towards Central Park West, in a hurry to get away. Good thing, too, as I didn't have any money on me to give him a tip.

Inhaling their heady fragrance, I wondered why a florist hadn't delivered the flowers. Tall stalks of purple irises and stems of larkspur in white and sky blue were softened by the graceful droop of deep blue lisianthus; bright yellow gerbera daisies added punch. It was an expensive and attractive assortment, and I felt a ripple of excitement, wondering who had sent them.

Not Jake. He was married and in Germany and hell could freeze over before I'd take him back. O'Malley? His kind of expensive touch, I'll admit that. But why would he be sending me flowers?

I turned back to the sound stage with my bounty, closing

the door quietly behind me as Ron was giving the cast notes before taping commenced. Holding the large spray in front of me, I searched for a card but couldn't find one. A sharp sting hit my lower leg. I pitched forward, unable to stop my forward momentum. The flowers flew from my arms and I fell forward, the hard cement floor rushing up to meet me.

CHAPTER TWENTY THREE

"Back off! Give her some air—"

"She's coming around—"

"I've got the ice."

I recognized Meg's voice and felt someone lightly press an ice bag against my right cheek and eye. I slowly opened my left to see a circle of concerned faces around me. O'Malley peered over Meg's shoulder. Li and Eva looked on as Frank brought a blanket from the hospital set and draped it across my feet and legs. A woman I knew as part of O'Malley's team stood at the foot of the couch I found myself stretched out on. The rest of the cast ringed around me.

"Wrap that ice in this," Gary Knowles said, taking the ice pack and wrapping it in a soft, clean towel, replacing it gently. "There you go, Trudy."

I was lying on a sofa that had been pushed to the back wall where pieces from dismantled sets waited to be taken back to storage. Ron Dowling disengaged from the ring of people.

"As Frankenstein said: 'She's alive!' And obviously going to live, people. So can we ignore Nancy's clumsiness and get back to work?" His churlish voice commanded knots of cast members back toward their pews at the opposite end of the studio.

Meg sat on the edge of the sofa and brushed my hair away from my forehead. "You had us frightened, Trudy."

Ned pulled a chair next to me, folding his lanky frame down. "I still think we should call EMS," he told Meg.

"No!" I insisted. "I'm embarrassed enough already. Didn't you hear Dowling? 'My clumsiness' must have made a great show for everyone."

"Meg said you'd be embarrassed, and I've listened to her. But I still feel you should be checked out," Ned persisted.

"Just give me a minute to catch my breath and sort out what happened, please." I shifted on the sofa and squinted up at him from under the heavy ice bag. He set his mouth in an unattractive line, and I giddily thought of what my mother would say: "You keep making that face, one day it will stay that way." I resisted the urge to laugh.

"Can you tell me what happened?" he said.

I nodded. "Reece told me there was a delivery for me outside. When I went to the lobby there was young boy on the stoop, holding this enormous bouquet of flowers. I know I brought them inside . . . then there was this sharp pain across my tibia . . . that's all."

With an effort I sat up and Meg helped me pull up my pants leg. A thin red line, just starting to turn purple, ran across my tibial plateau.

"Damon, search the area where Trudy fell," Ned instructed. The young officer nodded and slipped away.

"These are the flowers, right?" Ned pointed to a vase standing a few feet away on the floor. My bouquet had come apart from its ribbon, but someone had deftly fixed them in a tall cylinder filled with water.

"The kids picked them up and Gary arranged them for you, but we couldn't find a card," Meg said.

"I never found one, either, " I said.

"Can you describe the boy?" Ned had his pen poised over his notebook. "We might get his face off the CCTV out front."

I decided he must sleep with that notebook under his pillow, but dutifully gave him a description and the direction in which the boy had run, realizing even as I did how impossible it would be to find one specific Hispanic youth who had been swallowed up by the city.

Damon returned and motioned to O'Malley. "Sir, I think you'd better see this."

They disappeared deeper into the studio and I slumped back against the couch pillows. My face throbbed and I had a killer headache. Lifting the ice, I probed the area around my right eye. "Is it turning blue already?" I asked Meg. There was tenderness on the edge of my cheekbone and on the brow bone above my eye, but no one point of exquisite pain that pointed to a fractured orbit.

"Getting there," Meg said. "You must have a bad headache. I've got some Tylenol upstairs."

"Good idea, Meg." O'Malley had returned.

With my good eye, I could see Damon, gloved and kneeling down near where I'd fallen. I did note it took something like this for Ned-O to call us all by our first names. When Meg darted away, O'Malley took her place on the sofa.

"I still think you should be seen by a professional. The studio probably has a rule about it. At the very least you must have a concussion—" He was the voice of reason.

"Which just needs time and meds to go away." I could be firm, too. "I'm the professional in this, remember?" I knew any loss of consciousness meant a concussion, but I'd only been out a minute or two. "What did you find?"

He hesitated and my annoyance flared. I tried to sit up. "O'Malley, this happened to me—I need to know if I was clumsy or not."

"Don't get your dander up. Your head won't thank you." He settled me back down against the pillows. "You can be highly annoying, you know that?"

I nodded. I knew I was, but I didn't care. I raised my chin stubbornly. "You found something."

He brushed his hair back off his forehead before answering. "Damon found remnants of fishing line tied around the leg of a couch, across from where you fell. The skirting hid it but she got down on her knees to search."

"Very thorough," I admitted as I absorbed what this meant in connection to my stinging leg. "Someone waited for me to walk past, knowing that huge bouquet would hide the fishing line, then raised it to make me fall on that cement floor?" In my mind's eye I could picture a shadowy figure crouching behind scenery, hidden in the dark shadows across from the couch O'Malley pointed out.

I couldn't hide a shudder. "This person cut the line and just walked off, leaving one end tied around the leg? If I hadn't turned my head as I fell I'd have broken my nose at the very least." I didn't add that a fall on a hard surface like cement could have forced bone shards into my brain, killing me instantly. "But who'd do that?"

O'Malley leaned forward and adjusted the ice bag on my cheek. "Someone you've upset with your prying—or who just thinks you're getting close to the truth."

Ned's cell phone rang; it was Borelli.

"Meg called, told me about Trudy. You want me back there?"

"Anything on your end?"

"Only tired eyes," Borelli said. "I've gone through everything we've got on both the beatings and the murders and can't see a pattern we've missed anywhere. And the doorman at Griff's building said he didn't recall seeing Misty there."

"Damon's team pulled a zero here, too. Apparently no one bothers to look out their windows in Manhattan."

"Nothing on the shop canvass either?"

"Misty and Griff had each been to the corner coffee shop, but no one could recall seeing them in there together, or if they'd been with anyone else." Ned ran his fingers through his hair. "Bring a team and start with the florists in a ten block radius." With Trudy's help, he described the flower assortment. "When you get here, take Damon and search for this delivery boy. Set things in motion and I'll see you then."

Ned flipped his phone shut. Meg was helping Trudy sip water to get pills down.

"Want me to take her home?" Meg asked.

"Trudy, can you handle that couch a little while longer? You might be safer under my watch for now," he said. "And if we find that delivery boy I'll need you to identify him."

"No problem," Trudy murmured. "And it's an old wives' tale about not letting me sleep." She adjusted the ice bag and closed her eyes.

"I can finish up and leave soon," Meg said. "How about if I run home and pack a bag to stay with Trudy tonight?"

She smiled charmingly at Ned, her hand on Trudy's arm, and he could see why his partner was so attracted to this woman. She was nice to look at, and kind, too. "Thanks. I'll get Borelli to take her home later," he said.

Meg gave Trudy a quick hug. "I'll be over with dinner. You get some rest."

Damon reappeared with an evidence envelope as Meg left the sound stage. "All set, sir."

"Good job, Damon. How about waiting by that chapel set until there's a break in the action. Corner Reece Hunter and get his story about the kid." He explained what he wanted her to do when Borelli got there. She beamed and hurried off, and Ned felt she'd forgiven him for his rudeness this morning.

"Don't trust me, Ned?" Trudy's voice was soft, her eyes still closed.

Ned sat on the edge of the sofa, scrutinizing her pale face. Her full lips looked ruddy in the dim light against the whiteness of her skin. "Of course I trust you. I want to see if Hunter has any ideas where this kid came from, that's all."

Trudy's voice was sleepy. "You mean you want to find out if he's the one who got the kid to give them to me."

Ned unfolded the blanket and covered her with it. "Just rest, Trudy. Stop trying to out-think me."

M.K. GRAFF

CHAPTER TWENTY FOUR

I sent Borelli to buzz Ned in when he rang my apartment. Catching Meg's eye through my good one, I listened to the men's exchange at the door. After a trawl through my medicine cabinet, I was feeling just fine at the moment, determined not to let Ned's disapproval bring me down if he figured out I had narcotics on board.

"Hi, boss. Got Trudy settled and stayed to make sure she didn't remember anything else pertinent . . . "

"My idea, exactly," Ned grunted.

I lounged on my rocker, wrapped in a thin blanket. The bruises around my eye and cheekbone were a deep violet, darkening to black under the eye in places. My lid had swollen closed. I figured I looked like Quasimodo at this point, but didn't much care.

The coffee table was littered with open Chinese take-out cartons, gingery sweet and spicy scents heavy in the air. With the help of several heavy-hitter pain pills I'd scoped out, I had a healthy appetite, despite my sore face, and carefully chewed a spring roll.

"Join the party, O'Malley," I said. "You must be famished.

Grab a paper plate. Meg's treat." I concentrated on my food, hoping he wouldn't notice my glazed look. Borelli had dragged over my desk chair for him, and as Ned was settled in, he resumed his own seat next to Meg on the futon.

After only a slight hesitation, Ned piled his plate with fried dumplings, boneless spareribs, chicken lo mein, and a crispy spring roll. Once he dug in, the tension in the room abated and everyone started eating again.

"How's the headache?" Ned asked, dipping a dumpling in soy sauce.

I decided to come clean. Ned O'Malley wasn't my keeper or my conscience. If I'd listened to him and gone to the ER I'd have even more meds in me. "What headache? A visit to the nurse's medicine cabinet and everything's under control." Someone in the room giggled. "Leftovers from Jake Forster's sprained ankle came in very handy." I loved the blissful feeling from the pills, understanding for the first time how people could become hooked on the stuff.

"Is it safe to take narcotics with a concussion?" Ned asked, balancing his full plate on his lap.

I watched Borelli shrug his shoulders as he bit into a fried wonton. "Beats me. She looks kinda happy."

"I'm sitting right here, Borelli," I protested. "Don't talk about me in the third person. I'm perfectly fine." I didn't miss the look Borelli and Meg shared.

"I'll keep an eye on her," Meg promised.

I felt myself try on a pout for size. "It's just a conk on the head. Don't get snarky, Ned-O."

Borelli choked on his wonton. Meg sipped her glass of water and looked away. So what—I was the injured party, right?

Who deserved drugs tonight more than I did? Ned carefully wound a lo mein noodle around his fork. Through my drugged buzz, I imagined his thought process. Acknowledge or ignore, accept or censure? With Borelli looking on, too. What fun. Ned met my look and I beamed at him with a grin that felt lopsided, as only one side of my face wanted to move.

He smiled rakishly in return. "I've been talking to everyone at the studio, Trudy. You certainly are well liked; everyone is worried about you. But it seems you developed a recent habit of eavesdropping on people's conversations that didn't go unnoticed." He let the comment hang in the air as he forked a sparerib.

I frowned. "You've been talking about me?" What nerve.

"Let's see, what are the words that spring to mind? "Nosy" was one comment and then the word "meddlesome" was used a few times."

Meg smothered a laugh. I thought I had been very careful to appear nonchalant in my quest for the truth.

Ned stuffed the sparerib in his mouth. "You don't seem to understand this is not a game."

"I like games," I said defiantly. "And I know it's not a game. I'm trying to solve these murders."

"But wait, before I forget, what was the nickname someone gave you? Oh, yes, I remember now: *Thornfield Place*'s very own Miss Marple." He looked smug and satisfied.

My glance roved from face to face while anger rose through my chest and through the hazy high of Vicodin. Ned might think he was being amusing but he was spoiling my floaty feeling. "Miss Marple, indeed. She was a spinster!" I announced with great indignation, which was met with a round of chuckles from my audience.

I had to get back at Ned, and even though a very tiny bit of my brain proclaimed this a childish maneuver, most of it thought it highly appropriate. "Would you mind settling a little bet for me, O'Malley?"

"What kind of bet?" he asked, dipping a wonton in orange sauce.

"Speaking of games, Meg and I play this game—" I started.

"Trudy, no!" Meg insisted.

"—and we have a bet going," I continued. "Help me win this one."

Meg covered her face with her hands. Borelli raised his eyebrows.

"Okay, I'll be a sport and play along," Ned said, a mischievous grin on his face.

"Great! What kind of underwear do you favor? 'Cause I bet Egyptian cotton button-fly boxers, probably from Brooks Brothers, monogrammed."

Sudden silence. I thought Ned looked stunned, but maybe that was just my imagination.

"Did you do me?" Borelli addressed Meg. "What did you guess for me?

Meg's voice was smothered and I noticed she didn't look up. "Trudy, you have totally mortified me."

Borelli nudged her. "Yeah, but what did you guess for me?"

Ned rose, putting his empty plate down. "Thanks for the food, Meg. And don't be embarrassed. Trudy can't help being childish and meddlesome, it's obviously her nature."

Well, that was better, wasn't it? He turned to me somberly but I was sure I saw a glint of humor sparkle in his eyes.

"Miss Marple, I hope you feel better soon." He started to leave the room, stopped at the doorway, and hooked his head back inside to announce: "Not monogrammed—you lose."

Hours later I woke up on the futon, the quilt thrown over me. The lamp on my desk glowed and I sat up, blinking in the dim light as my eyes adjusted. My face was sore, the skin hot over the bruises. A large glass of water sat on the table in front of me with a note from Meg and three Tylenol: "I'm in your bed. Take these if you wake up—you've had enough of the hard stuff! M."

The evening was a blur. I knew O'Malley had arrived, there was too much Chinese food, and that my head had been floating, but that was all. So why did I have this acute feeling of humiliation? I must have passed out soon after eating since I had no memory of O'Malley or Borelli leaving.

Wilkie jumped up on the futon and curled around my feet. I swallowed the pills with half of the water and snuggled back under the quilt. Just before dozing off I thought I heard low voices coming from my bedroom. Maybe one of the detectives hadn't left after all.

Ned tossed the latest report back on his desk and turned off his desk light. He had to be up early to attend Misty Raines' autopsy, postponed due to a backlog at the ME's office after a bus accident by the Queens Midtown Tunnel. It was almost nine, and for once his stomach was full. He decided to stop into Art's Bar and Grill to recoup before going home. He usually didn't linger there, but he liked to feel he was a part of his neighborhood. The owner-bartender was a retired cop, Art Leonard. Ned liked that Art had kept the dark wood paneling and the booths smelling of spilt martinis, real ones without Kool-aid flavoring. Art also knew when to talk shop and when to leave a cop to his thoughts.

He thought back to his quick meal at Trudy's, her glassy eyes and silly demeanor, and had to stifle a laugh. He should be offended that as the lead detective in a double homicide his underwear was being discussed, but instead he worried that her questions and meddling had caught the murderer's attention and she was in more danger than an apartment break-in. Today's incident was a warning to her to stop interfering, and he had to decipher if that meant she'd uncovered a clue he'd missed or had just annoyed the offender with her prying.

The duty sergeant stopped him on his way out. "This young lady is looking for you, O'Malley."

The woman in question stepped forward, holding out her hand. She was slender with dark hair cut in a long pageboy. With a jolt, he noticed the scar running down her left cheek, half hidden by a swath of hair. He knew he'd met her before.

"Melissa West," she said as they shook hands. "I'm sorry to bother you so late, but when I call you're usually out. I live in the neighborhood and stopped in on impulse."

"What can I do for you, Miss West?" Ned asked, running the name through his memory bank. Bingo. One of the beating victims from earlier in the year was named West.

"I was wondering if you'd found anything out about the person who assaulted my brother. It's been so long with no news . . ."

"Let me walk you out." Ned escorted her down the hall toward the main door. "The case is still open, and we're openly and actively investigating, but I'm sorry to say I have no new information for you yet. How is your brother?" He held the door as she passed through.

"Dave's still in physical therapy. The hip is healing but he may always walk with a limp. At least he's walking, not like one of the other men." She stopped on the sidewalk and tilted her head to keep the scar out of view. "You didn't know my brother before this, but Dave is the sweetest guy. He's always been my biggest defender and supporter. I feel so frustrated I can't help him more."

Ned touched her shoulder lightly. "Please tell Dave we haven't forgotten him. And I promise to be in touch if we have any news at all."

"Thank you, Detective. Sorry to bother you."

He offered to get her a taxi, but she politely refused, reminding him she lived in the neighborhood, and walked away on the dark street. Watching her until she reached Broadway, he waited until she turned the corner before he turned for home. No stop at Art's Bar and Grill for him tonight.

He wondered how Melissa West had gotten that scar. Dave West came to mind as he'd first seen him in the Emergency

Room, barely able to speak, with multiple fractures and internal injuries. Then in rapid succession came the faces of the other two victims, all three men under thirty, with no previous history of trouble with the law, gangs, or drugs.

Once home, Ned switched his bedside light on and pulled the three files from his briefcase, plumping up his pillows and settling down for one more trawl through the statements and reports, looking for anything that linked these three assault victims to their perpetrator. He knew he was driven in some ways, committed to a job that would never be over, and could never be won. His own personal demons involved Luke Romano, a young cop he'd mentored, then let down spectacularly. More and more he pushed these memories aside. If he allowed his thoughts to dwell there, he'd get nothing accomplished.

The snick of the apartment door closing roused me and I sat up. My face felt hot, the bruises throbbing. Meg came into the room with a fresh ice pack.

"I heard you moving around. I hope we didn't wake you. How about some fresh ice for that face of yours?"

In the dim light I reached for the offered pack.

"Mmmm, feels good. Thanks, Meggie. Was that Borelli leaving?"

She nodded. "He stayed to talk a while. Trudy, I really like him. He has these wonderful stories about his family and growing up. They sound so warm and normal." She sat on the edge of the futon.

"Oh." I couldn't think what to add. "He does have nice eyes," I finally said.

Meg jumped right on it. "Yes, and a very caring nature. And he can cook!"

I sensed anything but agreement was going to get me into trouble with my friend. "Were we at least right on his underwear?"

"Trudy, I don't know! We just mostly talked, you know."

I nodded. "He must be a great kisser, romantic Italian and all."

Meg stood. "Enough. Can I get you anything else? Want to move to your bed?"

"No, I'm fine here, go get some sleep." Meg had turned away when I added: "Meg, was I a real jerk tonight?"

Meg halted in the hallway and turned back to me. "Trudy, you had a scary and painful accident today, plus you had drugs on board tonight. No one's upset with you."

I took that in. "Just no more Miss Marple jokes, all right?"

"I promise," she said solemnly.

Chapter Twenty Five

Tuesday, May 11th

Today's music was "Shooting Star," one of Bad Company's anthems. Byron Burknikoff riffed on his air guitar after removing the young actor's organ block to the dissecting table. The autopsy room had lost its shiny, sterile look and taken on the garish semblance of a butchery over Misty's flayed-open body. The metallic smell of raw meat hung heavily in the air, mixed with the noxious odor of decay. The music's beat throbbed in Ned's temple. He wondered why he had come here instead of sending Borelli.

Last night's review of the three beatings had been an exercise in futility. He should have slept more instead of letting the open cases gnaw at him. His sinuses stung as he shoved more menthol rub up his nose in preparation for Byron opening the intestinal tract. The bright greens and yellows of the young woman's interior glistened in the harsh overhead light. Handing a length of intestine to his diener for cleaning, Byron continued his dissection, whistling along with the next track, one Ned recognized: "Feel Like Making Love."

"How do you do that, Byron?"

"Use a very sharp scalpel and it's just like cutting butter," the pathologist explained.

"No, I mean, how do you cut apart a body and enjoy music at the same time? You sing and whistle, play air guitar, actually seem to enjoy it." Ned shook his head. "I don't get it."

"Ah, the detective is shocked that I should be singing about making love when I have reduced this lovely specimen to tickybits?"

"Tidbits. Is it some kind of protective mental thing you have going on?"

Byron shrugged. "The human body is mysterious to me, and I am the guardian of unlocking its secrets. It fascinates me and gives me tremendous *sila*—what you say strength or power—to read it well. I find it beautiful and enthralling, and—hel-lo!"

Despite his misgivings, Ned shuffled closer to the table. "What?"

Byron spread out the small pear-shaped organ he'd opened, displaying the endometrial lining of the uterus. "Someone felt like making love. I'd say this lady had an abortion in the last six weeks."

After she showered, Meg insisted I take one while she was still there, in case I got dizzy. She stayed in the bathroom with me, fixing her hair and makeup, talking to me on the other side of the shower curtain. I reveled in the hot water, gingerly letting the shampoo suds run down my face with my eyes closed.

"My upper teeth ache today on that side," I said as I rinsed off.

"I'll make us some oatmeal and tea before I leave, no chewing."

I turned off the taps and pulled back the curtain. Meg handed me a towel. "Thanks again for the dinner and for staying last night." I wrapped the bath sheet around me and twisted a smaller towel around my hair.

"You sure you'll be okay alone today?" Meg asked, sliding on hoop earrings.

"Absolutely. I need you to be my eyes and ears at the studio. See what the reaction is to my accident from an unbiased point of view. Look for gloating."

Meg gathered her cosmetic bag. "You must admit O'Malley was pretty funny last night. He might actually have a sense of humor."

"Yeah, he's real scream."

After breakfast Meg hugged me on her way out. "Don't forget to ice up again later." She shouldered her purse and overnight bag.

"Will do. Call me with breaking news." I shut the door behind her and slid the new dead bolt home, glancing at my shelf. Today's Word of the Day was "hyperbole." I didn't need to use that one three times; I'd been the epitome of exaggeration last night.

It took me all of three minutes to clean up after our quick breakfast. Meg had brought some groceries last night, so I wouldn't have to leave the apartment today. I folded the quilt and wiped the coffee table in the main room, then carried my pillow and sheet back into the bedroom. Meg, excellent guest that she was, had stripped the sheets and remade the bed with a clean set, throwing the used set in the washer. I threw mine in and turned it on, letting Wilkie out the window. Chores done, there was nothing humming in the fax machine, and the unexpected day off loomed in front of me. Now what?

Wandering back to the living room, I spotted my violin in the corner. After dusting the case off, I took it out, enjoying the glow of the maple wood grain, the carved scrolls and the familiar silhouette. I tuned it and ran a few scales to limber up my fingers, then warmed up with a few easy pieces, getting comfortable with the instrument I'd ignored lately. Finally I propped up the last piece of music I'd been trying to learn, John Williams' theme from "Schindler's List."

I'd taken violin lessons all through school, playing in the orchestra and enjoying it the way others enjoyed team sports. Rehearsing with a combination of instruments to produce a recognizable piece, following the conductor to bring forth the piece's emotion, all filled me with delight. The fact that a composer could figure out the notes each individual would play to achieve that effect was nothing short of miraculous in my humble opinion. Now I played for myself, to keep up a hard-won proficiency I didn't want to lose, and occasionally, for solace.

This piece was difficult. But after working my way through it, my face started to ache too much and I put the instrument down. It would take me months to get that piece sounding anything like the soundtrack version. I realized that was what I needed. I wanted to hear Itzhak Perlman, his violin an extension of his arms, coax feeling and emotion out of wood and strings and hear the piece played the right way.

I loaded my iPod with the soundtrack and settled on the window seat overlooking West 98ᵗʰ Street, opening a window. Facing north, I could see the leafy trees at Riverside Park, a few strollers, and a variety of dogs gamboling with their walkers. I knew if I walked down there the serpentine park would give me majestic views of the Hudson River and across to the Palisades of New Jersey. Past that narrow oasis the Henry Hudson Parkway carried travelers north to Morningside Heights and Columbia University, then on into Westchester.

The music blotted out the rush of parkway traffic noise. Images from the movie rose, of the little girl in the red coat flitting in and out of scenes as she tried to hide from the Nazis. Perlman was at the height of his talent, beguiling, capturing with rising emotion not just the loss of life, but the loss of innocence and trust in fellow man.

When that track ended, I had tears in my eyes, and let the disc play on. I ruminated on the murders, on what would lead one person to murder another. These were not the acts of uncontrolled Hitler-like megalomania. These crimes, even my own accident, displayed a level of careful planning and consideration that spoke of a deeply-felt personal pain eating away at someone until the acts taken had felt like a rational solution. But what could deeply scar one person might be better shouldered by another—look at my own mother and her behavior when my father had died.

My eyes grew drowsy from the sun coming in the window,

and I let the door in my mind open on that day, one that had started out like so many other summer days in the countryside of upstate New York, sunny and bright.

I was going over plans with my mother for my Sweet Sixteen party the next week, an evening barbecue, complete with a sheet cake my mother would bake, iced in pale green frosting with blue roses. I wanted paper lanterns hanging from some trees and fairy lights wound around others. There were to be bunches of green and blue balloons, my two favorite colors, tied here and there. "Like Christmas in July without the red," my mother said, and I was pleased she understood my vision.

A college friend of Ben's was donating his time to practice his talents as a budding disc jockey. There would be plenty of boys to dance with, as my school friends were invited, and several of Ben's and my other brother, Rick's, too. When my mother called out Benedict, Riccardo or Gertrude, we knew something was out of order.

As the birthday girl, I would have John Maydan—he of the sleepy dark brown eyes—dance the first dance with me, hoping to set the tone for a romantic evening. We had had three dates so far, and in the back of the movies Saturday night he'd darted his tongue inside my mouth when we kissed, an experience that thrilled me to my toes every time I thought about it.

DEATH UNSCRIPTED

"That's settled then," my mother said, closing her folder. My own love of lists and organization developed from years of watching Hilda Genova handle any event, from holidays to parties to the family store, with pre-planning that kept chaos to a minimum.

Mom glanced at the apple-shaped kitchen clock and frowned. "Where in heavens is your father? It's almost time to open the store."

At the height of summer the Genova orchard store would be packed by late morning with tourists and locals alike. When the apples were not in season, we brought in other fruits and vegetables from area farmers, the freshest produce available. Mom made the baked goods we sold, and the hearty sub sandwiches Ben had started making for lunches were proving to be a big draw for the area, something different from the local diner or fast food stands in town.

My father had gone to Albany early to pick up supplies we needed for the lunch crowd and was to stop in town on his way back for the rest. If he didn't return soon, Ben would be without some of the raw materials he needed to back up his growing clientele.

"Do you want me to run down and hurry him up? He's probably at the hardware store talking with Mr. Ames," I offered, hoping to be taken up on it.

"No, dear, you only have your permit, you know you shouldn't drive alone yet. I'll get your brother to chase him down." Mom left the kitchen, the door slapping shut as she crossed the yard and strolled down the drive to the roadside store.

Well, I'd tried. Driving was something that came easily

to me. I'd been driving tractors at the farm since the age of twelve. Mom returned and set me to vacuuming and dusting the living room. I heard the old Ford station wagon start up as I dusted, debating which of my nail polish colors would best suit the green sundress I'd bought with babysitting money for my party. When Mom removed the last batch of cookies for the shop from the oven, the delightful aroma of cooked brown sugar enticed me to snatch one when Mom's back was turned. I was munching the cookie and winding the cord around the vacuum cleaner when the phone rang.

"Whatever do you mean, Benedict?" Mom said.

Uh-oh, Benedict. That caught my attention. I shut the broom closet door and reached for another warm cookie.

"Mrs. Dunbar? I expect she would . . . police? Is that necessary? . . . All right, dear." Mom hung up and immediately redialed.

The cookie hit my stomach and began roiling around. "Mom, what's happening?"

"Ben says—oh, hello, Kathy. Can you give me a lift into town? Ben's down there and he's found the pickup but no sign of Mario. I need to bring the wagon back here—thanks."

My mother hung up and explained the situation to me as she took her apron off and nervously fluffed up her hair. "The pickup's parked in the railroad station lot, all the supplies in the back, but no sign of your father. Benedict thinks we should call the police." A frown creased her brow.

"I'm coming with you," I insisted, handing Mom her pocketbook.

In ten minutes Kathy Dunbar was dropping us at the station beside Ben. A Manhattan train pulled out, the blast of its horn cutting through the air as we thanked our neighbor and scrambled out. Diesel fumes hung in a cloud behind the departing train.

Ben met us, his anxiety making him break out in a sweat despite the cool morning. "No sign of him. I asked in the station and no one's seen him, but it's busy this time of day. And look at this—"

He brought us to the bed of Dad's truck, pulling back a tarp covering its contents on one side. The cold cuts and lunchmeats were packed neatly inside an iced cooler, submarine sandwich rolls and loaves of fresh bread stacked in paper bags alongside it.

Two large cartons were on the other side, both covered with an old blanket usually kept in the truck bed for our dog, Max. A patrol car pulled into the lot as I drew the blanket back and sucked in my breath. Stacks of bright blue and green paper napkins, plates, and cups, plus two large candles, numbers "1" and "6" stared back up at me.

The patrolman had gone to Schoharie High with Ben. I watched my brother talk to his former classmate, his arms gesticulating and temper rising when Ron Hanson explained they couldn't file a missing person report yet, but suggested we should visit our bank. The young cop was clearly uncomfortable.

"That might give you a clue if this was, um, a planned departure or if you should worry about foul play, although there's no sign of that yet. And then you should search at home for any note he might have left there, or anything that's missing."

Ben nodded briskly and piled us into the wagon. Half an

hour later the bank manager confirmed our worst fears. My father had been in the day before and closed out my parents' savings account, leaving the business accounts intact and my mother's housekeeping checkbook balance untouched.

"I'm sorry, Hilda," the banker told her. His sons had grown up with my brothers and he looked stupefied. "I wasn't here and the teller is new. She said he filled out the appropriate withdrawal slip and showed ID. She never questioned it."

Mom looked dazed. "What about our retirement account?"

The banker frowned, clicking buttons on his computer. "Was that the money market, not an IRA?" At Mom's nod, his expression grew even graver. "Closed out, too, I'm afraid."

Ben pounded the desk. "Let's go home. We have to let Rick know."

We stood and I saw Mom's hands tremble when she thanked the banker, who apologized again. I wondered how long it would take for the entire town to know my father had wiped out the family's finances. Where was he? What had he been thinking?

I heard a throat being cleared. Ron Hanson stood at the manager's door, his expression one of deep sorrow. He held us there with one hand. "Ben, could I speak with you a minute?"

Mom sank back into her chair. I stood by her, watching Ron put his arm around Ben's shoulder, talking earnestly. Ben drew back suddenly, throwing Ron's arm off. His head dropped to his chest. Ron kept talking and gestured toward me and Mom. He gripped Ben's arm and steered him back to us.

I knew then that my father was dead. What I didn't know was that he'd been murdered.

DEATH UNSCRIPTED

Hours later Ben forged ahead of us in the pickup truck, squealing the tires as he left the station in a churned up puff of dust. In just a brief time my entire family structure had cracked apart. I must be in a dream, I thought. This happened to other people, not the Genovas. I wanted to cry but couldn't find tears.

We drove home with Ron Hanson's partner. Ron followed us in the station wagon with Rick, who had closed the store when he heard the news and gotten a lift to the police station. Mom's hands twisted a sodden tissue. She stared out the window in mute shock. The familiar landscape blurred by as we climbed the hill from town up to the orchard, past the homes and farms of my friends and the people I saw every day. Green sloping hills, clumps of wildflowers in the gorse, cows and sheep and pigs, wire fences. Ron's partner hit every one of the potholes we knew to avoid on the dusty road, jarring us around in the back seat where the criminals usually sat. Mom grabbed my arm and held on tightly, her fingers digging into my flesh. I welcomed the pain, the only point of feeling I had.

How could this happen? How could my father leave this morning and be dead before lunch? He'd been found behind the train station, apparently dying where he'd fallen next to an empty utility trailer. At first glance, a heart attack was assumed. He had a gash on his head, and it was decided he'd hit the metal trailer as he fell. But how did that tie in with him withdrawing all of that money? Had he been planning to leave us? And if this was an accident, where was the money now?

I knew my parents argued at times, fighting often over what seemed like small matters. My father could go for long periods of silence after one of those bouts, his expression dark. My mother would ignore him as though nothing had happened, and after a few days his ire would wear off and things would return to normal. On reconsideration, maybe those bouts of silence had become more frequent recently, but everyone was used to Dad's moodiness and had taken it in stride.

I helped my mother upstairs to lie down before the house filled with neighbors as the news spread. I knew by local custom food would start to arrive, clogging up our table and overflowing the pantry and refrigerator. Mom's sister was flying up tonight from Florida to help with the funeral and its immediate aftermath. There would be an investigation, an autopsy, an inquest, events discussed in front of me or overheard in the coming days.

I paused before the dresser photo of two impossibly young people: Dad in a brown tuxedo with a yellow ruffled shirt, his wavy hair and droopy mustache jet black, grinning as though he'd won a prize; Mom, wearing an Empire-style dress, long ribbons of lace running from neck to hem, a circlet of white and yellow daisies framing her waist-length reddish hair, a match to the round bouquet she clutched.

My mother sat down heavily on the bed. "Thirty-four years, and I have no idea why he took that money. What could he need it for?" Her voice was hollow and low. "If he were right here in front of me, I'd shake him and shout my questions at him. And now he's gone I'll have no answers to any of it."

I ran to my mother and put my arms around her. Our eyes met. The anguish and betrayal I saw reflected on my mother's face would be burned in my memory. And then the dam broke and the tears finally came and we clung tightly to each other.

I shook my head to climb out of the past, sniffling heartily on my way to grab a tissue from the desk. It was time to concentrate on the present. The music had moved on to the sexy tango from "Scent of a Woman" and, tears dried, I felt my face ache anew. Rooting in the freezer for ice cubes, I filled a plastic baggy, wrapping it in a dishtowel. I sat back on my window seat with the soothing ice against my face.

On the street below I glimpsed a wheaten terrier skipping his owner down the street towards the park. Dogs were so uncomplicated, always happy to see you and the best practitioners of unconditional love. Unlike humans. I should go to the park and improve my mood once my face felt numb enough.

Over the years I'd become convinced the gash on my father's head was caused by another person stealing the money that was never recovered. This person had some kind of hold over my father, must have threatened or tried to blackmail him. It was the only explanation that made sense to me. The autopsy had shown some narrowing of the arteries to his heart but no acute infarction. Still, the coroner had judged it to be an accidental death, one that let my father's life insurance policy tide us over, one that everyone else in my family was relieved to believe. For months my mother kept expecting the delivery of a big surprise my father had planned, maybe a new sedan he'd been eying, or perhaps that John Deere tractor he'd finally decided he couldn't live without. The issue of the missing money was never resolved and eventually stopped being discussed in the family. To my mind, the police had never dug deeply enough to find out what had really happened. We got on with our lives, as the adage told us to, and stopped trying to find answers to questions. Except for me. I was the only one who kept the questions burning in one compartment of my mind.

The lack of resolution affected me in other ways. The emotional betrayal felt huge, affecting my dating throughout high school and nursing school. I rarely let anyone get close to me—until Jake. Despite my misgivings, I'd let my guard down, only to have Jake Forster reconfirm my fears.

Today when I examined the memories of that awful experience, I grasped what my introspection had shown me: I admired the extraordinary strength and courage my mother had shown after that first day.

But I also speculated on the reverse: What if my mother had succumbed to her pain, become suicidal, let her life be destroyed by her husband's death? What if my brothers hadn't rallied to keep the family business going and we had become destitute? Our world had been changed, but we'd managed to fashion a new one. What if we hadn't? Who would have been around for me to blame?

Old wounds cut deep. Pain could be buried, but never totally overcome. It could be compartmentalized, as I had mastered, and trotted out on occasion when I was feeling sorrow or fear, as I was now.

DEATH UNSCRIPTED

I sat up with a jerk, the ice pack falling to the floor. I was convinced this feeling of not overcoming deep psychic pain must apply to the person or people responsible for two deaths and a bad fall in the last week.

If I allowed myself to admit it, I knew if my father's killer appeared before me right now, I would have no difficulty cheerfully putting my hands around his neck and choking the life out of him.

CHAPTER TWENTY SIX

Tony Borelli sat at Ned's desk, a stack of reports in front of him, a dreamy smile on his face. Ned didn't know why Tony was at his desk, nor what had gone on after he'd left Trudy's apartment last night, but it didn't bear thinking about.

Ned recalled his own smart-ass parting shot, and that he'd left without helping to clean up the meal, but didn't think Tony and Meg had a great deal of trouble throwing out paper plates and closing cartons.

"Can I have my desk back?" Ned asked.

Tony sat up with a start.

"And wipe that stupid smile off your face," he continued, placing a fresh Starbucks coffee in front of Tony. "Don't say I never gave you anything." Ned had noted Tony was less twitchy these days. Maybe hormones were substituting for caffeine.

"Thanks, boss." Tony stood up and Ned sat. "One piece of good news. The bike thief's out of business."

Ned took the cover off his own coffee. "What happened?"

"Remember that call Phil's team got the other day—the guy who said his shed windows were broken by a gang?" Borelli perched on the end of Ned's desk. "Turns out the "gang" were kids whose bikes this guy had stolen. When Phil checked the guy's garage, he found all the stolen bikes and then some."

"A nice sideline, reselling?" Ned blew on his coffee.

"Nah, the guy's got a wheel fetish. Liked to go out there and just spin them at night. Gives me the creeps. Didn't he think they'd check there when he called in the broken windows?"

"Who knows? I wonder what kind of sexual connotation a psychologist would come up with for that."

"Ugh. Don't make me even think about it. How was the autopsy?"

Ned glared at him in answer. He drank from his cup and put it down carefully without splashing. "Actually, there was one interesting development. Misty Raines recently had an abortion."

"Whoa—guess there's no way to know the father?"

"None, but keep it in mind." Ned flipped back through his notebook, bringing his partner up to date, including his review of the beating files last night. "One other thing. The sister of one of the assault victims stopped by last night, Melissa West. Wanted to know of any progress. That's why the review, fruitless as it was."

"I remember her. Dave West's sister, brunette with a scar across her cheek, right?" Tony drained his coffee. "I interviewed her in the ER the night of her brother's beating."

"Any idea how she got that scar?"

"Yeah. When I interviewed Dave for any description he could piece together, he was worried about how his beating would affect her. She'd been through an ugly rape outside a club, about ten months before. Went out for air, got dragged into an alley, fought the guy pretty hard. That's how she got the scar; he had a knife. After he cut her, she stopped struggling and just let him finish. When she didn't return, her friends found her in the alley, hysterical and covered in blood."

"Poor kid," Ned said, remembering the young woman's pretty face, now permanently marred.

"That sounds like her. Tough gal, Dave said . . . " Tony's eyes opened wide. "Jeez, boss."

"Spit it out Borelli, what?"

"She ended up pregnant from the rape and was afraid she'd hate the kid. Dave went with her when she had an abortion."

Ned felt a tingle in his stomach. What were the chances of this just being a coincidence? But then Melissa West had said she lived in this neighborhood. He jolted upright, slamming his chair into the desk, moved into action. "Give Dave West a call. Find out exactly where his sister had her abortion."

PBJ NEWS TICKER: THE LATEST HEADLINE NEWS...
DEMS VOW TO WIN WHITE HOUSE BACK IN NOVEMBER NO MATTER WHO IS ON TOP; STOCKS STABLE FOR FIRST TIME IN TWO WEEKS; HOUSING MARKET ON THE RISE? SEE TONIGHT'S 6PM BROADCAST WITH BRETT HAME; TP'S MURDERER: A HIT AND A MISS? SECOND DEATH AT SOAP STUDIO IS FOLLOWED BY SUSPICIOUS ACCIDENT TO CREW MEMBER, COPS BAFFLED; KILEY SIGNS NEW TWO-YEAR CONTRACT TO HOST WITH KING THROUGH 2010; IS COLIN FIRTH THE REAL DAD ON FILM IN "MAMMA MIA" OR

DEATH UNSCRIPTED

WAS HIS SPOT TAKEN BY PIERCE BROSNAN? SEE ENTERTAINMENT NEWS WITH JILL RODGERS AT 11.

My violin was looking beautiful, the maple and spruce grain warmed, the boxwood fingerboard and tailpiece glowing after the careful cleaning I'd given it. My music teacher had said I should see the violin as an extension of myself if I ever wanted to play it well. I'd named her Clare because it was my favorite name at the time, one I'd wished were mine instead of old-fashioned Gertrude.

Clare had turned out to be a good friend to me and I'd repaid her camaraderie by largely ignoring the instrument lately. I was replacing the violin in her dusted case when the tag line on the local news caught my eye. I saw "TP's murderer" and read along. So I was a crew member and the police were baffled. I wondered what Ned would have to say about that. The phone interrupted my thoughts; the caller ID showed the studio's office number—Meg.

"How's the face feeling this afternoon? You sound rough."

"Too much introspection. The face is colorful. Iced it before and I'm just back from a walk in the park, some nice dogs today. I wore my sunglasses and no one seemed to notice me at all." I described an encounter with a boisterous Labradoodle and a mellow basset hound. "The hound kept nudging me for more petting while the doodle kept trying to leap in my lap. I did manage to keep him from dislodging my sunglasses."

"I'm glad you got some air. Edith came up to see how you were, and everyone else sends their regards." She paused.

"Why do I have the feeling there's something else you want to say and are hedging?"

"It's just—I know you don't like the idea of me seeing Tony, but honestly, the chemistry just crackles between us."

"I'm concerned, that's all. You couldn't be more opposite in upbringing or demeanor," I pointed out.

"Last night we talked about how scared I was for you. I am, you know, Trudy."

"I know. Go on."

"I'd held my feelings in all day. It was such a relief to have him there to soothe me, knowing the entire situation. He rubbed my shoulders and my back."

"At first," I prompted. Now we were getting to the good stuff.

"When we finally kissed, it seemed natural. He has lovely soft lips . . . "

"And?"

"And nothing. You know I don't take lovers lightly, and after all, we were on *your* bed! He was the perfect gentleman when I demurred, just went back to holding me and cuddling until he left."

"What a guy." Meg is the only person I know who would use "demurred" in her normal speech. "What about your parents?" The Pitmans were a formidable pair for anyone to meet. I recalled my own nervousness the first time Id been introduced to them.

"I think I'll start introducing his name into conversations, casually," Meg said. "A friendship, developing around the investigation."

"Your mother will see right through that," I said.

"Yes, but my father won't. He'll be polite and oblivious to the undercurrent. I'll bring them together when the timing feels right, when we know each other better."

"You mean when he ceases to be overwhelmed by either your parents or your birthright," I added.

"It's a plan, but we'll see," Meg acknowledged. "Do you think you'll be up to coming to work tomorrow? There's something going on here you wouldn't want to miss."

"I'm all ears. What's happening?"

"*Soap Opera Journal* wants to give Griff Kennedy a posthumous Lifetime Achievement Award. Nikki Olivier's decided to combine the ceremony with a memorial service on the sound stage for him, 'his true home' she put it today. It should be quite a scene."

"I've got my cover-up makeup at the ready. See you tomorrow."

Ned was at the *Thornfield Place* studio to see Reece Hunter. He cooled his heels in the lobby, waiting for the young man to finish taping a scene. Ned had to cross one more suspect off his list to whittle it down.

Hunter's story to Damon checked out. He'd been signing autographs outside on his way in for the taping of the funeral scene, when the boy with the flowers asked him to send Trudy Genova out to get them. Several witnesses, including the lobby guard, had borne out this version of events. No one had seen the youth before, and Ned felt continuing any search for him was a waste of time and resources without added information to pinpoint his identity.

The inquiries at local florists had not turned up orders for that kind of extravagant bouquet, so Ned had extended the search before leaving the precinct house.

He saw the taping light shut off over the stage door and a few seconds later it opened. Several cast members streamed out, one more scene crossed off the shooting schedule. Frank Resnick's voice pealed over the loudspeaker: "Everyone on set for Scene Six, Nikki's living room. Places, everybody, Scene Six."

The crush of actors rushing upstairs from their dressing rooms met those coming down. In the confusion, Ned almost missed Reece Hunter, but the young man paused to chat up a young woman carrying a camera who must have sprayed her jeans on that morning. He'd seen her on the sound stage and Trudy had explained she was "Continuity," the person responsible for taking photos of the actors dress and hair on set at the end of a scene if that scene was to be continued. Even if the next scene was taped on a different day, the actors' hair and dress and all the details would match up, down to the time on the clock in the room."

"Mr. Hunter—if I might have a word?"

"Uh, sure, detective. See ya, Kayla." Hunter watched the girl amble back to the sound stage, his gaze locked on her posterior.

DEATH UNSCRIPTED

"Is there somewhere private we can talk?" Ned asked. And without so many distractions, Ned thought.

"Um, my dressing room." The actor led the way downstairs past Wardrobe and down the hall to his room, opening the door with a key.

"Always lock up when you're upstairs?" Ned asked. He didn't remember Hunter unlocking the door at their first interview.

"Just this week, stuff going on. Can't be too careful." He ushered Ned into the small room, pointing to the love seat.

Helping himself to a diet soda from a dormitory-sized refrigerator, he offered one to Ned, who shook his head. Hunter popped the top and gulped down half the can, wiping his mouth off with the back of his hand. "So?"

"We need to discuss the depth of your relationship with Misty Raines."

"Told you. We were attracted."

"Just how far had the attraction gone?"

Hunter shrugged his shoulders. "On stage or off?"

"Stop screwing around, Hunter. Or was that the real nature of your relationship with Misty?"

The young actor reared back, hands up. "Told you, hadn't gotten there—yet." He nodded, as if to reassure himself. "Definitely headed there, though."

Ned brushed his fingers through his hair. "I think you've missed your chance."

CHAPTER TWENTY SEVEN

Westside Women's Clinic was located just off Broadway on West 63rd Street, a few streets over from the Passion Broadcasting Junction complex. Ned had left Tony calling the other two beating victims when he left to speak to Reece Hunter. He was to find out whether either victim had ties in the last year to the clinic Melissa West had used, which specialized in "abortion and gynecological care for New York women to fill the increasing need for affordable, quality health care," according to their advertisement in the yellow pages.

Ned returned to the precinct house, blood pumping. "Get me a copy of the background Casting sent us on Misty Raines, please," he called out to Damon before shutting his office door.

He felt the rush of scattered puzzle pieces coming together. Looking out his office window, Ned tried to keep his bubble of excitement at bay. This could prove to be the link they'd needed between the three beatings, and if there was also a link to Misty Raines, they'd struck gold and might tie in the two murders as well, although how Griff Kennedy fit in was yet to be seen.

Ned's precinct sat between Amsterdam and Columbus Avenues. As he watched, a bicycle messenger in a tight black and purple outfit and helmet adroitly moved between the slow-moving line of traffic and the multitude of parked squad and unmarked cars. Three young girls in matching navy blazers and plaid skirts from the nearby private school licked massive ice cream cones as they strolled down the street, backpacks plastered with Day-Glo stickers and dangling charms.

Ned felt a rush of emotion toward the nameless girls. So many dangers awaited them around every corner. Christ, these weren't even his own kids—what a nightmare that must be, to worry incessantly over your child, day in, day out. How did parents let them out without going crazy inside? You'd do anything to protect your child, wouldn't you? Or for that matter, a brother or sister. He'd never had one, his solitary childhood blanketed by aunts and uncles and friends of his parents. He recalled the time his anxious mother had asked him if he missed having a sibling. Somehow at the age of fourteen, he knew the answer she needed.

"I have my books and movies, do stuff with my school friends."

"And you go to museums and have the fencing team," she'd added, more to console herself. "You always say it's like chess on foot." Her wide smile had affirmed his answer had been correct.

Ned had reminded his mother of that conversation when she'd strenuously objected to him joining the police.

"A different kind of chess on foot, with tons of strategic thinking, quick steps and fast decisions. It's perfect for me." He'd silenced her but not convinced her, and now he felt he had a better understanding of why.

She'd relaxed when he'd made detective, as though he was

free of being in danger, a misconception on her part he hadn't corrected; at some point he had to live his own life. Ned's sense of responsibility toward his parents strengthened as they aged. Thankfully, they were both relatively healthy and enjoying retirement. Thoughts of what lay ahead for them haunted him at times; he usually managed to thrust those into a dark corner of his consciousness. He was good at managing to avoid unpleasant thoughts, like those memories of Luke Romano and the debacle that had cost the young cop his badge and his friendship with Ned. Why was he thinking of that now?

Ned had been stationed at Midtown South, the precinct around the revitalized area of Times Square, when post-9/11 vigilance was at its height. The area covered Madison Square Garden, the Theatre, Garment and Fur Districts, and the Empire State Building, on strict alert since the Twin Towers had tumbled down.

A seedy apartment building off Eighth Avenue near the Port Authority Bus Terminal was the site of a huge cocaine sting. Ned had been in charge. His team included a cop he liked and trusted, Luke Romano, anxious the last few weeks as his wife's difficult-to-achieve pregnancy moved into its final trimester.

The planned bust had come off with six collars, over a kilo

of cocaine, and $65,000 in cash found on the premises. It had been a night to celebrate, and indeed, some of the team had already gone to the corner bar when Ned brought the cash to log in with the duty sergeant—and found five thousand dollars missing.

He remembered his initial disbelief, counting out the money a second time, then asking the sergeant to do it. "Sixty thousand even," the sergeant tallied, wrapping the money and filling out an evidence deposit form. "Something wrong, O'Malley?"

Ned was lost in thought. "Maybe—not sure. I'll get back to you."

Alone in his office he checked back through his ever-present notebook. "$65K" stared back at him, hastily written in his own handwriting. His stomach started a spiral descent of dread as he made his way to the car he'd ridden in with Romano, who'd taken charge of the money. A quick search through the front seat became a more thorough search throughout the entire car. He even checked the trunk, although he knew they hadn't opened it.

Ned slammed the lid and looked up at the precinct door. Luke Romano, dressed in his civvies, stood on the stoop, ready to leave for home.

"My office," Ned barked. "Now!"

By the time they sat across from each other, Ned's anger had grown to the size of giant fireball, blazing red in front of his eyes.

"You want to tell me where the five thousand went, Romano?" he seethed.

Luke looked at the floor. His olive skin paled and he

refused to make eye contact with his superior and friend. He opened his mouth and closed it once before finally speaking.

"What if I said I don't know what you're talking about? You counted wrong," Luke finally muttered.

Ned stood, slamming his hand on his desktop. "Then I'd say you're a damn liar, Romano. What the hell's going on?"

Luke raised his head. Ned saw him wince at the fury written on his partner's face, until his own temper rose.

"You really telling me it matters a few thou either way? We've shut down a huge cocaine op, gotten those scumbags off the street, and scored over a kilo of coke in one night. Whose side you on, O'Malley?"

Ned slumped back in his chair. "Yours, Luke. I've always been on your side. But we do things by the book here." He steepled his fingers in thought. "If that money is on my desk when I get back from the men's room, we discuss what happened and how to handle it—together—and salvage your career. If it's not, I'll have your shield." He shoved his chair away from the desk and strode down the hall without looking back.

In the men's room, washing his face, Ned found his hands were shaking with rage. This was a man he'd trusted with his life, a backup he counted on. What the hell was Luke doing stuffing bills in his pocket? Baby needs a crib wasn't going to cut it. He couldn't believe Luke, of all the cops on his team, could be trying to pull this off. He heard the creak of the hall door and almost ran back to his desk.

Romano's shield lay squarely on top of his desk, shining in the overhead light.

Ned had come to see that what followed had not been

his finest hour. Blinded by bitter feelings of defection and disappointment, he allowed Romano's resignation to stand for cause without explanation. The money never surfaced, and he never contacted Luke for a further explanation of his actions that night.

He'd kept track of the man through others in the precinct. Luke was managing his father-in-law's dry cleaning shop, eking out a living. There was talk of some kind of problem near the end of the pregnancy, but the baby was carried to full term and born healthy.

A few months after his son was born, Luke carried the infant proudly into the precinct house. Amid congratulations and pats on the back, he'd handed the boy to secretaries to ooh and aah over, cornering Ned at his desk.

"Good looking boy, Romano," Ned admitted, standing, hands in his pockets so neither of them would feel obligated to shake hands.

Luke looked him straight in the eye and pushed the door partly closed. "I owe you an explanation, and Michael's it. Cindy almost lost him at six and a half months. There was a drug that would give her the chance to carry him full term, but the bastard insurance wouldn't cover it, called it experimental." Sweat popped out on Luke's brow; he wiped it off with one hand. "We couldn't lose this baby, not after all the others, not after we'd seen him waving to us on the sonograms. I'm sorry, boss. I let you down. But if I had to do it all over again, I'd make the same choice."

Ned was stunned. He sat back heavily in his chair. "Luke, why didn't you come to me. I would have loaned you the money myself. You should've told me that night why you took it—I could have put it back and let you pay me off, if it was a pride thing. We could have worked something out."

Luke smoothed the front of his shirt. "I almost did, that night. But I couldn't take the chance. All I could see was that I had to save that baby. It was up to me. A man should be able to provide for his family."

"A man should be able to go to his friends for help. You let your pride get in the way, and look what it's cost you—" Ned gestured around the precinct.

"To be honest, Cindy's happier not worrying about me getting killed every time I leave for work. I miss it sometimes, but . . . my father-in-law's talking about expanding now he's got my help." He shrugged. "Things happen for a reason."

They could hear the baby fussing and Luke looked in his direction. One of the women brought him in to his father. "I think he missed his daddy," she said, handing him over to Luke, who laid the infant on the top of Ned's desk and unwrapped the receiving blanket.

Ned watched in fascination as Luke popped a few snaps on the baby's stretch suit, checking his diaper. He swaddled little Michael tightly and picked him up, slinging him over his shoulder in a practiced move, rubbing his back. The baby quieted down.

"Time to get home for a feeding. I just wanted to say . . . I know why you had to do what you did. But so did I." He saluted Ned and walked away without a backward glance.

"Boss!" Borelli brought Ned back from his reverie. "I think we've got our connection."

CHAPTER TWENTY EIGHT

After flashing their badges, Ned and Borelli were ushered immediately into the clinic director's office, through the waiting room filled with a few bored-looking men and a dozen women.

"Mrs. MacKenzie will be right with you," the young receptionist said, gently closing the door.

They sat on the metal and leather chairs that faced the pale wood desk, topped with wire In and Out boxes brimming with files and papers. A computer keyboard and monitor sat on the other side. Ned scrutinized the office.

Next to the leather blotter, a mug crammed with pens displayed the photo of a Forties siren, holding a cigarette. The caption next to her blood-red lipstick read: "She had not yet decided whether to use her power for good or for evil."

A poster on the sidewall featured the idealized outline of a woman holding an orchid. Its caption read "Your Body, Your Choices." Behind the desk a sleek pale wood credenza held a family photograph: brunette mother and father in their thirties, each one holding a young boy, the older sporting a gap-toothed smile.

Borelli put his folder on the desk and picked up a brochure from the stack in a plastic holder its corner. "Get this." He cleared his throat and read aloud: "'Westside Women's Clinic's caring, professional staff members recognize the importance of a woman's health and her own responsibility toward it. We are dedicated to providing the most complete information and highest quality care available to our clientele.' Jeez."

"Offend your Catholic sensibilities, Tony? Maybe I should have brought Damon along on this interview," Ned said.

"No, boss, it's not that. I mean, I know sometimes abortion is a reasonable solution, like Doug West's sister. But this is pure marketing. It's misleading."

"Fine, but that's not why we're here—" Ned broke off as the door opened and a short, gray-haired woman dressed in a well-tailored business suit stepped into the room. Petite, Trudy would tell him.

"Just why *are* you here, detectives?" the woman said, holding out her hand. "Regan MacKenzie."

After their introductions, Ned began. "I understand you have patient confidentiality issues here. You need to understand at the outset that we're not here to interfere in any woman's care or her decisions."

He briefly outlined the beatings and the fact that all three men had accompanied a woman to have an abortion at this clinic in the last eight months. "There is also the possibility that a young woman who was recently murdered and known to have had an abortion in the last six weeks may have been a client. I'm asking for cooperation in our investigation."

"Are you telling me someone has been targeting my patients or their relatives?" MacKenzie's eyes widened.

"A distinct possibility," Borelli answered, opening his folder. He handed a studio photo of Misty Raines to the Director.

"This is Misty Raines, AKA Della Lou Gibbs. Recognize her?"

MacKenzie took the proffered photo, shaking her head. "I rarely get involved with individual patients. My job is the administrative end of things: marketing, billing and community relations. But if she's dead, and others lives could be at sake . . . " She hit a button on her intercom. "Liz, can you see if we have a file on a Della Lou Gibbs in the last six months. Thanks."

Borelli continued. "These are the names of three women who had abortions here. One woman's brother sustained a severe beating, and the other two had boyfriends who accompanied them and were also assault victims, all within days of the procedures."

Ned jumped in. "Would there be any way to track back the staff on duty those days to see if anyone recalls a suspicious character loitering near the premises?"

MacKenzie pursed her lips, then nodded. "I'll pull the duty rosters from those days and see who was in. I can fax you the names and phone numbers when I collate them."

"Thanks for playing ball with us." Ned was pleased the woman wasn't obstructive.

The director's eyes flashed. "These women come here for more than a procedure, Detective. We do physical exams, provide counseling, do screenings and treatment for sexually transmitted diseases—we are more than just an abortion clinic. Each woman who comes in here for healthcare deserves to be treated with respect, and if there's some sleazebag out there terrorizing her supporters or targeting them for murder, I assure you I want to find them as much as you do." She paused to catch her breath. The door opened and a woman wearing peach scrubs handed her a file and left.

MacKenzie opened the file and scrutinized the face sheet. "It seems Della Lou Gibbs had a surgical termination at our clinic on March 18th."

The detectives shared a glance and Borelli made a note. Ned spoke up. "Does it say who came in with her?"

MacKenzie flipped a few pages and ran her finger down to the middle of a page.

"Unaccompanied. I'm afraid she came in alone."

Five minutes later the two men stood on the street outside the clinic, leaving with the director's assurance that by tomorrow she would have the roster of employees who'd worked on the four pertinent days faxed to the precinct house to their attention.

"That went better than I'd thought," Borelli admitted.

Ned agreed. "Of course, we weren't asking for any confidential information; we gave her information."

"You still don't look very happy."

Ned made a pinching gesture with one hand. "I'm starting to feel this close, but I'm worried about chasing the wrong thread." He knew valuable time would be lost if they went too far down the wrong investigative road. He trusted his instincts but Jellyroll and their Lieutenant would have his hide if his instincts proved wrong.

Beside him, Borelli started to tap one foot. "Any chance of a quick coffee, boss?"

Ned glanced across the street at the corner diner Borelli pointed out. He angled his head back to the clinic, measuring the sight lines from the diner's windows on this side of the street to the clinic.

"How about a Danish to go with that coffee? My treat."

I sat on the futon, finishing up leftover Chinese food and watching a favorite forensic show. It always amazed me how quickly TV labs could get results, which must annoy Ned and Tony. One hand teased circles on Wilkie's belly, the ginger cat on his back, eyes closed in satisfaction, all four paws bent limply in the air. A commercial came on and I was contemplating another dumpling when Meg called.

"How's my friend tonight?"

"Bursting in Technicolor—nice greens and violets. Only took Advil this afternoon, the pain is definitely better. And yes, I iced up and took a nap, too, before dinner. What's new?"

"They started to set up for the gala tomorrow. Big splash out, DeLucca's is catering, corporate's coming, too."

"Sounds like a cocktail dress event," I said. Why did women's thoughts always turn to what they had to wear?

"I haven't decided what I'm wearing yet." After a pause Meg took a breath and continued. "Tony sent me flowers, lovely pink roses."

"Sweet." Meg couldn't see me roll my eyes. "See either of them today?"

"No, but when I called to thank Tony for the flowers he and O'Malley were heading to the Westside Women's Clinic, following a lead, he said. So much detective work is tedious, it sounds downright boring."

"The clinic? Now that's food for thought."

"Probably unrelated to the murders, Trudy. I can hear your wheels turning over the phone. They do have other cases, you know."

"Of course. But I did have a question for you. Have any of the cast or crew had a relative working at the studio lately?" I moved to get my pen and pad from the coffee table, dislodging Wilkie in the process. He stalked off in annoyance.

"Let's see. Not right now, I'm certain. The housekeeper had his granddaughter here last summer, and we had Frank's nephew here then, too, doing an internship, remember? Skinny college kid with acne, Phil, I think, with an eye for the girls . . . hmmm. Last year when Kayla from Continuity was on maternity leave, Gary Knowles' sister filled in for eight weeks. Oh, and Egan had a niece work over Spring Break, but I seem to recall she spent most of her time in the Production Office. That's all I can think of right now."

I concentrated on Meg's memories. "Frank's nephew I seem to recall, thick glasses and the Resnick cheekbones, almost feminine. Egan's niece I missed, but Knowles' sister—thin gal, dark hair, very shy?"

"That's her, Wilhemina."

"I remember someone fading into the woodwork. But I didn't know she was Gary's sister. Doesn't he have a brother, too?"

"Not that I know of." Meg yawned. "I should go find something to wear for tomorrow."

"Me, too. See you then, Meg." I clicked off, contemplating the information Meg had just given me. I recalled Frank's nephew, a hormonal youth who couldn't believe his good luck, ogling the women and sneaking peeks of them trying on clothes in Wardrobe. Could Misty have seduced the boy, just because she could, and Frank found out about it? But then where did Griff's death fit in? And Gary talked to "Willy" on the phone, could that have been Wilhemina? But I could have sworn he told me Willy was his brother. And what would any of that have to with either Misty or Griff? It looked like another dead end.

Ned turned off the light hoping sleep would come quickly. He had the same feeling he'd had the day of Trudy's accident. Tomorrow would be a pivotal day. During any investigation a rhythm became established, and Ned could feel the ragged, disparate pieces starting to come together. With any luck, they'd have their murderer before the week was out.

The results from forensics on the white fibers had come in: no match to the undyed cloths from the Hair/Makeup Department, nor to any of the towels the actors used, or Edith Carlisle's glasses cleaner. Even the housekeeping rags he'd had tested weren't a match. That just meant he hadn't found the right sample yet, and he intended to look again tomorrow at the studio.

This farce of a memorial service for Griff Kennedy would mean all of the soap's society on its many levels would be in attendance, an excellent time to watch them interact. He would be on high alert, of course, along with Borelli and Damon for backup.

Borelli was working out well, and he thought Damon might become a permanent part of their team if she were interested down the road. Ned was amused by the attraction between Meg Pitman and his partner. He wondered how long it would last when the society gal learned Tony's "apartment" was his parents' remodeled garage.

Ned watched the interplay of beams on his ceiling, pale fingers of car headlights filtered by the alleyway between his building and the next. As his eyes got heavy, he had the nagging feeling he'd forgotten to do something. If he had a cat, he would have thought he'd forgotten to feed it. That made him think of Wilkie, and Ned realized the thing he'd forgotten had been to call Trudy and check on her. It would have been reasonable to see how she was feeling, but perhaps smarter to keep the fine line between them from being crossed. He didn't need a relationship to mar this investigation, didn't know if she was even interested. And he certainly didn't need a romance to color his life right now, although his mother would probably start to foist one of her friends' daughters on him again any day now. He shuddered when he thought of Lucilla. Ned compared her prim look and inability to pass a mirror without glancing into it with Trudy and her infectious laugh and optimism, her stubborn manner and fierce independence, those vibrant green eyes. No contest.

If he was going to have a relationship, and he certainly wasn't at this time, it would be much more likely to be with someone like a Trudy Genova. If he was . .

CHAPTER TWENTY NINE

Wednesday, May 12th

I took a swig of mouthwash and spit it in the sink, noticing my face hurt a lot less today, then stood back and checked my reflection one last time in the full-length mirror behind the bathroom door.

My teal dress was a comfortable jersey knit, wrinkle-free. According to Meg's color specialist, the blue-green color shot through with golden threads was a perfect compliment for my reddish-blonde hair and pale skin. I would never confess I'd bought it because it was on a clearance rack, and I liked the way it made me feel when I wore it. The surplice bodice and cummerbund waist fell to a bias skirt that swished when I walked and gave me the illusion I was taller, graceful and feminine. I added cream kitten heels and was set. Now if people just didn't look too hard at one side of my face, I thought I was pretty presentable, cover-up makeup doing its job.

Dumping my backpack on the table, I pulled out my wallet, keys and lip-gloss, adding my cell phone from its charger. I threw them all into a cream leather purse that matched my shoes. Of course, the purse would end up in Meg's desk drawer and my shoes eventually under it, but what the hell, at least I'd look put together when I arrived.

Ten minutes later I was waiting for the "1" train to take me down to Lincoln Center. The subway was its usual mix of people and I observed them all with interest. Character descriptions for my future book would be based on people I ran across, all that fictional food for free right at my fingertips. Three coffees, seven water bottles, six book readers. Nine perused today's paper. The girl opposite me had thick brown hair with bangs, a really good cut I admired. Idly playing with the ends of mine, I wondered how that cut would look on me. An older woman next to me wore short Capri pants displaying her bulging varicose veins, her mouth turned down at the corners by gravity and age. Not quite the fashion statement she'd planned, I expected. Next to me sat a young couple holding hands, both wearing glasses, neatly dressed in fashionable jackets and designer jeans, wearing two-hundred dollar Nike's and consulting a map. In front of me, a tall black youth, iPod ears in, stood swaying to the car's movements, keeping time with his head to the beat he was hearing.

Leaning on the door, something I would never do, a businessman with a pockmarked face studiously read his iPhone messages, his large hands delicately texting either a corporate takeover or a lunch hour assignation. He reminded me of the man with the Financial Times on the train the other night but I expect I'm starting to see people I think I know everywhere.

I loved people-watching, and remembered reading one of

Neil Simon's memoirs. My favorite playwright had described his routine at youthful bar mitzvahs, almost disappearing by standing against the wall, soaking up the way people used language, punctuated their speech with their hands, and interrupted each other. I determined I would be that sponge today, absorbing the telling detail, opening my eyes and ears to how people spoke to one another and reacted, along with their body language. There must be some way to ferret out a murderer.

Under the shade of the awning outside the Passion Broadcasting Junction's main entrance, Ned and Borelli stood with Damon, watching the spectacle unfold across the street at the red brick building that housed the *Thornfield Place* studio. The local papers had carried press releases about the day's activities and fans had responded with a showing that would have made Griff Kennedy proud. Several patrolmen kept the crowd controlled behind sawhorses framing the sidewalk. Roving cameras caught the stars' arrivals, most alighting from limousines, giving their practiced smiles and waves to bursts of cheers and shouts. To Ned, the actors looked so phony he didn't see how anyone watching could be taken in by any of it.

He was suddenly tired of this case, tired of these plastic people with their collagen-stuffed lips and artificial body parts, tired of pursuing a killer who seemed just outside his grasp. Loosening his collar slightly, his eyes searched the crowd, looking for the one face that didn't belong there but couldn't stay away.

Reece Hunter arrived and several women screamed when he stepped out of his Lincoln Town Car. He paused at the sawhorses to sign papers and magazines thrust at him. Ned wondered if the women would swoon as hard if they knew there was air between the actor's ears, then reflected again that the man was a trained actor and could appear any way that suited his purposes. Perhaps he'd crossed him off his list a bit precipitously.

He saw Ron Dowling pay a taxi and slip in, ignored by the crowd, but Nikki Olivier's limo brought a whoop from the fans, many surging forward to clamor for autographs, waving books and her photo even before the door opened. She stepped out behind the two young women who played her daughters, walking regally to the sawhorses for autograph signing, deigning to give her subjects a treat to remember, assuring their allegiance to her show and the network.

Borelli nudged Ned. They watched Trudy fight her way through the crowd to the front of the sawhorses nearest the studio steps, engaging the patrolman in conversation.

Ned saw her smile. He could picture her explaining she was a crew member, just not one requiring a limousine. The cop waved her through. It was only the second time he'd seen her in anything other than jeans and a shirt and sweater, but that gallery sighting had been brief. The clingy dress she wore accentuated her figure and revealed a nicely shaped pair of tapered legs. Sunlight glinted off the clean, bouncy hair Ned knew would smell of lemons. She saw them and gave a tiny wave and went inside.

"Trudy's looking good today," Borelli noted.

Ned grunted his reply.

I wove my way through clusters of people fighting for access to Nikki Olivier. The two gals playing her twin daughters led the way to the stairs. They wore matching silk shantung cocktail dresses, one in pale green, the other in soft lilac. More appropriate for a summer wedding than a funeral, but they looked pretty.

Nikki was over the top, as usual, in a shimmery gold sheath, hair and makeup done to perfection, a large diamond brooch holding a matching stole in place.

I'm always surprised at the range of ages of the people waiting outside the soap studio. Middle-aged men and women were almost falling over themselves to get Nikki's autograph. After pointing out my name on a list of crew to the patrolman, I glanced across the street, recognizing Ned in the shadows of the PBJ building. Borelli stood next to him with Officer Damon. I waved tentatively, a small acknowledgement that I'd seen them, and went up the stone steps into the cool studio, glad I'd worn low heels.

Inside I greeted the security guard and signed in. I decided to look for Meg on the sound stage before going upstairs. The door was propped open to allow access for the caterer's rolling tables. It seemed even more cables than usual snaked underfoot, criss-crossing each other on the cement floor, and I picked my way toward the main area, shuddering at the memory of my fall. I put a hand up to my face. The makeup I rarely used had done a decent job of covering the yellowing bruises, the swelling mostly gone.

There was an air of excitement. Sound crews adjusted microphones, saying "check" into them over and over until any screechy feedback was eliminated. The gaffer dictated minor adjustments to the lights to eliminate shadows. Three cameras set on markings would tape the ceremony to be aired on the Soap Opera Network later in the week after editing. Meg had told me the director for this show was not from the usual roster, but someone from PBJ's staff who had experience with specials such as this.

Glad I had no official duties today, I stood at the edge of the lit area watching the crew at work. The actors might garner the awards and the autographs, might create headlines and generate ratings, but the crew worked around the clock, piecing together or dismantling sets to be used in the next day's action, like some kind of magician's helpers. They formed the bedrock of any show, the unseen force that allowed everything else to occur.

I couldn't see any of them at the heart of these murders. For that matter, how did an abortion clinic fit in with any of them? Or was that another case entirely?

I didn't see Meg but became aware of a presence approaching behind me. I hoped it wasn't Ron Dowling breathing down my neck, or Reece Hunter down my dress. A familiar leather and citrus scent reached me, and I turned around, bumping right into O'Malley's chest, closer to me than I'd expected.

"Hi. I was just going to look for Meg." I peered up at him in the darkness.

"She's over there with Borelli." He pointed back toward the Prop Room, where the two stood chatting, shoulders touching.

"Pathetic, aren't they?" I said.

"Totally," he confirmed. There was a beat of silence, then: "Hope your face is feeling better You look very nice today."

I have to admit I was pleased, hoping the darkness hid the color rushing to my face. "Thanks, it is. I clean up well. You look nice, too."

He did look nice, standing tall. If I looked straight ahead, I was looking at his tie, a silk foulard of blue and green, my two colors. I flashed back to a pile of blue and green napkins and paper plates for a Sweet Sixteen party that never happened, and looked hastily down to where Ned's hands were clasped casually in front of him. Nice watch. And that gold ring on his right hand—family heirloom or college crest? The veins stood out on his hands, long fingers wrapped around each other. I flashed back to a dark movie theatre, dates of long ago, and wondered when a man's hands had become erotic.

"Where do you suggest we sit to be out of the way?" he asked.

I was relieved to have something to do and ushered him to the other side of the studio where several rings of chairs were set well behind the lit space.

"The peon seats for visitors and invited guests. Less chance of getting on camera, unless you want to be."

"No, I think I'd prefer to keep my mug out of the spotlight

and concentrate on the reason I'm here today." As he sat down, his cell phone rang.

I nodded, the awful reality of the murders rising between us. I walked back to the doorway, searching the studio with my eyes, thinking of Neil Simon and trying to discern a murderer by body language. What could someone exhibit that would signal to me they were a killer?

Frank Resnick was talking to the caterer, who was putting swags of kale and ivy on a large buffet table. Ron Dowling conferred with two of his director colleagues, gesturing at the dais. Edith Carlisle stood in one corner with Li, Eva, and an assistant brought in for the day, chatting. The main cast was downstairs, primping and waiting to make their entrances on cue. From somewhere offstage I heard a female voice call out in despair: "I hate this pink hat—it makes me look like a flamingo!"

Edith sent her assistant to solve the hat dilemma, and I became aware of raised voices. Turning, I saw Frank had cornered Ron Dowling, poking him with his index finger. Dowling shrank away from the pointing digit and Frank's very red face. I couldn't hear what was being said, but as I watched, Frank pushed Dowling, who stumbled into the buffet table. Eva and the caterer both ran over and separated the men before serious damage could be done. Eva took Frank away, shaking her head and talking rapidly, either reasoning or chastising him. Dowling shook off the caterer and left the room quickly.

Was this an example of the body language I should be looking for? And if so, did it mean more than a jealous snit? Before I could digest the situation, the stage door slammed, focusing everyone's attention to that area. Reece Hunter, wearing a robe and tooled leather cowboy boots, holding a shirt, seemed unusually agitated as he strode up to Edith.

"You screwed up!" he shouted at the tiny woman, pointing to the shirt. Edith looked unimpressed, taking him by the arm and escorting him out of the studio. Several people stifled laughter. Everyone seemed on edge today.

Frank, his color back to normal, moved to the microphone. He bellowed: "Testing—testing. All right, people. Take your seats. Three minutes to tape."

At those magic words, people started to file into the studio and take their places. The writers and directors sat with the producers in the second row of the lit area, leaving the front row empty for the cast. The emcee was a Soap Opera Network honcho in a stiff tuxedo. He'd combed his hair over his bald spot and nervously consulted a stack of index cards.

Edith returned and sat with Li and Eva in the peon seats. Frank ignored his seat in the second row and joined them, draping one arm around the back of Eva's chair. Farther back, Meg took a seat with Borelli and O'Malley. Damon stood near the entrance door, casually keeping an eye on the people entering. I went back to my seat.

The camera lights came on and everyone in the circle of light sat up straighter.

The emcee suddenly developed a personality, his wide toothy grin welcoming everyone to this "rare and special occasion." He introduced the producers, with Egan standing and taking a bow, then the writers and directors. I noted Ron Dowling had left his Birkenstocks home today, leather sandals being his idea of dressing up, along with chinos and a collarless linen shirt—the artistic look, as defined by Director Himself.

The cast streamed in, introduced in ascending order, making their entrances through the studio door to a smattering of polite applause. A good soundtrack overlay would soon punch that up in editing. The lesser players first, then the children to a gush of "ooh's" from the women in the audience, followed by the younger team, including Nikki's matching twins, capped off by Reece Hunter. Must have been a wardrobe malfunction that had been his problem with Edith. He looked stylish in a tailored navy Armani suit and cream shirt, worn, of course, with his polished dress boots. The emcee seated them all with a flourish.

I was tired of standing and wandered over to the peon seats and plunked down next to Meg. Only Nikki Olivier was left. A spotlight fell onto the closed stage door; a hush fell over the audience.

The door was flung open by unseen hands and Nikki Olivier walked grandly up to the dais, majestic in bearing, the lights catching the sheen from her gown and glinting off the sparkling brooch.

"Talk about grand entrances," I whispered to Meg. "Check out the bauble."

"Borrowed from Harry Winston," Meg breathed back.

Nikki soaked in her wave of applause, some of the audience standing for the actor. She offered them all a sad, beatific smile as she waited for the clapping to die down.

"Bet she's been practicing that one for days." Borelli whispered to Meg.

"Thank you. Thank you all. Please sit down, do sit down."

The queen was benevolent to her underlings.

When she was assured she had the audience's full attention, Nikki launched into an opening speech regaling them with Griff Kennedy's life, bravely holding her tears in check throughout. I noted no mention was made of his first wife and avoided glancing at Edith.

Nikki turned as a screen descended from the ceiling. "Now we will all be treated to highlights spanning Griff's career."

The actor walked to her chair next to Reece, who rose gallantly and held her hand deferentially until she was seated. The montage rolled, stills mixed with taped snippets from scenes of Griff's Broadway plays, narrated in a voice-over by Nikki.

I took the opportunity to scan the audience. Reece Hunter seemed in a daze now that his moment in the spotlight was over. Frank Resnick was restless, shifting in his seat until Eva's hand on his stilled him. Edith Carlisle watched the images through a screen of tears, dabbing her eyes with a lacy handkerchief she'd pulled from her sleeve.

"Did you hear from the waitress yet?" Borelli whispered to O'Malley.

I leaned back against my chair to pick up their muted conversation.

"Not yet," O'Malley answered. "But the white fibers didn't match any of the samples we'd sent."

"Damn! I was sure it was going to be from Hunter's towels. He's our guy, I just know it."

The montage ended with a blowup of Griff's best smiling head shot, with the caption "In Memorium," to a generous round of applause. Nikki returned to the dais, reminding the audience of the tragic death of another of their cast, the young starlet Misty Raines, whose body would eventually be returned to her native Georgia for burial. She explained that Griff's body would be cremated "in the near future," which meant when his body had been released from the Medical Examiner's Office. Then she and a "few others close to him" would be scattering his ashes throughout Central Park from a horse and carriage ride. I knew that scattering ashes is illegal in New York State and wondered how Nikki planned to get around that one. Sounded like a photo op to me, but then I knew I could be cynical. I had to wonder if Edith would be included in that ride.

"Griff originally wanted us to scatter his ashes from the top of the Empire State Building, star New Yorker that he was, but the City's Health Department has restrictions on that," Nikki explained.

Nothing about scattering ashes being illegal. I'd bet he'd be buried down the road like everyone else and Nikki was being her usual dramatic self.

"Jeez," Borelli whispered. "Griff bits are falling on my head," he sang softly. Meg elbowed him to shut him up.

The emcee handed Nikki a glass sculpture in the shape of a shooting star. "On behalf of dear Griff Kennedy, I accept this in his memory." Her voice cracked on a sob.

Tears glistened on her eyelashes but didn't spill over to ruin her makeup. I wondered how she managed to do that.

Nikki continued. "I know Griff would have loved to be here today to receive this in person."

"No kidding," Borelli muttered.

Ned felt his stomach clench. Sitting in the darkened studio, he sensed an imminent threat reaching out around him. His ran his eyes ran along the rows, picking out the people who interested him. He had to get this right before the killer struck again.

He'd finally dropped Nikki and Edith from his internal suspect list as he focused on the men, adding Reece Hunter back in, scrutinizing Ron Dowling and Frank Resnick. Frank definitely had a bit of a temper, and Ned wondered what would push him over the edge into full-blown rage.

Borelli muttered rude comments until Meg jabbed him. Ned envied their casual banter and the obvious attraction between them. Had they slept together yet? He pictured Tony bringing the patrician Meg home for Sunday dinner. Mr. Borelli would be gracious and press wine on her, the Borelli boys would fall over each other for her attention, and Mrs B. would urge Meg to eat while mentally designing her mother-of-the-groom dress. He couldn't for the life of him think what Meg Pitman's parents would make of Anthony Giovanni Borelli but he knew there would be a giant hurdle to jump there if those two stayed together.

The emcee gallantly escorted Nikki to her seat. Just as Ned hoped the emcee would wrap things up, a side door opened from the area of the Control Room, and with a lavish gesture, the emcee announced: "And now, ladies and gentlemen, the Harlem Boys Choir to serenade us."

"You've got to be kidding," Borelli said a bit loudly.

Meg whispered, "Nikki wanted something very New York for Griff."

The young boys, dressed in matching blue blazers and red bow ties, filed in silently and took their places on two risers set up behind the dais. On cue from their director, they launched *a cappella* into "Amazing Grace," their high voices suffusing the studio, stopping casual conversation—until they segued into "New York, New York." A studio still of Griff hung suspended on the screen above them. It was a bizarre, theatrical, yet moving moment, Ned decided, one that could only have been accomplished in Soap Opera Land.

When the cameras were turned off, I felt a ripple of relaxation spread through the room. An immediate line formed by the buffet table when the hot foods were settled in their chafing dishes, their delicious mixed aromas filling the air. The clink of china and silverware mingled with the scents of lemon chicken, stuffed shrimp and tortellini pesto.

I was on high alert, sipping a glass of champagne, standing with Meg and Borelli. He snagged a slice of prime rib on toasted garlic bread from a passing waiter and offered bites to Meg. I left them to it, walking toward the back of the studio. Something Ned had said to Borelli had struck a chord with me. White fibers had been found on the doctored carrot that killed Misty Raines, but apparently none of the crime team's samples had matched it. When the choir had segued from "Amazing Grace" into "New York, New York," I'd pondered where I'd seen something that would leave white fibers.

On a hunch, I ducked into the Prop Room, putting my glass down on the long worktable and walking behind it to the area where Gary Knowles usually stood or sat. He used white gloves to polish his precious silver. Anyone could have come in here and taken a pair of those gloves.

I bent down and looked at the bottom shelf where Knowles stored his supplies. Next to bottles of Tarnex, Brasso and Hagerty's Silversmith's Polish, a neat stack of clean white cotton gloves stood in readiness. I grabbed the top glove and rolled it around itself until it was a small tube. Now how could I get it out of here?

"Can I help you, Trudy?" Gary Knowles stood on the other side of the table by the door, champagne bottle in one hand, glass in the other. Today he wore a silky black turtleneck and soft, draped gray slacks held by a beautifully carved silver buckle on a black leather belt. Instead of his cross, today's amulet was a chunky silver rectangle, decorated in alternating squares of black enamel, resembling a chessboard.

I stood up, clutching my earlobe. "Dropped an earring." I made a show of adjusting the back of my pearl earring.

"It seems you found what you were looking for," Knowles said, pushing my glass toward me. "Should we toast our dear departed colleague?"

"Sure." I sipped from my glass. Could I pull this off? Did he know I'd taken the glove? Knowles stood between me and the doorway, which suddenly looked very far away.

"To Griff," the Prop Master said, tipping his glass.

Better stall for time until someone interrupted us. "To Griff and Misty," I answered, draining mine.

CHAPTER THIRTY

Gary Knowles pulled the door closed to retrieve a leather stool from behind it and sat down, blocking the door.

"Sit down, dear, there's one on your side," he said pleasantly.

My hands were clammy, my stomach turning to liquid as my anxiety rose. I pasted a smile on my face. Don't be silly. Everyone has access to this room; it's not even locked. Maybe he's just lonely and wants the company. Was I imagining the menace I felt from those dark eyes? Remember Neil Simon. This was my chance to ask the questions that had occurred to me, while I played the sponge and soaked up his answers. I decided to brazen it out. "I should get back out there soon," I said, pulling out the stool and sitting down at the head of the table.

"No rush," he said. "Your friends are all on a very long buffet line. I'd rather wait until the crush is over, wouldn't you? I've never understood why some people feel the need to be first in line." He arranged the drape of his trousers so the sharp creases fell straight. "They certainly aren't going to run out of food."

What an absurd idea. "No way." I said, giggling. Now why did I do that?

M.K. GRAFF

Knowles had refilled my glass. "Drink up."

I drank obediently. My mouth was so dry, like sawdust had been sprinkled in it. I cast around for a subject to get him talking. "Your flowers are just lovely."

He visibly preened. "Thank you. I like to do them myself, especially for the special occasions. The ones on the tables today will be featured in the opening credits as a backdrop for the crystal star award. They've already filmed that."

"The ones you arranged for me are still lovely." What was there about flowers that I should find out? There was something about flowers, but what was it? And something else, something I had to find out from him. My head ached with the effort of remembering. Then my eyes lit on his necklace. "Unusual charm."

"Hand made by a SoHo silversmith. I like a game of chess, don't you? Such strategy, moving pieces backward and forward to their best effect. Not unlike how some people play their lives."

"Never played," I said. Now that was a profound statement. There was a buzzing in my ears that had become highly annoying. Was someone hissing in the microphones onstage? I squinted to clear my focus, trying hard to retrieve what it was I needed to ask Gary about. I glimpsed a framed photo on a shelf, Knowles with his arm around a dark-haired thin woman. Yes, that was one of the things. I wanted to ask him about his sister, but the words stuck in my throat. Instead I swallowed more champagne to wet my mouth and pointed at the photo. Gary followed my line of sight.

"My sister, Willy. Lovely girl, but not much common sense. You may have met her when she worked here last year." I found myself nodding and draining my glass again. So thirsty. Gary refilled it instantly. I drank half down. Was he still on his first glass? I pushed the rest of mine away. I never drank like this.

What was it I was going to ask him about his sister? Or was it a brother? I flashed on *Chinatown*, Faye Dunaway repeating "My sister, my daughter, my sister, my daughter." Why did I think of that?

"Bro-" I got out. What was wrong with my mouth? This was so frustrating. Why did Gary unexpectedly have such a huge head? But Gary seemed to understand me. Good thing, because I couldn't understand myself.

"No brother, just the two of us." He leaned closer to me, his voice dropping to a whisper, his face tight with a rigid smile. I leaned over, too, waiting to hear his secret spill from that big head and tight mouth. "I told you a little white lie, to let you think I had a brother, Trudy, because you are an evil, snooping bitch."

I had difficulty following what he was saying, but eventually the words sunk in. I tried to open my mouth to protest but it had totally stopped working. And I was seriously dizzy. Was I falling off the stool? I clutched at its sides and tried to stand.

"Did you really think I wouldn't notice you chatting people up, trying to find information? Who do you think you are, poking into everyone's business—Nancy Drew?"

At least he hadn't called me Miss Marple. I thought of a humorous reply. A small voice from somewhere over my shoulder garbled: "Nora Char-" before choking on the words.

"Ah, wife of the fictional detective Nick Charles. Did you know *The Thin Man* actually refers to the missing gentleman in

Hammett's book? Hollywood deemed the Thin Man should be Charles himself. Just like Hollywood to screw things up. Show business at its heart is an awful, terrible thing."

I nodded, but then again, I might have laughed or not moved at all. The shelves on the walls nodded along with me, though, so maybe I did nod after all. When in doubt, move your head.

Now the shelves were leaning toward me and moving away. I was in Wonderland, waiting for the Red Queen to appear to chop off my head.

Gary's face stayed close to mine. "Having difficulty focusing? You should see your eyes. They're zipping all over the place, quite amusing to watch."

I understood that but didn't even try to reply. Nystagmus, that's what he was talking about. That meant something to Nurse Nancy, finally. Gary drugged my drink and here I'd been slugging it down. No wonder he wasn't drinking his.

My limbs felt stuck in molasses. My throat was thick, with air stuck in my chest. I hoped I wouldn't vomit all over my best dress. I loved this dress, good with my eyes and hair and skin, skin on fire, eyes closing. I desperately needed to lie down, and slumped across the table, resting my sore face on the cool Formica top.

"Ready for some rest now? I can help with that."

Oh, good, he was going to help me. There was a dragging noise behind me, shifting, Gary moving about. I felt myself being lifted off the stool like a rag doll and set down. That was better, but I couldn't stretch out. My legs were bent and cramped, my arms folded across my chest. Smell, there's a musty smell. I hoped I didn't sneeze. I sneezed when there was too much dust around. I wanted to protest, to tell Gary about my bent legs and my sneezes, but sleep was enfolding me like a dark, thick blanket.

A slam. I was enveloped in total darkness, except for a tiny hole near my shoulder letting in a speck of light. My head whirled, my body felt leaden. Lethargic. Now I knew what that word meant.

Must stop this awful suffocating feeling, something about that speck of light, need to focus on that speck, need air to breathe, need to get to Ned. Where's a cop when you need him? Not Nora Charles or Miss Marple, just Trudy. No sister just brothers. Ask about his sister, no brother.

God, I need to sleep, need to give in to the comfy thick darkness all around me, but need to use that speck of light before I let myself sleep, to let Ned know, need, need to get Ned to the speck of light and to the white glove. The hand that holds the glove. Maybe I should just go to sleep. The horse and carriage rode through the park and Cinderella wore long white gloves and sprinkled her ashes.

CHAPTER THIRTY ONE

Ned watched the knots of people, clustered in chairs pulled together, eating off their laps or using other chairs as tables. The elite sat chattering away at nightclub tables set up for their use. Some stopped at Nikki's table to see the award and pay their respects. Beside him, Borelli wolfed down a plate of tortellini but Ned was too distracted to eat, lost in his deliberation.

"I looked in the ladies room and there's no sign of her," Meg said, concern creasing her brow.

"Did you check downstairs?" Borelli asked. His knee bobbed. "No coffee yet?"

"Tony, would you please put that plate down and help me look?"

Meg's anxious tone caught Ned's attention. He turned to the couple. "What's wrong?"

"Trudy's missing," Meg said, grabbing his sleeve. "We need to find her."

"What do you mean missing?" Ned glanced around the studio. "She was right here during the ceremony."

"I haven't seen her since. She never got on the food line and that's not like her."

Ned's cell phone rang. He propped it up between his chin and shoulder, walking a few steps away, jotting in his notebook, then motioned to Borelli to join him.

"You're certain? Yes, you've been very helpful. I'll send an officer right over to take your statement—thank you." He snapped the phone shut. "The waitress at the diner across from the women's clinic describes a man matching Gary Knowles' description taking a window seat in the last year, a regular." He punched in a number on his phone. "Detective O'Malley—get me Director MacKenzie—tell her it's urgent."

"What about Trudy?" Meg broke in.

"Check downstairs and call her cell. Damon!" Ned called the officer away from her post at the door, holding his hand over the phone. "Trudy Genova's missing. Have you seen her?"

"She ducked into the Prop Room half an hour ago."

"I'll handle that. You and Borelli search the sound stage." Goddamn his premonitions. Then MacKenzie came on the line and a minute later he had the answer to it all.

Ned pushed open the door to the Prop Room. Gary Knowles sat at his worktable, staring at a framed photograph.

"We need to talk, Knowles," Ned said, stepping into the room. He looked around the workroom; there was no other exit. "Seen Trudy Genova recently?"

"Trudy? Sure, she was at the ceremony, sitting right by you." Knowles nodded, a smirk raising his eyebrows.

Cool character, Ned thought. "You're a regular at the West 63rd Diner, like to sit in the same booth where you watch the clinic across the street. Now, why would you do that?"

"Does 'I like their food' suit you? I rarely cook at home and they make a mean burger." He stroked the heavy charm around his neck.

Ned reached out and took the photograph from the table. He'd erase that smug smile. "Your sister, Wilhemina? She had an abortion at that same clinic. You didn't accompany her that day, did you?"

Knowles' face darkened. "Medical records are supposed to be confidential. She could sue you." He closed his eyes briefly. "I never knew about it or I wouldn't have let it happen."

"Those records are private, except when murder and assault are involved. Care to tell me about your sister? Or should I interview her myself? I can have a detective over there in less than twenty minutes." Ned pulled out his cell phone.

"You can't!" Knowles stood up. "She's much too fragile, heavily medicated most of the time. She went into a deep depression after . . . afterward." His voice rose. "She's tried to commit suicide once already. Leave her alone!" He collected himself and sat stiffly back on his stool.

"Who was the father?" Ned asked, his agitation growing. In a second he'd be tapping his foot just like Borelli.

Knowles twisted his hands and his eyes grew bright. "He ruined her! She was so starved for attention she believed every lie. When she got pregnant he said his precious career couldn't handle a baby, it wasn't the right time for them, as if there ever would be a right time. She didn't want to get rid of it, but she'd do anything he told her at that point." He lowered his head to his hands. "The bastard was afraid if Nikki found out he'd lose his precious role and lifestyle. It was horrible. *He* was horrible."

"Griff Kennedy? Reece Hunter?" Ned's fists tightened when Knowles remained silent. In one second he was going to punch this guy. To keep his calm, he placed his cell phone on the table, the unspoken threat to his sister between them.

Knowles looked at the phone for a long minute. "It's like the game of 'Clue'—the illustrious Griff Kennedy, dead on the hospital set, instead of Colonel Mustard in the drawing room."

"You have access and knowledge about flowers—which provided the poison that killed him." Ned held his breath. Would Knowles deny his part in it? Or try to blame it on his sister? He picked up the photo of sister and brother, toyed with it, put it down facing the Prop Master. "Looks like a nice gal to me. Shame to drag her into this if she had nothing to do with it."

Knowles regarded the picture with sadness.

Borelli appeared at the door, out of breath, Damon on his heels. "No sign of Trudy anywhere."

Ned saw something pass Knowles' face, the briefest whiff of triumph. "Where is she, Knowles?"

"I've shared enough secrets with you for one day, Detective," he taunted, his façade back in place

Ned moved aside to let Borelli in. "Arrest him for the murder of Griff Kennedy."

Borelli slapped his cuffs on Knowles, reading him his

Miranda rights, while Ned's eyes searched the workroom for a place that could hide Trudy.

There were stacked paintings in bubble wrap, some leaning against shelves filled with silver pieces, china vases, candelabras; a low trunk heaped with an assortment of drapes; books no one had ever read to line shelves. Ned could feel his heartbeat in his ears. There was no way out of this room. Trudy had to be in here or Damon would have seen her leave. Then the briefest flash of teal color caught the corner of his eye, pushed through the lock hole on the trunk.

Borelli marched Knowles toward the door. "You're too late, Detective," the man cackled in a gleeful voice.

Ned threw the pile of drapes off the trunk and raised the heavy lid. Trudy lay stuffed on her side, curled in a fetal position, arms folded across her chest. She was unconscious, her lips blue.

"Damon, help me get her out of here!" Together they lifted Trudy out onto the floor. Ned knelt beside her, feeling for a pulse as Damon tilted her head back. Meg appeared in the doorway.

"What's happen—Trudy!"

"Call 911!" Ned barked, starting mouth-to-mouth on Trudy's inert form, noticing two incongruous things between breaths: that same statement had started his involvement in this whole mess, and that one sleeve of Trudy's dress was torn off.

DEATH UNSCRIPTED

It was strange being up here, watching those people scurry around my body as I lay complacently on the Emergency Room gurney. The overhead lights were bright, the conversation tense.

"Another hundred of Atropine!" A nurse noted the meds on an arrest record. The crash cart drawers stood open, debris piling on the floor as the staff worked on my body. Monitors beeped loudly and erractically.

I felt extremely calm and peaceful up here, wherever here was, in direct contrast to the flurried activity going on around me down below. Oh, crap—they'd had to slice my best dress right down the middle to attach leads and put the subclavian line in. At least my bra and panties were a matched set today. My mother would be happy. The cubicle curtain ripped open, rings clanging, admitting a bearded man in a white lab coat. I noted his pink shirt and blue tie strewn with pink whales.

"Respiratory arrest?" The Beard consulted the monitor, then a clipboard with lab slips.

"Probable drug ingestion mixed with alcohol," the ER doc answered. "Glasgow 3, no gag, we tubed her. Not much response to Narcan."

"Put an NG in, give her a hundred g's of charcoal. And try another hundred migs of IV lidocaine." The Beard shook his head. "Shame, nice looking girl." He stalked out.

I wanted to tell him I wasn't a drug-taking party girl but it didn't seem important enough to yell at him. It was like watching a movie unfold right in front of me, and I was the star. I didn't want it to end.

CHAPTER THIRTY TWO

Friday, May 14th

A deep blackness covered me, but occasionally something would pull at its edges, as if a blanket were being lifted, letting in small flashes of sound or awareness. I heard a rhythmic beeping. Once I thought I heard my mother crying. Hushed voices spoke just beyond me at different times, but I couldn't make out words. Someone raised my left eyelid and shined a light in. I shied away from it and gratefully sank back into the black.

A deeper male voice spoke soothingly, sounding familiar, holding my hand. Back to blackness.

The next time the blackness lifted, I felt cool liquid on my hands. Meg, I registered, smelling her lavender cream, panacea for all things. I floated off again. Later I smelled the heavy scent of flowers. That was definitely my mother's voice, stronger now. And the aroma of strong coffee. It smelled so good, I wanted a cup. Maybe if I opened my eyes? But they were trapdoors, snapping shut against the light as I struggled to lift them. Later I heard a moan—was that from me? I tried again to open my eyes, this time glimpsing my mother fast asleep on a chair next to my bed before my lids fell. Knowing she was there made me happy.

There was a thin slit of warmth crossing my face, annoying and soothing at the same time. This time when I tried to pry my eyes open, I blinked several times to clear the gauzy film that seemed to adhere to my lids. My mother clutched one of my hands as she slept heavily in a lounge chair pulled up next to my bed.

A shaft of sunlight had woken me and, as my sight steadied, I took in the crush of colorful flowers lined up on the windowsill. One large arrangement sat on the floor in a basket, a huge Styrofoam thermometer stuck in it. I dozed off.

M.K. GRAFF

When I opened my eyes again the sun was fully up. I looked at my mother, searching for the thick cluster of gray hairs that ran over one temple. Gone. But surely this was Hilda?

My arm jerked convulsively, waking my mother, who stood up, clasping the errant arm, smoothing the muscles as her face broke into her familiar smile.

"Trudy! You're awake! Thank God—" My mother continued to smooth my arms as one jumped again. "They said you might have these—they'll pass."

"Myoclonus," I automatically replied. What had been happening? My leg gave an involuntary twitch. I wanted to throw the covers off.

My mother smoothed the tangle of hair at my forehead, crying softly. "I'm so glad you're awake, Trudy. Losing your father—I couldn't go through that again."

"What day is it?" I said through dry lips.

Mom helped me take a tiny sip of water through a straw. "Friday, my birthday—a wonderful gift."

"Happy Birthday—guess I missed your birthday call—sorry." I took another sip. Cold water had never tasted so good. "What's been going on?"

"Your friends will catch you up, dear. They got the murderer thanks to you. He tried to kill you, too—" Mom's voice caught. She rang the bell for the nurse. "Your brothers have called three times a day. I made them stay home to run things. I told them 'I'm the mother and it's my place to be here.'" She blew her nose into a tissue and brightened. "Guess what? I'm going to be a grandmother and you're going to be an aunt!"

"See what happens when I turn my back for a few days," I said, and promptly dozed off again.

DEATH UNSCRIPTED

By that night I was already tired of lying in bed. In the afternoon I'd been for a brief walk, delighting the nurses caring for me, then had a quick shower with Mom's help. It was the best shower of my life. I'd eaten soup for lunch and taken a long nap after all of that activity. No dreams of dancing Griff's, either.

At dinnertime Meg, O'Malley, and Borelli crowded into the room. The men brought in extra chairs from the hall and I insisted my mother leave for my apartment to shower and change clothes, maybe grab a decent meal on her way back.

"Did you see she's highlighting her hair?" I asked Meg after Mom left. "What's that all about?"

Meg shrugged. "She looks nice."

Everyone pulled their chairs closer and settled in a ring around my bed. I laughed, reaching a hand up to check my forehead. "What? Did I grow another eyeball when I was asleep? Stop staring at me."

"We've been here on and off the last few days, in rotation," Meg explained. "It's nice to have you back with us, that's all."

"I don't know—I was kind of getting used to you keeping your mouth shut," Borelli threw in, but he smiled when he said it.

"Please, tell me what happened before I go crazy. My memory is hazy at best and Mom didn't know the gritty details."

Ned spoke up. Today he was definitely off-duty. I saw

how different he looked in chinos and a blue button-collared Oxford shirt, open at the neck, sleeves rolled up. I'd bet Meg a vodka gimlet without looking he had on loafers without socks.

"Gary Knowles admitted to poisoning Griff Kennedy after I told him we knew about his sister's abortion and threatened to question her about it. She sank into a deep depression after it, had tried to commit suicide. He's been caring for her at his home each night, with someone coming in during the day. And Griff realized in his final moments he was poisoned. He was pointing his finger at Gary, standing behind you.

"A few months ago Gary started hanging out at the diner across from the women's clinic. First he tried to take out his rage at Griff by attacking some of the men he saw waiting for clients there, in the mistaken impression they were the fathers, all repeats of Griff Kennedy out to ruin another woman's life."

Borelli interrupted. "In fact, one of these men was the woman's brother."

My head bounced back between the two detectives as they explained the entire story of the string of beatings. Something was still missing.

"But what about Misty?" I asked. "Did he kill her, too?"

Ned leaned forward. "We have you to thank for that, Trudy. He wouldn't admit to that at first, not until we found his white glove rolled inside your bra—"

"My bra!"

"Relax, the ER nurses brought it out to me when they found it. I knew what it was straight away. The fibers matched the ones found on Misty's doctored carrot. Once we had that, Knowles caved the next day. Not only had Misty also had an abortion, which he knew from watching the clinic, she saw Knowles leaving Griff's dressing room after he'd doctored that Emmy cup with poison. She was dangling blackmail in front of him."

"And it was Gary who searched your apartment, trying to see what you'd figured out, afraid Misty had confided in you," Meg said.

"He ordered your flowers from his supplier to set up your accident," Ned added; "Thought he was so clever with that one, paying some kid to deliver them."

"Totally crumbled finally," Borelli said, sipping a Coke. "Cried like a baby, admitted it was GHB he'd put in your champagne."

"GHB? Isn't that made from cleaning fluid?" I asked.

Ned explained. "Now it's being used as a date rape drug, a clear liquid that can be lethal when mixed with alcohol. He planned all along to get to you that day. You made it easier when he found you in his room."

I nodded. I knew of Rohypnol but had not paid close attention to the newer class of drugs. "I remember drinking champagne, Gary calling me an evil bitch, then lying down. That's about it. So who saved me?" I looked from one to another.

"Actually, you saved yourself." Ned said. "You tore your sleeve and pushed it through the lock hole on the trunk. We would have eventually looked there, but it caught my eye before it was too late."

"What trunk?" I asked. I saw the others share a look.

"Enough information for one night. Do you want to take a walk? What can we do for you?" Meg asked.

I directed my comments to Ned. "I want you to find that bearded doctor in the pink shirt and tell him I'm not a druggie."

"Pink shirt?" Meg asked, looking quizzically at the men.

"Yes, white lab coat, pink button-down Oxford shirt, a blue tie with little pink whales all over it," I insisted. "O'Malley, you have a shirt just like it."

"Methinks the lady hallucinated. The drug causes that, you know," Borelli said.

Ned leaned forward and touched my foot through the sheet. "No, she's right. There was a consultant, a respiratory guy they called in. I saw him come out of her cubicle." He frowned. "He was dressed just like she said," he told Meg and Tony, then looked back at me. "But Trudy, you were unresponsive then, there's no way—"

"Glasgow coma scale 3, no gag reflex, full respiratory arrest. I remember all of that bit in the ER," I insisted, and had the satisfaction of seeing all three of them momentarily speechless. Then they all started to speak at once.

"Oh, my God," Meg whispered. "You had a near-death experience."

"Did you see a bright light?" Ned asked sheepishly.

Borelli got so excited he almost spilled his soda. "Wait till my mother hears about this!"

Chapter Thirty Three

Friday, May 21ˢᵗ

Since coming home from the hospital, I'd been surprised at my weakness. I remembered in nursing school we'd learned it took only three days of complete bed rest for a body's muscle tone to start breaking down, and I wholly believed it.

Today, though, right after lunch I'd ventured with Mom down the block to the park, greeted with great joy by all of my doggie pals. The air never smelled fresher; the trees were never greener. I knew it would take time to process my very close brush with death, but for now, I enjoyed noticing everything around me with new eyes.

Even the river traffic had become interesting. I'd never paid attention to the barges before, piled with equipment, or the little red and black tugboats puffing behind them. And the birds, circling in the air, landing in the trees, squawking and fighting. Everything was lit from within. Everything looked sparkling and new and very, very meaningful.

After a half-hour outside petting my pals, I was ready to trek the one block back, and fell asleep quickly after Mom promised me a decent dinner. I realized my appetite was coming back when I woke to the scent of my mother cooking chicken and dumplings simmering with herbs, and my stomach began to growl.

I stretched deliciously, rubbing the sleep from my eyes. I'd insisted my mother sleep in the bedroom and had been sleeping on my old friend, the dependable futon, usually with Wilkie beside me. Before I knew it, I'd nodded off again.

My mother sat at the opposite end of the table, set with my new placemats and napkins, and as we ate, she discussed the new baby on its way. I was relieved to hear she believed Ben and Gail should choose the baby's name themselves, so there were no fears of a little Hilda or Giovanni. I planned to go home for a visit with Mom when she left, and when I felt strong enough and had the doctor's permission.

Filled with love for this strong and capable woman, I watched Mom load the dishwasher. How much did I resemble her, if at all? When I asked about her new highlights, she blushed like a girl and explained she'd started dating.

"Dating!" I tried unsuccessfully to keep the censure out of my voice.

"And too bad if you don't approve." My mother smiled. "I didn't know I needed my grown daughter's approval."

"No, of course you don't. I'm just surprised. You never

said . . . " But why not? My mother was a gracious, attractive woman who'd kept her family together, financially and emotionally.

"Even mothers are allowed a few secrets."

"Sure, the more I think about it, that's really great. Really. You deserve . . . companionship." No way as I going to discuss my mother's sex life or play the underwear game with her. "Who are you seeing?"

Her blush returned. "You remember Bob Riley?"

Bob Riley, Bob Riley, now who—oh, no! "As in Mr. Riley, my high school English teacher?" I knew I looked shocked and hastened to recover. "That's wonderful." I guess. A picture of Bob Riley and my mother holding hands rose before me.

"You always said he was a good teacher and the one who turned you on to mysteries with Conan Doyle and Dorothy Sayers. Trudy, you're looking pale, let's get you back to lying down."

For once I didn't argue.

Hilda Genova admitted Ned to the apartment. Sal had given him Trudy's mail after trying out a few jokes on him. There was a stack of cards and a small package at the back of the rubber-banded bundle, and he resisted his desire to scrutinize the sender.

"Lovely to see you, Ned. Trudy's in the living room resting.

Go ahead in and I'll bring you both some coffee."

At the hospital it hadn't taken Hilda long to call Ned by his first name and he realized he appreciated her easy way. He'd stayed away during Trudy's first days at home, deluged with interviews, reports and meetings with the District Attorney about the case against Gary Knowles. He'd heard from Tony through Meg that she'd had visitors almost every day from *Thornfield Place*. Even the producer had stopped by with an admonition to take as much time as she needed to recover.

Trudy had deep circles under her eyes and her face was thinner, but her facial bruises were gone. She sat nestled on the futon in a sea of pillows, surrounded by a stack of books on the table in front of her. A plethora of colorful flower arrangements on the wide window ledges gave off their sweet scent.

They exchanged greetings, awkwardly he thought, although he couldn't say why. Ned handed her the bundle and she tucked it next to her. Maybe she was annoyed he hadn't visited sooner. He'd clarify that. He sat in the rocker, glad he didn't have to deal with the futon today.

Hilda brought in a tray with two mugs of coffee and fixings, and two thick slices of homemade pound cake. "I thought I'd run to the grocery store while Ned is here, dear."

"Go ahead, Mrs. Genova. I can stay. It's my first day off in weeks, getting the case settled." That should settle any questions, Ned decided. "You look well, Trudy." He tried to find a comfortable way to fold his long legs under the rocker. Maybe the rocker was not as good a choice as he'd thought. He settled for placing both feet on the floor, leaning forward, elbows on knees.

The apartment door closed and they were left alone.

"I'm much better, thank you," Trudy said, not meeting his eyes.

This is going well, Ned mused. "Is anything wrong? I'm sorry I haven't been here before but there was so much paperwork and meetings—"

"Did you have me followed right after Misty Raines died?" she burst out.

Apparently Trudy's memory had returned full blast. "Maybe for a few days here or there. I meant to tell you earlier but things kind of got away from me."

Trudy exploded. "A few days! I thought I gave him the slip at Zabar's."

"You did," he admitted. "I sent a more experienced man after that." He could see Trudy wasn't pleased.

"Why would you think I'd kill Misty? Or Griff? Don't tell me just because I was the one who found her—"

"Calm down." He put up one hand to stop her tirade. "I never really thought you murdered anyone."

She sat up straighter. "The *Financial Times* man! Then why have me followed?"

"Because I knew you wouldn't willingly let me give you protection. You weren't being tailed, you were being watched." Ned spread his hands. "I was afraid you were in danger, especially after the second murder. You were too close to both victims at the time of their murders, and your snooping hadn't gone unnoticed, as evidenced by your apartment break-in. I thought the murderer might suspect you'd been privy to information, or unearthed something that was close to the truth."

"Oh." Trudy fell back against her pillows, silent for a moment, then: "Sorry."

"Apology accepted."

Trudy appeared to be in deep thought. "You send mixed messages, you know. I can't decide if you're my friend or my foe."

On that score she was right, and she deserved his honesty "Certainly not your foe, Trudy. And as long as we're being honest with each other, when I saw you at the Fitzpatrick Gallery, I was escorting my cousin, I wasn't checking up on you."

I knew my moods were labile; grouchy at times, giddy at others. It was from the concussion, the coma, the drugs—all I'd been through, catching up with me. Still, it felt good to know I had thought Ned was suspicious of me when all the time he'd been trying to protect me. Hmph. And Horseface was his *cousin*—Meg would get a kick out of that. I let out a big sigh. "If we're being honest, if I'd known you were trying to protect me, I'd have been—"

"Annoyed? Irritated? Pissed off?" Ned's smile was easy.

I held up a hand in surrender. "You've got me there. I seem to have . . . issues with men revolving around trust."

"I know." Ned's voice was soft.

I looked at him sharply. "You don't really. Something like

Jake happens, it undermines your self-esteem. You think it's your fault you couldn't measure up." I saw his raised eyebrow. "See how I can't even talk about it without removing myself? *I* thought I didn't measure up, and that the great low rent I pay is because Jake feels sorry for me, not because I deserve it because he treated me like crap. And there was my father's murder—another man with a hidden agenda."

Ned leaned forward, his expression earnest. "Murder? I thought his death was an accident. Wasn't there an investigation?"

"There must have been, but there were loose ends that were never tied up. I was planning my sixteenth birthday party with Mom when my father died." Once I started talking about that day, the words flowed. I described the day in detail, finding the paper goods for my party in the abandoned truck, the bank visit, and my father's body being found. "The missing money was never recovered and never explained. I can't help but attach a sinister explanation to that. It still haunts me. I believe he was murdered and his killer got away with it. I feel the police screwed up at the time and didn't fully investigate and that hasn't left me with the best taste in my mouth for men in blue, either. No offense to you and Borelli."

Ned nodded in understanding. "How did your mother handle it?"

"After that first day she never cried over him in front of us, although I heard her cry herself to sleep at night in the beginning. She counted pennies, learned how to do the books, gave my brothers more and more responsibility as they matured." I sighed, a deep heavy sigh, and went on to describe how Ben's marriage four years ago had been an unexpected bonus to the orchard and the store.

Gail increased the inventory and the store started selling the herbs she grew, along with homemade jams, jellies and honey. She'd added antiques in one corner that threatened to take over the shop, supplementing their stock with handcrafted consignment items from local potters and artisans. Genova's Orchard Store had expanded once, and there were plans for a conservatory-type tearoom in the future.

"And your other brother?"

I sipped my coffee. "Rick's the agriculture maven, met his partner at ag school. He manages the orchard operations, employs the seasonal workers." I laughed. "You should see his eyes glow discussing fertilizers and pest control."

"Sounds like a nice family," Ned said. "Your mom was good at not letting anyone wallow in depression. I like her."

"She's a mean cook, too. And guess what? After all these years, she's started dating, and it seems she's seeing my old English teacher." I explained about Mom coloring her hair and we had a good laugh together. I was more relaxed now in Ned's company than I'd ever been, and that package he'd brought in was starting to call to me. "It's strange being taken care of by her, like when I was child."

"I'll tell you what's strange. We never found out who was the father of Misty's baby."

I arched my eyebrows. "Once again, the amateur gets the goods. It was Emilio, the thick-necked grip who looks like he takes steroids." I enjoyed Ned's surprise.

"Who told you that?"

"Edith Carlisle, keeper of secrets, when she visited me. You just have to know the right person to ask." I stretched back against the pillows with a languid gesture. "You might remember that in future investigations. I'll be sure to remind you."

"I'll bet you will." Ned's smile lit up his eyes.

It was time to own up to my sneaky deed, now that I felt assured Ned was on my side. Meg had been my conspirator in the order and I would have to cough up the details to her later on this one.

"I've got something here for you," I told him, bringing out the package and ripping the mailing envelope open. "This is for helping to save my life."

Ned had a questioning look but took the small Brooks Brothers blue box from me and opened it. I felt a sense of great delight bubbling up inside, and this time it wasn't from drugs or a near-death experience.

He parted the tissue and brought out a pair of pale blue, Egyptian cotton, button-fly boxer shorts. One leg was embroidered in dark blue: "Ned-O."

ACKNOWLEDGEMENTS

Death Unscripted is based on my favorite nursing job from my varied thirty-year career. I worked for Cinema World Studios, still in operation in Greenpoint, NY, which supplies authentic medical equipment and nurse medical consultants in addition to its own soundstage and backlot. The job is just as Trudy describes it. Some days I worked on faxed script pages from Hollywood movies and shows at home. On-set days were for medical scenes filming in New York City, shows like the original "Law and Order," but the most frequent calls were to soap operas. I became a regular on ABC's "One Life to Live" as a medical consultant and baby wrangler. OLTL is where I met skilled and talented actors like Marilyn Chris, who along with her husband, actor Lee Wallace, also worked in theatre and film. We remain great friends and I thank her for her close reading of several drafts to ensure my memories from the soap opera world remained accurate.

The OLTL studio was an old armory building directly across from the ABC Broadcast studios and headquarters that still take up an entire city block and contain the attractive cafeteria where Trudy dumps pie on Griff Kennedy's head. The interiors and functioning of each place were as I've described them. The major difference is that the cast and crew I worked with were hard-working professionals; my characters are all from my imagination. At the same time I was doing this job, I wrote feature articles for *Nursing Spectrum*, the magazine Trudy reads. Yes, that story about the Resusci Annie doll is real, as is the story when I attached a string to the toe of an actor to tell her when to breathe.

Dr. Daisy Miller Armus used to live in the Upper West Side apartment I've borrowed for Trudy and was an early champion of the book. And while Ned's 2-0 precinct is on West 82nd Street, I've never been inside it. Thanks to Detective Mark Rawdon, formerly at the 20th Precinct, NYPD, for his information and explanations.

Sean C. Burk, paramedic and police officer for Plymouth, NC, provided research and background in both fields of his expertise. Forensic details were confirmed by Dr. Mary G. F. Gilliland, Professor, Brody School of Medicine, Forensic Pathology.

This book had several outings, first work-shopped with my own writing group and then sent out to beta readers. My grateful thanks to those who read and commented on the various drafts: Toni Amato, Mariana Damon, Barbara Ebel, Dorothy Halmstad, Julia Shaw-Kokut, Anne Jacobs, Barbara Jancovic, Anne Marie and Dave Koschnick, Robin J. Minnick, Nina Romano, Lauren Small, Melissa Westemeier; and to UK author Margaret Murphy who gave advice on the opening pages. Thanks, too, to authors Helen Smith, Edith Maxwell and Triss Stein for the reads and cover blurbs.

Paul Bauer did a great copyedit on the final manuscript with several suggestions I adopted. Beth Cole was patient as I dithered over the cover and layout design, wanting this series to be distinctly Manhattan at first glance and different from the English Nora Tierney Mysteries. Thanks to both for their contributions and hard work. A special nod to Lauren Small, publisher, and her work at Bridle Path Press.

Thanks to the readers who support me and leave reviews, and to the many friends and family who help me on tours by sharing their guest rooms. I appreciate each and every one of you.

I need to thank my family—here in North Carolina, in New York and in Minnesota—who never tire of supporting my writing. A very special thanks to Arthur, for always believing, always sustaining, always caring. I couldn't do it without you, Doc.

Death Unscripted had its genesis when I was transitioning from nursing to full time writing, studying various forms of writing and conducting interviews for *Mystery Review* magazine. During a course at Oxford concentrating on Gothic mystery writers like Wilkie Collins and Daphne Du Maurier, the magazine arranged for me to train down to London to interview the reigning Queen of British Crime, P. D. James. I could scarcely believe my good luck. James was my hero and I was going to meet her at her Holland Park townhouse.

The Baroness had just turned eighty when she opened the door and invited me into her antiques-filled home. Two hours later, after my questions were exhausted and I couldn't in all good conscience take up more of her time, I prepared to leave. Instead, she asked if I would like to come down to her kitchen for a coffee before my train back. *Would I?*

We talked more personally then, and she asked about the English mystery series I'd been making notes for on this trip. I was enthralled, knowing I was sitting at the table where this legend created her stories in longhand. She approved of my planned story arc, and of moving Nora around England, too. Talk turned to my nursing history and my unusual consulting job, achieved because I knew screenplay formatting. Then she insisted I write this book.

DEATH UNSCRIPTED

"Readers love a behind-the-scenes look at a world they don't know," she said. "Promise me one day you'll write a mystery that revolves around someone who does that."

That day started a wonderful fifteen-year relationship between us that only ended with her passing in November of 2014. P. D. James became my mentor and friend, and encouraged me through seeing three English mysteries in print. Phyllis was gracious and kind, generous and warm. I was blessed to know her.

Finally the book she wanted me to write is in print. I'm only sorry she isn't here to see it. Promise kept.

M.K. GRAFF